Hermann Sudermann, Bertha Overbeck

Dame Care

Hermann Sudermann, Bertha Overbeck

Dame Care

ISBN/EAN: 9783741112577

Manufactured in Europe, USA, Canada, Australia, Japa

Cover: Foto ©Andreas Hilbeck / pixelio.de

Manufactured and distributed by brebook publishing software
(www.brebook.com)

Hermann Sudermann, Bertha Overbeck

Dame Care

THE CONTINENTAL CLASSICS

VOLUME X

DAME CARE

BY

HERMANN SUDERMANN

TRANSLATED FROM THE GERMAN

BY

BERTHA OVERBECK

HARPER & BROTHERS PUBLISHERS

NEW YORK AND LONDON

Meinen Eltern

zum 16. November 1887.

Frau Sorge, die graue, verschleierte Frau,
Herzliebe Eltern, Ihr kennt sie genau,
Sie ist ja heute vor dreißig Jahren
Mit Euch in die Fremde hinausgefahren,
Da der triefende Novembertag
Schwerathmend auf nebliger Haide lag
Und der Wind in den Weidenzweigen
Euch pfiff den Hochzeitsreigen. —

Als Ihr nach langen, bangen Stunden
Im Littauerwalde ein Nest gefunden
Und zagend standet an öder Schwelle,
Da war auch Frau Sorge schon wieder zur Stelle
Und breitete segnend die Arme aus
Und segnete Euch und Euer Haus
Und segnete die, so in den Tiefen
Annoch den Schlaf des Nichtseins schliefen.

Es rann die Zeit. — Die morsche Wiege,
Die jetzt im Dunkel unter der Stiege,
Sich freut der lang verdienten Rast,
Sah viermal einen neuen Gast.
Dann, wenn die Abendgluth verblichen,
Kam aus dem Winkel ein Schatten geschlichen

Und wuchs empor und wankte stumm
Erhobenen Arms um die Wiege herum.

Was Euch Frau Sorge da versprach,
Das Leben hat es allgemach
In Seufzen und Weinen, in Noth und Plage,
Im Mühsal trüber Werkeltage,
Im Jammer manch' durchwachter Nacht
Ach! so getreulich wahr gemacht.
Ihr wurdet derweilen alt und grau,
Und immer noch schleicht die verschleierte Frau
Mit starrem Aug' und segnenden Händen
Zwischen des Hauses armen vier Wänden,
Vom dürftigen Tisch zum leeren Schrein,
Von Schwelle zu Schwelle aus und ein,
Und kauert am Herde und bläst in die Flammen
Und schmiedet den Tag mit dem Tage zusammen

Herzliebe Eltern, drum nicht verzagt!
Und habt Ihr Euch redlich gemüht und geplagt
Ein langes, schweres Leben lang,
So wird auch Euch bei der Tage Neigen
Ein Feierabend vom Himmel steigen.

Wir Jungens sind jung — wir haben Kraft,
Uns ist der Muth noch nicht erschlafft,
Wir wissen, zu ringen mit Noth und Müh'n,
Wir wissen wo blaue Glücksblumen blüh'n
Bald kehren wir lachend heim nach Haus'
Und jagen Frau Sorge zur Thür hinaus.

DAME CARE.

CHAPTER I.

JUST when Meyerhofer's estate was to be sold by auction, his third son Paul was born.

That was a hard time indeed.

Frau Elsbeth, with her haggard face and melancholy smile, lay in her big four-post bed, with the cradle of the new-born child near her, and listened to every noise that reached her in her sad sickroom from the yard and the house.

At each suspicious sound she started up, and each time, when a strange man's voice was heard, or a vehicle came driving along with a rolling sound, she asked, clinging with great anxiety to the bedposts:

" Has it come to the worst? Has it come to the worst?"

Nobody answered her. The doctor had given strict orders to keep every excitement from her, but little he thought, good man, that this constant

1

suspense would torment her a thousand times more than the most terrible certainty.

One morning, the fifth day after her child's birth, she heard her husband, whom she had scarcely seen during this trying time, pacing up and down in the next room, swearing and sighing. She could only understand one word, only one; that he repeated over and over again: the word "Homeless."

Then she knew. It had come to the worst.

She put her feeble hand on the little head of the new-born child, who with his little serious face was quietly dozing, hid her face in her pillow and wept.

After a while she said to the servant who attended the little one,

"Tell your master I want to speak to him."

And he came. With loud steps he approached the bed of the sick woman, and looked at her with a face that seemed doubly distorted and desperate in his endeavor to look unconcerned.

"Max," she said, timidly, for she always feared him—"Max, don't hide anything from me; I am prepared for the worst, anyhow."

"Are you?" he asked, distrustfully, for he remembered the doctor's warning.

"When have we to go?"

As he saw that she took their misfortune so calmly, he thought it no longer necessary to be careful, and broke out, with an oath:

"To-day—to-morrow—just as it pleases the new owner. By his charity only we are still here, and, if it pleased him, we might have to lodge in the streets this very night."

"It won't be as bad as that, Max," she said, painfully striving to keep her composure, "if he hears that, only a few days ago, a little one arrived—"

"Oh, I suppose I shall have to beg of him—shall I?"

"Oh no; he will do it without that. Who is it?"

"Douglas, he is called. He comes from Insterburg. He seemed to swagger very much, this gentleman—very much. I should have liked to have driven him from the premises."

"Is anything left us?" she asked, softly, looking hesitatingly down on the new-born child, for his young, tender life might be depending on the answer.

He broke out into a hard laugh. "Yes; a wretched pittance: full two thousand thalers."

She sighed with relief, for she almost felt as if she had already heard that terrible "Nothing" hissed from his lips.

"What good are two thousand thalers to us?" he continued, "after we have thrown fifty thousand into the swamp? Perhaps I shall open a public-house in the town, or trade in buttons and ribbons. Perhaps you might help me, if you were to do the sewing in some aristocratic houses; and the children might sell matches in the streets. Ha, ha, ha!"

He thrust his hand through his gray and bushy

hair, and inadvertently kicked the cradle with his foot, so that it swayed to and fro violently.

"Why has this brat been born?" he murmured, gloomily. He knelt down near the cradle and buried the tiny little fists in his big red hands, and talked to his child: "If you had known, my boy, how bad and vile this world is, how impudence triumphs, and honesty goes to ruin in it, you would really have stayed where you were. What fate will yours be? Your father is a sort of vagabond, a ruined man, who has to roam about the streets with his wife and his three children till he has found a place where he can completely ruin himself and his family."

"Max, do not speak thus; you break my heart!" called out Frau Elsbeth, crying, and stretching out her hand to lay it round her husband's neck; but her hand sank down without strength ere it had reached its destination.

He sprang up. "You are right; enough of these lamentations. Yes; if I were alone now—a bachelor, as in former days—I should go to America, or the Russian Steppes—there one can get rich; or I should speculate on the Exchange—to-day up, to-morrow down. Oh, there one could earn money; but so tied as one is!" He threw a lamentable glance at his wife and child; then he pointed with his hand towards the yard, from whence resounded the laughing voices of the two elder children.

"Yes; I know we must be a burden to you now," said the woman, meekly.

"Don't talk to me of burdens," he answered, gruffly; "what I said was not meant angrily. I love you, and that's enough. Now the question only is, Where to go? If at least this baby had not come, the chance of an uncertain existence might be borne for some time. But now, you ill, the child requiring careful nursing, the end of it is there is nothing for it but to buy a farm, and to give the two thousand thalers for a premium. Hurrah! that will be a nice sort of life: I with the beggar's wallet, you with the knapsack; I with the spade, you with the milk-pail."

"That would not be the worst, after all," said the woman, softly.

"No?" he laughed, bitterly. "Well, that I can get for you. There is Mussainen, for instance, which is to be sold—the wretched moorland on the heath yonder."

"Oh, why that of all places?" she asked, shuddering.

He immediately fell in love with the idea.

"Yes; that would be emptying the cup to the dregs. The lost magnificence always in view—for, you must know, the manor-house of Helenenthal exactly overlooks it. It is surrounded by moor and fen—wellnigh two hundred acres. Perhaps one could cultivate some of it—one might be the pioneer of progress. What could people say?

'Meyerhofer is a brave fellow,' they would say;
'he is not ashamed of his misfortune; he looks at
it with a certain irony.' Pah, really one *should*
look at it with irony; that is the only sublime view
of the world—one should whistle at it!" and he
uttered a shrill whistle, so that the sick woman
started up in her bed.

"Forgive me, my darling," he pleaded, caressing
her hand suddenly in the rosiest of humors; "but
am I not right? One should whistle at it. As long
as one has the consciousness of being an honest
man, one can bear all adversity with a certain relish.
Relish is the right word. The ground is to be sold
any day, for the owner has lately gained a rich estate by marriage, and leaves this rubbish entirely
uncultivated."

"Think well over it first, Max," the woman
pleaded, in great anxiety.

"What is the good of hesitating?" he replied,
violently. "We must not be a burden to this Mr.
Douglas, and we cannot lay claim to anything better
with our miserable two thousand thalers; therefore,
let us seize upon it promptly." And without taking
time to say good-bye to the sick woman, he strode
away.

A few minutes later she heard his dog-cart driving away through the gate.

In the afternoon of the same day a strange visitor
was announced. A beautiful, distinguished lady
was said to have driven into the yard in a smart

carriage, who wished to pay a visit to the mistress in her sick-room.

"Who was it?" She had refused to give her name.

"How strange!" thought Frau Elsbeth; but as in her grief she was beginning to believe in special providences, she did not say no.

The door opened. A slender, delicate figure, with gentle, refined features, approached the bed of the sick woman with gliding steps. Without speaking a word she seized her hand and said, in a soft, slightly veiled voice:

"I have concealed my name, dear Mrs. Meyerhofer, for I feared you would refuse to see me if I had given it beforehand. And I should like best even now to remain unknown. Unfortunately, I fear that you will not look at me with kindness any longer when you know who I am."

"I hate no one in the world," replied Frau Elsbeth, "least of all a name."

"I am called Helene Douglas," said the lady, gently, and she pressed the invalid's hand closer.

Frau Elsbeth began at once to cry, while the visitor, as if she had been an old friend, put her arm round her neck, kissed her on the brow, and said, with a soft, comforting voice:

"Do not be angry with me. Fate has ordained that I should drive you from this house; but it is no fault of mine. My husband wanted to give me a pleasant surprise, for the name of this estate is identical with my Christian-name. My joy vanished directly when I heard under what circumstances he had acquired it, and how you, especially, dear Mrs. Meyerhofer, must have suffered in this doubly trying time. Then I felt compelled to unburden my heart by asking your pardon personally for the sorrow which I have caused you, and shall still have to cause you, for your time of suffering is not over yet."

Frau Elsbeth had bent her head on the stranger's shoulder, as if that was the most natural thing in the world, and went on softly crying to herself.

"And perhaps I can also be of use to you," she continued; "at least, so far as I can take part of the bitterness from your soul. We women understand each other better than those hard, passionate men. The common sufferings that weigh on all of us bring us nearer to each other. And, above all, one thing: I have spoken to my husband, and beg you, in my name and his, to look on this house as your property for as long as ever it pleases you. We generally pass the winter in town, and we have another estate besides which we intend to let an inspector manage. You see, therefore, that you do not in any way disturb us, but, on the contrary, do us a favor if you will stay on here as before for another half year or longer."

Frau Elsbeth did not thank her, but the tearful glance she gave the stranger was thanks enough.

"Now be cheerful again, dearest Mrs. Meyerhofer," she continued, "and if in future you need advice or help, always remember that there is some one who has to make amends to you for much— And what a splendid baby!"—she turned towards the cradle—"a boy or a little girl?"

"A boy," said Frau Elsbeth, with a feeble smile.

"Has he found any brothers or sisters already? But why do I ask? The two little stalwart fellows outside, who received my carriage—may I hope to know them better? No, not here," she interposed, quickly; "it might excite you still more. Later on, later on. This little citizen of the world interests us most for the moment."

She bent over the cradle and arranged the baby-clothes.

"He has quite a knowing little face," she said, jestingly.

"Care stood at his cradle," answered Frau Elsbeth, gently and sadly; "that's why he has that old face."

"Oh, you must not be superstitious, dear friend," answered the visitor. "I have been told that new-born babes often have something old in their features; they soon lose that."

"Surely you, too, have children?" asked Frau Elsbeth.

"Oh, I am still such a young wife," answered her visitor, blushing. "Scarcely six months married. But—" and she blushed still more.

"God be with you in your time of trouble," said Frau Elsbeth; "I will pray for you."

The stranger's eyes grew moist. "Thanks, a thousand thanks," she said. "And let us be friends, I entreat you, with all my heart. Shall I propose something? Take me as godmother for your youngest child, and do me the same favor when Heaven blesses me."

The two women pressed each other's hands silently. The bond of friendship was sealed.

When the visitor had left her, Frau Elsbeth looked round with a shy, sad look. "Just now everything here was bright and sunny," she murmured, "and now it has become so dark again."

After a short time, in spite of the nurse's opposition, the two eldest boys rushed into the sick-room with joyful clamor. Each had a bag with sweets in his hand.

"The strange lady has given us this," they shouted.

Frau Elsbeth smiled. "Hush, children," she said, "an angel has been with us."

The two little boys opened anxious eyes, and asked,

"Mamma, an angel?"

CHAPTER II.

So Mrs. Douglas became Paul's godmother.

Meyerhofer, indeed, was not a little indignant at the new friendship, for "I don't want the pity of happy people," he often used to say; but when the mild, gentle woman appeared in the manor-house for the second time, and tried to persuade him, he did not dare to say "No" any longer.

He also gave his consent to their prolonged stay in the old home, though he did it with repugnance. The farm Mussainen, which in fact he had bought that same day, was in so desolate a condition that it seemed dangerous for wife and children to stay there in the cold autumn days. Above all, the most needful repairs had to be made. Carpenter, mason, and builder had to be fetched ere it was possible to think of moving.

Nevertheless, Frau Elsbeth, through her husband's obstinacy, was forced to move into the new dwelling long before the arrangements were finished. One day when an inspector from the new master appeared with a number of workmen and asked for shelter in his name, he declared this proceeding to be an intentional insult, and was firmly resolved not to stay a day longer on the ground which once had been his property.

It was a cold, dull November day when Frau Elsbeth and her children had to say farewell to the dear house. A fine, drizzling rain came from the sky, making everything damp.

The heath, shrouded in gray mist, lay desolate and comfortless before their eyes.

The youngest at her breast, the two other children crying near her, she stepped into the vehicle which was to lead her towards her new fate, which, alas! seemed so dark.

When they drove out of the gate, the cold winds from the heath whipped their faces with icy scourges. Then the little one, who for so long had been lying peaceful and quiet, began to cry bitterly. She wrapped him closer in her cloak and bent down low over the shivering little form, in order to hide the tears, which were streaming down her cheeks incessantly.

After half an hour's drive over the heavy rain-soaked clay roads, they reached their destination. She could have shrieked aloud when she saw the new house before her in all its desolation and ruin.

Wretched mud farm-buildings; a swampy yard; a low dwelling-house with a shingle roof, from the walls of which the chalk had crumbled down and showed the bare wall underneath; a wilderness of a garden, in which the last sad remains of the summer asters and sunflowers stood among half-decayed vegetables, round about a gaudy painted fence, which seemed to have received extreme unction just before its end—this was the place where the family of the ruined squire had to live henceforth.

This was the place where little Paul grew up, and to which the love of his childhood, the care of half his life was devoted.

He was in his early years a delicate, sickly creature, and many a night his mother trembled lest the feeble light of his life should be extinguished before dawn. At such times she would sit in the dark, low bedroom, leaning her elbow on the edge of his little bed, gazing with feverish eyes at his little thin body, which was painfully convulsed by spasms.

But he passed all the crises of his early childhood, and at five years old, though pale and weak of limb and almost careworn in face—for he had really retained the old look—he was a healthy boy, who gave promise of long life.

At this time his first recollections begin. The earliest, which in after-years he often recalled, was as follows:

The room is half dark. Icicles are clinging to the windows, and through the curtains shines the red glow of the sunset. The elder brothers have gone skating, but he is in his little bed—for he has to go to bed early—and near him sits his mother, one hand encircling his neck, and the other on the edge of the cradle, in which the two little sisters sleep, which Master Stork brought a year ago, both on the same day.

"Mamma, tell me a fairy tale," he pleads.

And his mother told him one. What? He could only remember very faintly, but there was something in it about a gray woman who had visited his mother in all her sad hours, a woman with a pale and haggard face, and dark, tear-stained eyes. She had come like a shadow, like a shadow she had gone, had extended her hands over his mother's head, she knew not whether for a blessing or for a curse, and had spoken words which had reference to him—little Paul. In them there was the question of sacrifice and of redemption; the words he had forgotten again—probably he was too stupid to understand them. But one thing still remained clearly enough: while he listened to his mother's words, breathless with terror and expectation, he suddenly saw the gray figure of whom she spoke, bodily standing at the door—exactly the same, with her arms uplifted, and her pale, sad face. He hid his head on his mother's arm; his heart beat, his breath began to fail him, and, in deadly terror, he screamed out,

"Mamma, there she is, there she is!"

"Who? Dame Care?" asked his mother.

He did not answer, but began to cry.

"Where, then?" continued his mother.

"There, at the door," he replied, raising himself and clutching her round the neck, for he was dreadfully frightened.

"Oh, you silly little one," said his mother; "that is papa's long travelling-cloak." And she fetched it, and made him feel the lining and the stuff, so that he should be thoroughly convinced; and he gave in. But inwardly he was all the more firmly persuaded that he had seen the gray woman face to face. And now he also knew what she was called.

"Dame Care," she was called.

But his mother had grown thoughtful, and was not to be moved to tell the end of the fairy tale. Neither would she in later times, however urgently he might plead.

He had only a vague remembrance of his father in those days: a man with high Wellington boots, who scolded his mother and whipped his brothers, while he overlooked him altogether. Only at rare times he got a look askance, which did not seem to bode any good. Sometimes, especially when his father had been in the town, his face was dark red in color, like an overheated kettle, and his steps swayed from side to side when he crossed the room. Then the same thing was always enacted over again.

First he fondled the twins, whom he seemed to be particularly fond of, and rocked them in his arms, while his mother stood close beside him, following each of his movements with anxious looks. Then he sat down to eat, turned over what was in the dishes, pushed them aside, calling them poor and

unsavory food, only fit for beasts. Occasionally he
would hit Max or Gottfried with the rod, was angry
with their mother, and finally went out to pick a
quarrel with the servants. His bullying voice resounded in the yard, so that even Caro, chained
up, hid his tail between his legs, and retired to
the farthest corner of the kennel. If after a while
he returned to the room, his humor had generally
changed from anger to despair. He wrung his
hands, lamented the misery in which he had to live
there, talked to himself of all sorts of great things
which he would have undertaken if one thing or
another had not prevented him, and if heaven and
earth had not conspired together to ruin him. Then
he would often go to the window, and shake his fist
at the White House yonder, which looked so at-
tractive in the distance.

"Ah, the White House!"

His father abused it and knitted his brow if he
only glanced in that direction; and he himself—he
loved it, as if part of his soul lingered there. Why?
He did not know. Perhaps only because his mother loved it. She, too, stood often at the window,
gazing at it; but she did not knit her brow, not
she; her face grew soft and melancholy, and from
her eyes there shone a longing so ardent that he,
standing near her, often felt a sensation of awe
steal over him.

Was not his little heart filled with the same longing? Did not that home, ever since he could think

at all, appear to him as the embodiment of everything beautiful and magnificent? Did it not always stand before him when he shut his eyes and
even creep into his dreams?

"Have you ever been in the White House?" he
asked his mother one day, when he could restrain
his curiosity no longer.

"Oh yes, my son," she answered, and her voice
sounded sad and unsteady.

"Often, mamma?"

"Very often, my boy. Your parents once lived
there, and you were born there."

Ever since then the "White House" was to him
what "Paradise Lost" is to mankind.

"Who lives in the White House now?" he asked
another time.

"A beautiful kind woman, who loves everybody,
and you especially, because you are her godchild."

He felt as if an endless fountain of happiness
streamed upon his head. He was so excited that
he trembled.

"Why do you not drive, then, to the beautiful
kind woman?" he asked, after a while.

"Papa won't let us," she answered, and her voice
had a strangely sharp tone which struck him.

He did not ask any more, for his father's wish
was regarded as a law of which nobody had a right
to ask the reason, but from that day the secret of
the White House formed a new tie between mother
and son. They could not speak about it openly.

2

His father was furious if one only hinted at its existence, and his brothers also did not like to talk about it with him, the younger one ; very likely they feared that he would repeat it in his foolishness. But his mother—his mother trusted him.

When they were alone together—and they were nearly always alone during school-time—she would open her mouth and her heart, too, and the White House arose higher and brighter before his eyes from her description of it. Soon he knew each room, each arbor in the garden, the pond, surrounded by green bushes and shrubs, before it the shining glass balls, and the sundial on the terrace : only fancy, a clock on which the sun itself had to mark the hours.

What a marvel !

He could have walked about in Helenenthal with his eyes closed, and not have lost his way.

And when he played with his bricks, he built a White House for himself with terraces and sundials —two dozen at a time. He dug ponds in the sand and fastened pebbles on little posts to represent the glass balls. But, of course, they did not reflect anything.

CHAPTER III.

At this time he made the plan to pay a visit to the White House quite on his own account. He put it off till spring, but when spring came he did not find the necessary courage; he put it off till summer, but even then all sorts of hinderances came between plan and execution. Once he had seen a big dog roving alone in the meadow—who could know whether it might not be a mad one? and at another time a bull had made straight for him with his horns lowered.

"Yes; when I am big like my brothers," he consoled himself by thinking, "and when I go to school, then I'll take a stick and kill the mad dog, and the bull I'll seize by the horns so that he cannot harm me any more." He put it off until next year, for then he was to begin going to school, just like his big brothers.

These brothers were the objects of his veneration. To be like them seemed to him the brightest aim of all earthly wishes—to ride on horses, on big real ones, to skate, to swim quite without the help of either floats or bladders, and to wear shirt-fronts, white starched ones, which were fastened with ribbons round the waist—oh, if he could do all that! But for that one must first grow big, he comforted himself by thinking. He kept these thoughts quite to himself; he did not like to tell his mother, and, as to his brothers, they occupied themselves with him very little.

He was a little manikin in their eyes, and when their mother told them to take him with them any-where they were angry, because then they had to take care of him, and on account of his silliness could not play so many tricks. Paul felt that very well, and in order to escape their angry faces and still more angry blows, he generally said he wanted to stay at home, however sore his heart might feel. Then he seated himself on the pump-handle, and, rocking himself to and fro, dreamed of the time when he could do as his brothers did.

In learning, too, and that was no small matter; for both of them, Max as well as Gottfried, were always the highest in their school, and always brought home for the holidays excellent testimo-nials of good conduct: how excellent they were was quite evident, for their father always gave them a silver groschen and their mother a honey-cake in consequence.

On such joyful days he used to hear his father say:

"Yes; if only the two eldest could go to a good school, something might be made of them, for they have clear heads; but beggars as we are, I suppose we shall have to bring them up like beggars."

Paul reflected a good deal about this, for he already knew that Max was born to be a Field-marshal, and Gottfried to be Chief Master of the Ordnance.

The fact was that once a Ruppin picture-book, with pictures of the Austrian army, had found its way into the Haidehaus, and on that day the brothers had agreed to divide the two highest dignities in the army between themselves, while to him, the younger, the place of a non-commissioned officer was assigned. Since then, indeed, there had been periods when one of them had inclined to the voca-tion of a trapper, and the other to that of an Indian chief, but Paul's thoughts clung to those gold-braid-ed uniforms, with which the wooden spears, and the patched rag sandals, which the brothers wore in their games—the latter they called moccasins—could by no means bear comparison; also, why they afterwards wanted to be naturalist and super-intendent was incomprehensible to him; the new Ruppin pictures always remained the best.

At this time the twins began to walk; Katie, the elder one—she was born three-quarters of an hour before her sister—made the beginning, and Greta followed her three days after.

That was an important event in Paul's life.

He suddenly found himself in a round of duties from which he could not easily get free. Nobody had ordered him to watch his little sisters' first steps, but just as it had always been natural to him

to clean his boots in the evening, and his brothers'
into the bargain, to fold his little frock in a square,
and to put it at the head of his bed, with his stockings across it, never to make a spot on the table-
cloth, and to receive the punishment from his father when the self-same accidents happened to his
brothers—so it became just as natural that he
should henceforth look after his little sisters, and,
with premature care, watch over their most rash
attempts to stand and walk.

He appeared to himself so full of importance in
this office that even the longing to go to school became less, and if by a lucky chance he had only
been able to whistle, there would have been no
wish left him.

Ah! to be able to whistle, like Jons, the farm-
servant, or like his elder brothers; that was now the
goal of all his wishes, the object of incessant prac-
tice. But however much he might point his lips,
however much he might moisten them to make
them flexible, no sound came forth. If he drew in
the air, then accidentally he would do it. Once he
had even succeeded in producing the first notes of
"Ist ein Jud im Wasser gefallen" (A Jew Tumbled
into the Water); but each professional whistler
knows that the air must be blown from the mouth,
and this was just what he could not learn.

Here also the thought comforted him: "When I
am big."

Christmas this year brought glad tidings. There

arrived a big box from his "good aunt" out of the town, a sister of his mother's, with all sorts of beautiful and useful things: books, linen for his brothers' shirts, little frocks for his sisters, and for himself a velvet coat—a real velvet coat, with military braidings and big shining buttons. That was a delight. But the most beautiful Christmas-box was contained in the letter, which his mother read aloud with tears of emotion. The good aunt wrote that she had seen from Elsbeth's last letters that it was her husband's dearest wish to be able to give a better education to his two eldest boys, and that in consequence she had decided to receive them in her own house, and to let them go to college at her expense. His brothers shouted with joy, his mother cried, his father walked up and down the room, passed his hand through his hair, and muttered excited words.

He meanwhile sat quietly at his sisters' little bed, rejoicing inwardly.

Then his mother came to him, buried her face in his hair, and said,

"Will *you* ever have such luck, my boy?"

"Oh, he," said his father—"he never understands anything!"

"He is so young still!" answered his mother, stroking his cheeks; and then she dressed him in his beautiful velvet coat, and he was allowed to wear it till night because it was a holiday. And his brothers came and fondled him, partly because their hearts were so full of joy, partly on account of the beautiful velvet coat. They had never been so good to him before.

Ah, that was a Christmas!

And as spring drew near a great deal of sewing and embroidering for the outfit began. Paul was allowed to help with the cutting-out: to hold the yard-measure and to hand the scissors; and the twins lay on the ground, rummaging among the white linen. The brothers were fitted out like two princes. Nothing was forgotten. They even received neckties, which his mother had manufactured from an old silk bodice.

The brothers meanwhile were immensely proud. They already played at being gentlemen in every possible way. Max rolled cigarettes by putting the tobacco from his father's canister into little paper bags, which he lighted at the thick end, and Gottfried put on a pair of spectacles, which he had purchased at school for six trouser buttons.

" Does this suit me ?" he asked, strutting up and down before Paul, and as the latter said " Yes," he was caressed ; had he said " No," he would have had a box on the ear.

Soon after Easter the two brothers went away. There was much weeping in the house, but when the dog-cart had rolled out of the yard gate his mother pressed her tear-stained face against Paul's cheeks and whispered,

"You have long been neglected, my poor child; now we two are together again as before."

"Mamma, tiss me, too!" screamed little Kate, stretching out her tiny arms, and her sister did the same.

"Yes; of course you are there as well!" their mother cried, and bright sunshine lighted up her pale face.

And then she took one on each arm and approached the window with them, and gazed a long time at the White House.

Paul hid his head in the folds of her dress and did the same.

His mother looked down upon him, and as she met the prematurely wise look in the child's eyes she blushed a little and smiled, but neither spoke a word.

When his father came back from the town he wanted Paul to begin going to school.

His mother grew very sad, and begged that he might be left at home for one half-year longer, so that she should not miss the two eldest ones too much. She would teach him herself, and surely get him on more than the school-master would do. But his father would not listen to anything of the sort, and called her "a weeping fool."

Paul was terrified. The longing for school that he had formerly felt had now quite disappeared; but then of course the brothers, whom he wished to emulate, were no longer there.

The following day his father took his hand and
led him into the village, the first houses of which
were a few hundred yards from Meyerhofer's farm—
at all events, a tolerable distance for such a little
fellow.

But Paul kept up bravely. He had such fear of
a thrashing from his father that he would have
marched to the end of the world.

The school was a low, thatched building, not
very different from a peasant's hut; but near it
there stood all sorts of long poles, ladders, and
scaffoldings.

"That's where lazy children are hanged," explained his father.

Paul's anxiety rose still higher; but when the
teacher, a kind old man with a white stubby beard
and greasy waistcoat, took him on his knee and
showed him a beautiful, many-colored picture-book,
he felt calmer; only the many strange faces that
stared at him from the benches seemed to forebode
no good to him.

He had to take the lowest place, and during two
hours made pothooks on a slate.

During the time for recreation the big boys came
up to him and asked about his luncheon, and when
they saw that it was a sausage sandwich they took
it away from him. He quietly yielded, for he
thought it must needs be so. On the way home
they beat him, and one stuffed some nettles inside
his collar. He thought that, too, was only to be

expected because he was the smallest; but when he had left the village behind him and was walking alone across the sunny heath, he began to cry. He threw himself down underneath a juniper-tree and gazed up at the blue sky, where the swallows flitted to and fro.

"Oh, if only one could fly like that, too," he thought. Then the White House came into his mind; he raised himself up, and strained his eyes to look for it; it shone from afar (like the enchanted castles of which his mother spoke in her fairy tales); the windows sparkled like carbuncles, and the green bushes surrounded it like a hedge of thorns of a hundred years' growth.

A feeling of pride and self-importance mixed with his grief. "You are big now," he said to himself, "for you go to school. And if you were to undertake your pilgrimage now, nobody could say anything against it."

And then fear overcame him again. The wicked bull and the mad dogs—one never knew. He resolved to consider the matter till next Sunday.

But henceforth the White House left him no peace. Each time when he went across the heath he asked himself what could really be in that road more than on the road to school. The high-road, indeed, ran across a dark fir-wood, and in such woods all sorts of goblins and witches live; even wolves are no rare occurrence, as the story of Little Red Ridinghood clearly shows; but if he were to

go over the fields he could always keep his home
in view and be sure of the way back.

It seemed to him he was in honor bound to undertake this journey, because he was "big" now,
and when his fears arose anew he called himself a
coward. This word in school was considered a
great insult.

When Sunday came he resolved to risk the ex-
pedition. He crept along the fence, and ran as
quickly as he could across his father's meadows, in
the direction of the White House.

Then came a stile which could be easily climbed
over, and then a piece of unknown heath-land, on
which he had never yet been. But there was nothing dangerous here, either. The heath glittered in
the sun, the withered hawkweed crackled at his feet,
a warm wind blew softly towards him. He tried
to whistle, but still he had to draw in the air to
produce any sound. At that he was ashamed, and
a feeling of despondency seized him. Then came
a swampy moor that again belonged to his father.
Of this the latter often spoke; he meditated the
idea of cutting peat there, but he only wanted to
begin on a large scale, and for that he lacked the
necessary capital. Paul sank up to his ankles in
the marsh, and now for the first time the thought
occurred to him that he might, perhaps, dirty his
new boots. He was terrified, for he remembered
his mother saying: " Be very careful of them. my
boy; I have saved them from my milk money."

He was also wearing his beautiful velvet coat, because it was Sunday. He looked down at the shining silk braid, and for a moment hesitated whether he had not better return, not for the sake of the velvet coat, but only in order not to grieve his mother.

"But perhaps I shall get through unhurt," he consoled himself by thinking, and began to run on. The ground gave under his feet, and at every step a squashy sound was heard, as if the handle were being draw out of a churn.

Then came a black morass, at the edge of which stood white-haired cotton-grass, and on which swam a layer of dissolved iron, shining like verdigris.

He carefully avoided it, though he got into the morass after all, but finally struggled back to dry land. The boots were ruined, but he thought perhaps he could wash them secretly at the pump.

He marched on. He was no longer in the mood to whistle, and the clearer the White House rose from the bushes, the more embarrassed he felt. He could already distinguish a kind of rampart, which was surrounded by trees, and through a breach in the foliage he saw a long, low building, which from a distance he had never noticed; behind that another one, and in a black hollow a high flame which quivered up and down. "That must be a forge; but did they work even on Sundays?"

An incomprehensible desire to cry seized him, and while he blindly ran on tears gushed from his eyes.

Suddenly he saw a wide ditch before him filled to the edge with water. He knew very well he could not get across, but obstinacy compelled him to prepare for a spring, and the next moment the thick and dirty water closed over him.

He reached land wet to the skin, covered with a layer of morass and weeds.

He tried to let his clothes dry, sat down on the grass, and looked over at the White House. He had grown quite despondent, and as he began to shiver very much, he turned sadly and slowly homeward.

CHAPTER IV.

THE summer which followed brought nothing but grief and care to Meyerhofer's house. The former owner wished to have the mortgage paid off, and there was no prospect of any one lending the necessary sum.

Meyerhofer drove to the town three or four times weekly, and returned home late at night dead drunk. Sometimes he stayed away for the whole night.

Frau Elsbeth meanwhile sat upright in her bed and stared into the darkness. Paul often woke when he heard her low sobs; then for a while he would lie as quiet as a mouse, because he did not want her to know that he was awake, but at last he would begin to cry, too.

Then his mother became quiet; and if he could not stop crying she got up, kissed him, and stroked his cheek; or she said,

"Come to me, my boy."

Then he sprang up, slipped into her bed, and went to sleep on her shoulder again.

His father often beat him — he seldom knew why; but he took the blows for granted.

One day he heard his father scolding his mother.

"Do not cry, you blubbering fool," he said; "you are only here to make my misery worse."

"But, Max," she answered, softly, "will you prevent your family from bearing your misfortune with you? Must we not keep closer together when we are so unhappy?"

Then he was moved, said she was his brave wife, and called himself bad names.

Frau Elsbeth tried to pacify him, bade him confide in her, and be brave.

"Yes, be brave—be brave!" he cried, getting angry again. "It is all very fine for you women to speak so; you sit at home, and spread your apron out, waiting humbly for fortune or misfortune to fall into your laps, just as kind Fate may send it. But we men must go forth into hostile life; we must struggle and strive and fight with all sorts of rogues. Away with your warnings! Be brave; yes, indeed, be brave!"

Then he walked out of the room with heavy steps, and ordered the trap to be got ready, in order to set off on his usual pilgrimage.

When he came back, and had slept off his intoxication, he said:

"There, now my last hope is gone. The d—d Jew, who wanted to advance the money at twenty-five per cent., declares he will have nothing more to do with me. Well, let him do the other thing. I don't care a straw for him. And at Michaelmas we may really go a-begging, for this time nothing remains to us but what we stand up in. But this I tell you: this time I shall not survive the blow. An honorable man must set some value on himself, and if one fine morning you see me swinging from the rafters, don't be astonished."

The mother uttered a piercing cry, and clung with both arms round his neck.

"Well, well, well!" he calmed her; "it was not meant so seriously. You women-folk are all the same deplorable creatures, a mere word upsets you."

The mother started and stepped back from him, but when he had gone out she seated herself at the window, and looked after him anxiously, as if she feared he might already be thinking of doing himself a mischief. From time to time a shudder ran through her frame, as if she were cold.

In the following night, Paul, waking, observed that she got up, put on a petticoat, and went to the window from which the White House could be seen. It was bright moonlight—perhaps she really gazed at it. For wellnigh two hours she sat there, looking out fixedly. Paul did not stir, and when, with the approach of dawn, she came back from the window and stepped to her children's bedsides, he closed his eyes firmly and feigned to sleep. She first kissed the twins, who were sleeping with their arms entwined; then she came to him, and as she bent down over him he heard her whisper, "God give me strength. It must be." Then he guessed that something extraordinary was in preparation.

3

When, the following afternoon, he came home from school, he saw his mother sitting in the arbor in her hat and cloak and Sunday clothes; her cheeks were paler than usual; her hands, which lay in her lap, trembled.

She seemed to have been waiting for him, for when she saw him she breathed more freely.

"Are you going out, mamma?" he asked, wonderingly.

"Yes, my boy," she answered, "and you shall go with me."

"To the village, mamma?"

"No, my boy"—her voice quivered—"not to the village. You must put on your Sunday clothes; the velvet coat, of course, is spoiled, but I have taken the stains out of your gray jacket—it will still do; and you must polish your boots quickly."

"Where are we going, then, mamma?"

Then she laid her arms round him, and said, softly,

"To the White House."

He felt a sudden fever of excitement. The exultant joy which welled up from his heart nearly choked him; he jumped on his mother's lap and kissed her impetuously.

"But you must tell nobody," she whispered—"nobody; do you understand?"

He nodded, full of importance. He was such a clever fellow. He knew what it was all about.

"And now dress yourself quickly."

Paul flew up-stairs to the room where his clothes were kept, and suddenly—he never clearly knew on which step it was—a long-drawn shrill sound escaped his mouth; there was no doubt any more—he could whistle! he tried for the second, the third time—it went splendidly.

When he came back to his mother in all his finery he shouted, jubilantly, "Mamma, I can whistle!" and was astonished that she showed so little interest in his art. She only pulled his collar straight and said, " You happy children !"

Then she took his hand, and their pilgrimage began. When they reached the dark fir-wood in which the wolves and goblins lived he had just finished his studies for " Kommt ein Vogel geflogen " (A Bird Comes A-flying), and when they came out again into the open field he could be sure that " Heil Dir im Siegerkranz " (God Save the Queen) went without a flaw.

His mother looked down at him with a sad smile ; each shrill note made her start, but she said nothing. The White House now stood close before them. He no longer thought of his new art. All his faculties were absorbed in what he saw.

First there came a high red-brick wall with a gate in it, on the posts of which stood two stone heads ; then farther on a large grass-grown court ; whole rows of wagons stood in it, and it was flanked by low gray farm buildings, forming a big square. In the middle lay a sort of pool, surrounded by a low hedge of may, in which a troop of quacking ducks were making merry.

"And where is the White House, mamma?" asked Paul, whom this did not please at all.

" Behind the garden," replied his mother.   Her voice had a strange, husky sound, and her hand clasped his so firmly that he almost screamed with pain.

Now they turned the corner of the garden fence, and before Paul's eyes lay a simple two-storied house, closely shaded by lime-trees, and having little or nothing remarkable about it.   It did not look nearly as white, either, as from the distance.

" Is this it?" asked Paul, drawling out the words.

"Yes; this is it," answered his mother.

"And where are the glass balls and the sundial?" he asked.

A desire to cry came over him suddenly.   He had imagined everything a thousand times more beautiful: if they had cheated him regarding the glass balls and the sundial as well, he would not have been surprised.

At this moment two Newfoundland dogs, as black as coal, came rushing up to them with suppressed barks.   He took refuge behind his mother's dress and began to scream.

" Caro! Nero !" called a sweet childish voice from the house door, and the two monsters, howling joyfully, rushed off in the direction whence the voice came.

A little girl, smaller still than Paul, in a pink-flowered frock, round which a kind of Scotch sash was tied, appeared before the house. She had long, golden curls, which were drawn back from her forehead by a round comb, and a small, delicate little nose, which she carried rather high.

"Do you wish to speak to mamma?" she asked in her gentle, soft voice, and smiled at the same time.

"Are you called Elsbeth, my child?" inquired his mother, in return.

"Yes; I am called Elsbeth."

His mother made a movement as if she wanted to clasp the strange child in her arms, but she mastered herself, and said,

"Will you lead us to your mother?"

"Mamma is in the garden: she is just drinking coffee," said the little girl, with much importance. "I would rather lead you round the front of the house, because if we open the door on the sunny side so many flies come in directly."

His mother smiled. Paul wondered that this had never struck him at home.

"She is much cleverer than you are," he thought.

Now they entered the garden. It was much larger and more beautiful than the one at Mussainen, but there was nothing to be seen of a sundial. Paul had formed a vague idea of it as a great golden tower, on which a round, sparkling disk of the sun formed the dial-plate.

"Where is the sundial, mamma?" he asked.

"I will show it to you afterwards," said the little girl, eagerly.

From the arbor came a tall, slender lady, with a pale, delicate face, on which shone an inexpressibly sweet smile.

His mother gave a cry, and threw herself on her breast, sobbing loudly.

"Thank God that I have you with me once again!" said the stranger, and kissed his mother on her brow and cheeks.

"Believe me, all will now be well; you will tell me what weighs upon your mind, and it will be strange if I cannot help you."

His mother dried her eyes and smiled.

"Oh, this is pure joy," she said; "I feel already so relieved and happy because I am near you. I have longed for you so much."

"And could you really not come?"

His mother shook her head sadly.

"Poor woman!" said the lady, and both looked for a long time into each other's eyes.

"And this, I suppose, is my godchild?" the lady exclaimed, pointing towards Paul, who clung to his mother's dress and sucked his thumb.

"Oh, fie! take your finger from your mouth," said his mother. And the beautiful, kind lady took him on her lap, gave him a teaspoonful of honey—"as a sort of foretaste," she said—and asked him after his little sisters, about school, and all sorts of other things which it was not at all difficult to answer, so that at last he almost felt comfortable on her lap.

"And what things do you know already, you little man?" she asked him at last.

"I can whistle," he answered, proudly.

The kind woman laughed heartily, and said, "Well, then, whistle us something."

He pointed his lips and tried to whistle, but the sound would not come; he had forgotten it again.

Then they laughed—the kind lady, the little girl, and even his mother; but tears rose to his eyes with shame; he struggled and kicked, so that the lady had to let him glide down from her lap, and his mother said, reproachfully,

"You are naughty, Paul."

But he went behind the arbor and cried, until the little girl came to him and said:

"Oh dear, you must not cry. God does not like naughty children." Then he was ashamed again, and rubbed his eyes with his hands till they were dry.

"And now I will show you the sundial," continued the child.

"Oh yes, and the glass balls," he said.

"They were broken a long time ago," she replied; "a stone I threw flew by accident into one of them, and the other was blown down by a storm." And then she showed him the spots where they had stood.

"And this is the sundial," she went on.

"Where?" he asked, looking round, wonderingly.

They were standing before a gray, unpretending post, on which was fastened a sort of wooden plate. The child laughed, and said that this was the sundial.

"Oh, fie!" he retorted, angrily; "you are mocking me."

"Why should I want to mock you?" she asked; "you have never done me any harm." And then she repeated her assertion that this was the sundial, and nothing else, and she also pointed out to him the hand, a miserable rusty piece of metal, which stuck out from the middle of the dial and threw its shadow just on number six, which was written there among other figures.

"Oh, this is too stupid," he said, and turned away. The sundial in the garden of the White House was the first great disappointment of his life.

When he returned to the arbor with his new friend, he found a tall, broad-shouldered gentleman with bushy whiskers there, who wore a gray shooting-coat, and whose eyes seemed to twinkle merrily.

"Who is that?" asked Paul, timidly, hiding behind his friend.

She laughed and said, "That is my papa; you need not be afraid of him."

And, shouting with joy, she jumped on the strange man's knee.

Then he thought to himself, would he ever dare to jump on *his* papa's knee, and from this he concluded that all fathers were not alike.

But the man in the shooting-coat caressed his child, kissed her on both cheeks, and let her ride on his knees.

"See! Elsbeth has got a playfellow," said the kind, strange lady, pointing towards Paul, who, hidden by the foliage, glanced shyly towards the arbor.

"Just come here, my boy," the man called out merrily and snapped his fingers.

"Come—here, on the other knee; there is room enough for you," called out the child; and when, with a questioning glance at his mother, he crept timidly nearer, the strange man seized him, put him on his other knee, and then they had a merry race.

He had lost all fear, and when freshly-baked cakes were put on the table, he fell to bravely. His mother stroked his hair and warned him not to eat too much. She spoke very softly, and kept looking down upon the ground before her. And then the children were allowed to go to the bushes and pick gooseberries for themselves.

"Are you really called Elsbeth?" he asked his friend, and as she said "Yes," he expressed his astonishment that she had the same name as his mother.

"But I have been christened after her," said the child; "she is my godmother."

"Why didn't she kiss you, then?" he asked.

"I don't know," said Elsbeth, sadly, "perhaps she does not like me."

But that she had not had the courage to do it never occurred to either of them.

It already began to grow dark when the children were called back.

"We must go home," said his mother.

He was very sorry, because he had just now begun to like it. His mother pulled his collar straight, and said: "There, now kiss the lady's hand and thank her."

He did as he was ordered, the kind lady kissed his forehead, and the man in the shooting-coat lifted him high up into the air, so that he thought he could fly.

And now his mother took Elsbeth in her arms, and kissed her several times on her mouth and cheeks, and said: "May Heaven some day reward you, my child, for what your parents have done for your godmother."

A heavy burden seemed to be taken from her soul; she breathed more freely and her eyes shone.

Elsbeth and her parents went with the two as far as the gate, when his mother took leave of them there over again, and stammered all sorts of things about compensation and divine blessings. The man interrupted her laughingly, and said the whole affair was not worth mentioning and did not require any thanks at all. And the kind woman kissed her warmly, and asked her to come again very soon, or at least to send the children.

The mother smiled sadly and was silent. Elsbeth was allowed to go a few steps farther; then she took leave with a little courtesy. Paul's heart was heavy; he felt there was still something he had to tell her, so he ran after her, and, when he had caught up to her, whispered into her ear,

" You know—I *can* whistle all the same !"

When mother and son entered the wood, night was closing in. It was pitch-dark all round, but he was not afraid in the least. If a wolf had come in their way now he would soon have shown him who had the best of it.

His mother did not speak; the hand which clasped his so firmly burned feverishly, and her breath came from her breast like a sigh.

And when they both stepped out onto the heath the moon rose pale and majestic on the horizon. A blue veil spread over the distance. Thyme and juniper sent forth their perfume, here and there a little bird twittered on the ground.

The mother sat down at the edge of the ditch, and looked across at their sad home to which all her care was devoted. The outlines of the buildings stood out clearly against the evening sky. One lonely light twinkled from the kitchen.

Suddenly she spread out her arms, and called out over the silent heath, "Oh, I am happy !"

Paul clung to her side almost anxiously, for

never yet had he heard a similar cry from her. He
was so much accustomed to her tears and her sorrow that this exultant joy seemed to him quite un-
canny.

And then it occurred to him: "What will father
say when he hears of this walk? Will he not scold
mother and be even more angry with her than
usual?" A sullen defiance took possession of him;
he set his teeth, then he stroked his mother's hand
consolingly, kissed her, and whispered,

"He shall not harm you!"

"Who?" she asked, with a shudder.

"Father," he said, softly and hesitatingly.

She sighed deeply but answered nothing, and silently and sadly they went on.

The gray woman had flitted across their path
and spoiled the moment of joy, and it was the only
one that Fate had still in store for Frau Elsbeth.

Next day there was a bad hour between herself
and her husband. He called her undutiful and dishonorable. By her begging she had added disgrace
to poverty.

However, he took the money.

CHAPTER V.

YEARS passed away.

Paul grew up a quiet, unpretending boy, with a shy look and awkward behavior.

Generally he kept apart, and, while he took care of the twins, would sit for hours working at some wood-carving without saying a single word. He was what one calls in his part of the country "fussy:" a nature inclined to worry about details and brooding anxiously by himself.

He had no intercourse with any boys of his age, not even in school. Not that he avoided them on purpose; on the contrary, he liked to help them, and more than one used to copy, in the morning before prayers, his arithmetic problems or his German composition; but their interests were not his, and therefore he could not befriend them.

He also got an abundance of thrashings; especially from the brothers Erdmann—two saucy, wild-eyed fellows, loved and feared as the strongest and most daring—he had much to suffer. They were inexhaustible in the invention of new tricks which imbittered his life: they threw his copybooks on the top of the stove, filled his satchel

with sand, and let his cap, in which they put a stick
for a mast, float down the river like a boat. Most
of these injuries he bore patiently; only once or
twice a blind fury came over him. Then he bit and
scratched like a madman, so that even those companions who were much stronger than he wisely
took to flight. The first time one of the boys had
called his father a drunkard, and another time they
wanted to lock him up in a dark cow-shed with a
little girl.

Afterwards he was ashamed, and came of his own
accord to beg pardon. Then they only laughed at
him the more, and the hardly-won respect was lost
again.

Learning went on with great difficulty. The task
for which his comrades hardly needed fifteen minutes he required an hour or two to finish. On the
other hand, his handwriting was like copper-plate
and there never was a mistake in his sums.

All the same, no work seemed done well enough
to satisfy himself, and often his mother surprised
him as he got up at night on the sly, because he
was afraid that what he had learned by heart had
escaped his memory.

That he should go to a better school, like his
brothers, was not to be thought of. His mother
had for some time cherished the plan of letting him
follow the two elder ones as soon as they had passed
their examination, for it pained her mother's heart
that he should be behind the others; but in the

end she gave in, and that was certainly for the best.

Paul himself had never expected anything else. He considered himself as a creature totally subordinate compared to his brothers, and had long since given up trying ever to be like them. When they came home for their holidays—velvet caps on their wavy hair, many-colored ribbons on their breasts, for they belonged to some forbidden school corporation—he looked up to them as to beings from a higher world. Eagerly he listened when they began to talk to each other about Sallust and Cicero, and the tragedies of Æschylus—and they liked to speak about them a great deal, if only to impress him. But the object of his highest admiration was the thick book, on the first page of which was written "Table of Logarithms," and which from the first page to the last contained nothing but figures —figures in long, close rows, the mere sight of which made him giddy. "How learned he must be, to have all that in his head," he said to himself, caressing the cover of the book, for he imagined that they had to do no less than learn all those figures by heart.

The brothers were unusually affable and condescending to him; when they wished to have anything in the house, when they desired a saddled horse or an extra stiff glass of grog, they always addressed him confidentially, and he felt highly honored to be allowed to help them.

As regards farming matters, he was as well acquainted with them as if he were the master of the house himself; to them were devoted all his efforts and his care.

What was it that had made him so prematurely serious?

Was it the helplessness of his lonely mother, who had initiated him so early into all her cares? Was it the brooding, striving spirit, ever looking to the future, which was peculiar to him?

Very often when he sat musing, his elbows leaning on the table—in his manners, too, he was quite like a grown-up person—his mother stroked his hair, and said,

"Let us see a bright face, my boy; be glad that you have no cares yet." Oh, he had cares enough! Care cleaved to him like his own flesh and blood: whether the hen which had strayed to-day would be found again to-morrow; whether the ointment which his father had brought from the town yesterday would agree with a dun-colored horse; whether the hay had been dry enough before it was turned; and how the starlings in the gutter on the roof would bring up their little ones without the cat getting at them.

And he had to care about everything. Care had been born with him; only for himself he never took any care.

The older and more reasonable he grew, the deeper, too, grew his understanding of the mis-

management which his father had allowed to pre-
vail, and often a deep sigh came from his breast:
"Oh, if I were only big already!" The fear of his
father's wrath did not let him express his anxieties,
and if ever he dared to speak his mind to his
mother, she looked with fearful eyes all around the
room, and said, anxiously, " Be quiet."

And yet his father saw very well whither his son's
thoughts tended. He had given him the nickname
of "Cotquean," and jeered at him whenever he saw
him. That naturally was in his good moments; in
his bad ones he thrashed him with the yard measure, with the handle of the whip, with the straps of
the harness—with whatever was nearest his hand.
Paul feared his hand itself most of all, the blows of
which hurt more than all the sticks in the world.
His father had a strange manner of boxing his
ears. He flung his hand into his face with the
knuckles outward, so that the nails and joints left
bruises on his cheeks. This kind of blow he called
his "cheek-comforter," and when he intended beating Paul he called out to him in the most affable
tone, " Come here, my son, I want to comfort you."

When he had received his beating he used to
run out trembling onto the heath in shame and
pain, and while he made faces and drummed with
his fists, to choke down his tears, he whistled.

In whistling he manifested not only all his longings, his childish dreams, but also his anger and
indignation. The feelings for which his uncouth

mind did not find any expression, for which he
lacked words or even thoughts, he dared in this
loneliness to pour forth unchecked by means of
whistling.   So his depressed, timid soul found an
outlet.   Whole symphonies he executed, shrill and
harsh at the beginning, growing softer and softer,
and at last melting away in sadness and resigna-
tion.

Nobody guessed the art he practised by himself,
and how much consolation and exultation he owed
to that same art—not even his mother.

Since he had seen her break into tears, one
winter's night, as he, without heeding her, had softly
whistled to himself—since that time he left off as
soon as she came near him; he thought it hurt
her. What power was given him in those sounds
he little knew.

Only at times he was proud—looking towards the
White House—that he had after all learned to whistle; and when some melody seemed to him especially good, he thought within himself, "Who knows
if you would laugh at me if you were to hear this?"

But never had he met any of them again.

CHAPTER VI.

For some time past Mr. Meyerhofer had gone about with great plans in his head. He had discovered that the turf moor which surrounded the farm in a wide circle was in a condition to afford a sure profit. Already, twice or thrice, when need had been sorest, he had, to make shift, ordered peat to be cut, and sent five cart-loads to the town.

Secretly, quite secretly—for he was too proud to be considered as nothing better than a common peat-cutting farmer. His people had each time brought home twenty to twenty-five marks clear gain, and said that there was far more to be gained still in this way, because black, firm peat was an article much in demand in the market.

But Meyerhofer was not to be induced to utilize the moor in this manner. "I have never bothered about such trifles," he said; "I'd rather be ruined wholesale than earn in detail," and then he drew himself up like a hero.

But the moor did not let him rest. It was in September, after an unusually favorable harvest, when Lob Levy, the complaisant friend of all farmers in debt, appeared on the farm twice or thrice weekly, and had much to negotiate with the master. Frau Elsbeth trembled with fear as soon as the Jew, in his dirty caftan, appeared at the gate. She seated herself at the window and followed untiringly every movement of the negotiators. If her husband assumed a thoughtful air she felt a cold shiver, and only when he smiled again she dared to breathe freely, too.

She anticipated no good, but did not venture to ask what kind of business her husband had to transact with this usurer.

She was soon to be enlightened. One afternoon Paul saw how a strange vehicle came rumbling along on the road from the town, which looked in the distance like an immense black copper on wheels. Something that appeared to be a chimney stuck out beyond it, and when the wheels staggered on the uneven ground bent to the right and the left like a man politely bowing. He gazed at the wonder for a while, then ran to his mother, whom he eagerly pulled to the door by her dress.

She shaded her eyes with her hand and looked down the road. "That is a locomobile," she said at last.

Paul knew as much as before. "What is a locomobile?" he asked.

"A steam-engine which can be moved anywhere, and which great land-owners use to turn their thrashing-machines; one can also harrow and plough with it, for such a thing has more strength than ten horses."

"But why is it drawn by horses, then?" he asked.

"Because by itself it cannot move anywhere," was the answer.

He did not understand that. "Anyhow," he thought, "it must be a great happiness to possess such a thing with that strange name, and if we ever become rich—"

At this moment his father came rushing out of the house in great excitement; he had a slipper on one foot, a boot on the other, and his necktie had turned to the back of his neck.

"They are coming! they are coming!" he cried, clapping his hands; then he caught his wife round the waist and danced with her into the middle of the road.

She looked at him with great anxious eyes, as if she wanted to say, "What fresh nonsense have you contrived now?" But he would not let her go, and when the twins in their pink cotton frocks and dark little pigtails came running out of the garden, he made for them, took them in his arms, let them dance on his shoulders, and pretended to throw them over the ditch, so that the mother could only stop this nonsense by most ardent pleading.

"There, you little rogues," he cried, "rejoice and dance. All poverty is ended now; next spring we shall measure our money by the bushel."

The mother looked at him askance, but said nothing.

The monster came nearer and nearer. Paul stood there motionless—all eyes. Then he looked up at his mother, whose face was care-worn, and a certain fear came over him as if now the devil had come into the house; but then he remembered how his wish of a moment ago was fulfilled, and he resolved to meet the black guest with full confidence.

Meanwhile all the farm-servants and maids came hurrying from the stables and kitchen. All the inmates of the Haidehaus stood in a row by the fence and gazed at the approaching wonder.

"But tell me, what do you want to do with it?" Frau Elsbeth at last asked her husband.

He threw a pitying glance at her; then he laughed shortly, and said, "Drive about in it."

Frau Elsbeth asked no more. Her husband, turning to the upper farm-servant, expounded his plans: how he would begin peat-cutting on a large scale; cutting and pressing machines were also on the way, and to-morrow, early, work could begin. Then he gave him orders to go to the village to engage the necessary workmen. Ten men would suffice for the beginning, but he hoped soon to need as many as twenty or thirty.

Frau Elsbeth mutely shook her head, and went into the house just as the locomobile arrived before the gate. Paul never tired of looking and admiring. Behind the yellow screws and crooked handles there seemed to lie a world of mystery; the place for the fire, with the grate and ash-box beneath, seemed to him like the entrance to that fiery furnace, in which the well-known three holy men had once intoned their song of praise; and the chimney above all, standing threateningly upright, with its wreath of pine soot at its mouth, which seemed to lead down into blackness and fathomless depths!

Paul did not heed the little basket-carriage that drove behind the monster, in which sat Lob Levy, with his shaggy, reddish beard, and his merry, twinkling eyes; he did not heed the screaming of the carmen, and the exultation of his two little sisters, who danced like mad round the wheels. He stood there dazed with wonder, as if he could not understand yet what was happening around him.

When, later on, he entered the big room, he found his mother crouching in the corner of the sofa, crying.

He put his arm round her neck; but she kept him gently off, and said, "Go and look after the little ones, so that they do not get under the wheels."

"But why do you cry, mamma?"

"You will see in time, my boy," she said, stroking his hair. "Lob Levy is in it—you will see in time."

Then he felt angry with his mother! When all were joyful why should she sit moping in a corner and cry? But the joy was now over for him; and when he saw Lob Levy loiter about the yard, in his long black "heel-warmer," he would have liked most to favor Caro with a hint towards his calves.

The twins were quite beside themselves with joy. They took a cord, and crying "gee" and "whoa," raced wildly through the garden. One of them was the locomobile, the other the horse, but each wanted to be the locomobile, because then she got father's black hat put on for the chimney.

Before going to sleep they had already given a name to the new monster.

They maintained that it resembled the fat servant-girl with a long neck, who a short time ago had been dismissed on account of her slatternliness, and they called it, after her, "Black Susy."

The locomobile kept this name forever after in Meyerhofer's house.

Next morning the noise began afresh. The ten hired workmen stood in the yard and did not know what to do. Meyerhofer wanted to have the engine heated, but Lob Levy, who had passed the night in a shed in order to be at hand the first thing in the morning, wanted first to receive his price, as it had been settled in the agreement, because the grain had to be delivered in town by noon.

"What grain?" the mother asked, turning pale.

Well, it could not be denied any longer: Meyerhofer had sold almost the whole harvest — the thrashed corn as well as the amount still to be thrashed—to the Jew for the old worn-out engine.

Triumphantly the latter drove away with the beautiful full sacks. And this was only a sort of premium; towards Christmas he would come and fetch the rest.

A feeling of discouragement overcame for a moment even the light-minded Meyerhofer himself when he saw the high-piled carts disappear behind the woods; but in the next he put his hands defiantly into his trousers-pockets, and ordered that the machine should be got ready without delay.

At the same time as the monster a man in a blue blouse and with a brandy-nose had come to the farm; he called himself "stoker," and distinguished himself by constantly eating onions; he said that this was good for the digestion. This man fancied himself the hero of the day. Puffed up with pride, he stood near the engine, called it his foster-child, and stroked the rusty iron walls with his black, knotty hand, that sounded as if two graters were rubbed together. With a great show of foreign words he explained to every one who came near him the inner arrangement of the "lookmanbile," as he called his foster-child, only he had to have some drink; otherwise he was abusive. But if he got the amount of brandy which he wanted, he was deeply moved, and swore he would rather have his hands and feet cut off than ever separate himself from his foster-child. He had got to love it like his own flesh and blood, and thought a thousand times more of it than of any human being in the world.

Meyerhofer walked proudly round him, for this pearl was now his property, too, and he declared over and over again that here one could see what German faithfulness meant.

But when the engine was to be heated, the very faithful man could nowhere be found. At last he was discovered on a hay-stack asleep. When he was awakened, he called this proceeding ill-treatment of human beings, and could only with great trouble be induced to come out of his corner.

The heating of the engine was a new festival. Paul stood before the fire, and stared with dreamy eyes into the glowing depths which opened yawning, as if it wished to swallow something alive. He thought of the old heathenish idol Moloch, about whom he had heard in his biblical history, and every moment he expected to see a pair of red, glowing arms stretch themselves forth. And then in the body of the monster there arose a mysterious singing, at times hollow, like the distant roar of a forest, then again delicate and high, like soft angels' voices. Then it began to hiss in the valves — steam clouds rose, the iron shovel clattered, and fresh heaps of coal sank rattling into the furnace. There was such a noise all round that one could hardly hear one's own voice. The stoker with the red nose stood there like a king; he drank from a flat-bodied flask, and from time to time he handled the valves, sending forth a loud, imperious bellowing like a tamer of wild beasts. And then the big wheel began to turn—surr, surr, surr—always quicker and quicker. One became quite giddy by merely looking on, and then there was a crack—a clatter—a hissing—the great wheel stood still forever.

At first the stoker gave himself great airs, and declared in half an hour the whole damage would be repaired, but when Meyerhofer, after two days' work, urged him to have done with his repairs, he became abusive, and declared that this old heap of rubbish could not be repaired any more, and that it was just good enough to be sold to the dealer for old iron.

"Foster-child?" he thanked you for such a foster-child; he was still a little too good to look after such a heap of rubbish. And then it came out: Lob Levy had picked him up three days ago in some low den, and had asked him whether he would like to live like a king for a week—longer the joke would not last, anyhow. And only on this assurance he had gone with him, for to stay in one place longer than eight days was against his principles.

Hereupon he was driven from the farm.

Next day Meyerhofer sent for the village blacksmith, that he might look at the damage. He again fumbled about the engine for a few days, ate and drank for two, and declared in the end that if it was not all right now the devil was in it.

The heating was repeated; but "Black Susy" was not to be brought to life again.

When, towards Christmas, Lob Levy came to the farm to fetch the rest of the grain, Myerhofer thrashed him with the handle of his own whip. The Jew screamed " Murder !" and drove away hastily. But soon a lawyer's messenger with a big red-sealed letter appeared. Myerhofer swore and drank more than ever, and the end of it all was that he was sentenced to pay all costs of the case and compensation money as well. Only with great difficulty he escaped the punishment of imprisonment.

Since that day he would not see " Black Susy " any longer. She was put into the farthest shed, and stood there in concealment many a year without anybody ever looking at her.

Only Paul from time to time secretly took the key of the shed and crept in to the black monster that he loved more and more, and which at last appeared to him like a dumb, ill-treated friend.

CHAPTER VII.

WHEN Paul was fourteen years old his father decided to send him to confirmation-classes.

"He will never learn anything decent in school, anyhow," he said; "time and money are thrown away upon him. Therefore, he shall be confirmed at once, so that he can make himself useful on the farm. He will never be anything better than a peasant, anyhow."

Paul was satisfied, for he was longing to take a part of the care which pressed on his mother upon his own shoulders. He thought of making himself a sort of inspector, who could at any time replace the absent master, and work himself where the farm-servants needed a good example. He hoped this activity might be the beginning of a new, prosperous time, and when he lay in his bed at night he dreamed of waving cornfields and brand-new massive barns. The resolution to use all his strength to bring the neglected Haidehof into good repute became stronger and stronger.

The brothers one day should be able to say of him : "He has been of some good, after all, even if he could not follow us in our brilliant careers."

Yes; the brothers! How tall and distinguished they had grown meanwhile. One of them studied philology, and the other had entered a big bank as clerk. In spite of their good aunt, both wanted money, much money—far, far more than their father could send them. Paul hoped that for them also, as a result of his beginning farming, a better time would come. All surplus money should be sent to them, and he! oh, he would save and scrape, so that they might strive for their lofty aims, free from need and care.

With these pious thoughts Paul made his way to the first confirmation class. It was a sunny spring morning at the beginning of the month of April.

The fresh grass on the heath shone in greenish lights, juniper and heather budded with new tender shoots, anemones and ranunculus were blooming at the edge of the wood.

A warm wind waved over the heath towards him; he could have shouted aloud, and his heart was quite filled with rapture.

"There must be something sad in store," he said to himself, "for on earth one may not feel so happy."

Before the rectory garden there stood a long row of conveyances, only a few of which he knew. There was also aristocratic carriages among them. The coachmen with their shining buttons sat on their boxes with proud smiles and threw contemptuous glances all around.

In the garden were assembled a big troop of children. The boys and girls stood apart. Among the boys were the two brothers from whom he had had to suffer so much formerly, and who had ceased going to school for the last year. They gave him a friendly greeting, and while one of them shook hands with him the other tripped him up.

Some of the girls walked arm in arm on the paths. Some also had put their arms round each other's waists and giggled. Most of them were strangers to him. Some seemed especially aristocratic; they wore fine gray ulsters, and had hats with feathers on their heads. The carriages outside must belong to them.

He looked down at his jacket, to assure himself that he had nothing to be ashamed of. It was made of fine black cloth, from an old evening suit of his student brother's, and looked as good as new, only that the seams were a little shiny. Taken altogether, he did not need to be ashamed of himself.

A bell sounded. The candidates were called into the church. Paul felt light-hearted and pious in the solemn twilight of the house of God. He did not think of his jacket any longer; the forms of the boys around grew shadowy.

At both sides of the altar benches were placed. On the right the boys were to have their seats, and on the left the girls.

Paul was pushed into the back row, where the little ones and the poor sat. Between two barefooted cottage children, who wore coarse, ragged jackets, he took his seat. Past the shoulders of the boys before him he saw how the girls on the other side ranged themselves: the most distinguished in front, and then the more poorly clad.

He was thinking whether in heaven the order of rank would be a similar one, and the verse occurred to him:

"Blessed are the meek and lowly, for they shall be exalted."

The vicar came.

He was a comfortable-looking man, with a double chin and light, spare whiskers. His upper lip shone from frequent shaving. He did not wear his robe, but a simple black coat; nevertheless, he looked very dignified and solemn.

He first spoke a long prayer on the text, "Suffer little children to come unto Me," and added an exhortation to consider the coming year as a time of consecration, not to romp wildly or to dance, for that would not be in keeping with a student of religion.

"I have never romped or danced," thought Paul, and for a moment he was filled with pride over his pious conduct. "But it was a pity all the same—" he thought afterwards.

Then the vicar praised as the highest of all Christian virtues: humility. None of these children should feel above the others because their parents happened to be richer and more distinguished than those of their humbler brethren and sisters, because before God's throne they were all equal.

"That's for you," thought Paul, and lovingly seized the arm of his ragged neighbor. The latter thought he wanted to pinch him, and said, "Ow, don't!"

Then the vicar took from his pocket a piece of paper, and said, "Now I will read you the order of rank in which you will have to sit henceforth."

"Why this order of rank," thought Paul, "if before God's throne we are all equal?"

The very first name startled Paul, for it was "Elsbeth Douglas." He saw a tall, pale girl, with a gentle face and fair hair smoothly combed back, rise and walk towards the first place.

"So that's you," thought Paul, "and we shall be confirmed together." His heart beat with joy, but also with fear, because he was anxious at the same time lest she should think him too much beneath her. "Perhaps she does not remember me any more," he thought.

•He watched her as she took her seat with downcast eyes and a kind smile.

"No; she is not proud," he said softly to himself; but to make sure he looked at his jacket.

Then the boys were called up. The brothers Erdmann came first. Without asking, they had already placed themselves comfortably on the first seats, and then his own name was called out. At this moment Elsbeth Douglas did exactly as he

5

had done before. She raised her head quickly and scrutinized the ranks of the boys.

When he had seated himself in his place he also looked down on the ground, for he wanted to imitate her humility; and when he looked up again he saw her eyes on him, full of curiosity. He blushed and picked a little feather from the sleeve of his jacket.

And then the lesson began. The vicar explained passages from the Bible and heard verses of hymns. It was Elsbeth's turn first. She raised her head a little, and repeated her verses quietly and modestly.

"Oh golly! the hussy has courage," mumbled the younger Erdmann, who was at his left side.

Paul felt sudden anger rise within him. He could have cudgelled him in open church. "If he calls her 'hussy' again I shall thrash him afterwards." He promised this solemnly to himself. But the younger Erdmann no longer thought of her; he was busy sticking pins into the calves of the boys sitting behind him.

When the lesson was over, the girls left the church first, marching in couples. Only when the last were outside, the boys were allowed to follow. Just outside the church he met Elsbeth, who was walking towards her carriage. Both looked a little askance at each other and passed on. An old lady, with little gray curls and a Persian shawl, stood near her carriage; she probably had waited for her at the vicarage. She kissed Elsbeth's forehead, and both seated themselves on the back seat. The carriage was the finest one in the whole row. The coachman wore a beautiful fur cap with a red tassel; he had also smart braid on his collar and cuffs.

Just as the carriage had started, Paul was attacked by the two Erdmanns, who thrashed him a little.

"You ought to be ashamed, two against one," he said, and they let him go.

He went home very contentedly. The midday sun glittered on the open heath, and in misty distance the carriage rolled before him ; it grew smaller and smaller, and at last disappeared as a black spot in the fir-wood.

When he arrived home his mother kissed him on both cheeks, and asked, "Well, was it nice?"

"Quite nice," he answered, "and, mamma, Elsbeth from the White House was there, too."

Then she blushed with joy and asked all sorts of things : how she looked, whether she had grown pretty, and what she had said to him.

"Nothing at all," he answered, ashamed; and as his mother looked at him surprised, he added, eagerly, "but you know she is not proud."

Next Monday when he entered the church he found her already sitting in her place. She had the Bible lying on her knee, and was learning the verses they had been given as their task.

There were not many children there, and when

he sat down opposite to her she made a half movement as if she meant to get up and come over to
him; but she sat down again immediately and went
on learning.

His mother had told him before he left just to
address Elsbeth. She had charged him with many
greetings for her mother, and he was to ask, too,
how she was. On his way he had studied a long
speech, only he was not quite decided yet whether
to address her with "*Du*" or "*Sie.*" "*Du*" would
have been the simplest; his mother took it for
granted. But the "*Sie*" sounded decidedly more
distinguished—so nice and grown up. And as he
could come to no decision he avoided addressing
her at all. He, too, took out his Bible, and both
put their elbows on their knees and studied as if
for a wager.

It was not of much use to him, because when the
vicar questioned him afterwards he had forgotten
every word of it.

A painful silence ensued; the Erdmanns laughed
viciously, and he had to sit down again, his face
burning with shame. He dared not look up any
more, and when, on leaving the church, he saw
Elsbeth standing at the porch as if she was waiting
for something, he lowered his eyes and tried to
pass her quickly. However, she stepped forward
and spoke to him.

"My mother has charged me—I am to ask you
—how your mother is?"

He answered that she was well.

"And she sends her many kind regards," continued Elsbeth.

"And my mother also sends many kind regards to yours," he answered, turning the Bible and hymnbook between his fingers, "and I was to ask you, too, how she is?"

"Mamma told me to say," she replied, like something learned by heart, "that she is often ill, and has to keep in-doors very much; but now that spring is here she is better; and would you not like to drive in our carriage as far as your house? I was to ask you, she said."

"Just look, Meyerhofer is sweethearting!" cried the elder Erdmann, who had hidden behind the church door, through the crack of which he wanted to tickle his companions with a little straw.

Elsbeth and Paul looked at each other in surprise, for they did not know the meaning of this phrase; but as they felt that it must signify something very bad they blushed and separated.

Paul looked after her as she got into the carriage and drove away. This time the old lady was not waiting for her. It was her governess, he had heard. Yes; she was of such high rank that she even had a governess of her own.

"The Erdmanns will get a good licking yet;" with that he ended his reflections.

The next week passed without his speaking to Elsbeth. When he entered the church she was

generally already in her seat. Then she would nod
to him kindly, but that was all.

And then came a Monday when her carriage
was not waiting for her. He noticed it at once,
and as he walked towards the church-yard he
breathed more freely, for the proud coachman with
his fur cap, which he wore even in summer, always
caused him a feeling of oppression. He had only
to think of this coachman when he sat opposite to
her and she appeared to him like a being from
another world.

To-day he ventured to nod to her almost familiarly, and it seemed to him as if she answered more
kindly than usual.

And when the lesson was ended she came towards him of her own accord, and said, "I must walk
home to-day, for our horses are all in the fields.
Mamma thought you might walk with me part of
the way, as we go the same road."

He felt very happy, but did not dare to walk by
her side as long as they were in the village. He
also looked back anxiously from time to time, to
see whether the two Erdmanns were lurking anywhere with their mocking remarks. But when they
went through the open fields it was quite natural
that they should walk side by side.

It was a sunny forenoon in June. The white
sand on the road glittered; round about golden
hawkweed was blooming and meadowsweet waved
in the warm wind; the midday bell sounded from

the village; no human creature was to be seen far and wide; the heath seemed quite deserted.

Elsbeth wore a wide-brimmed straw-hat on her head as a protection against the sun's rays. She took it off now, and swung it to and fro by the elastic.

"You will be too hot," he said; but as she laughed at him a little he took his off also and threw it high in the air.

"You are quite a merry fellow," she said, nodding approvingly.

He shook his head, and the lines of care which always made him look old appeared again upon his brow.

"Oh no," he said; "merry I am certainly not."

"Why not?" she asked.

"I have always so many things to think of," he answered, "and if ever I want to be really happy something always goes wrong."

"But what do you always have to think about?" she asked.

He reflected for a while, but nothing occurred to him. "Oh, it is all nonsense," he said; "clever thoughts never come to me, by any means."

And then he told her about his brothers, of the thick books, which were quite filled with figures (the name he had forgotten), and which they had already known by heart when they were only as old as he was now.

"Why don't you learn that as well, if it gives you pleasure?" she asked.

"But it gives me no pleasure," he answered; "I have such a dull head."

"But *something* you know, surely?" she went on.

"I know absolutely nothing at all," he replied, sadly; "father says that I am too stupid."

"Oh, you must not heed that," she replied, consolingly. "My Fraulein Rothmaier also finds fault with many things I do. But I—pah, I—" she was silent, and pulled up a sorrel-plant which she began to chew.

"Has your father still such sparkling eyes?" he asked.

She nodded, and her face brightened.

"You love him very much—your father?"

She looked at him wonderingly, as if she had not understood his question, then answered, "Oh yes; I love him very much."

"And he loves you, too?"

"Well, I should think so."

Now he also rooted up a sorrel-plant and sighed.

"Why do you sigh?" she asked.

Something was just crossing his mind, he said, and then asked, laughingly, if her father still took her on his knee sometimes, as on the day when he had been in the White House.

She laughed and said she was a big girl now, and he should not ask such silly questions; but afterwards it came out that all the same she still sat on her father's knee—"Of course, not astride any more!" she added, laughing.

"Yes, that was a nice day," he said, "and I sat on his other knee. How small we must have been then."

"And we were so pitifully stupid," she answered, "when I think now how you wanted to whistle, and could not."

"Do you remember that?" he asked, and his eyes sparkled in the consciousness of his present attainments in the art.

"Of course," she replied; "and when you went away you came running back and—do you still remember?"

He remembered very well.

"Now you can whistle, of course," she laughed; "at our age that is no longer an accomplishment —even I can do it," and she pointed her lips in a very funny manner.

He was sad that she spoke so slightingly of his art, and reflected whether it would not be better to give up whistling altogether.

"Why are you so silent?" she asked. "Are you tired, too?"

"Oh no, but you—eh?"

Yes; the walk through the sand and the noontide heat had tired her.

"Then come into our house and rest," he cried, with sparkling eyes, for he thought what joy his mother would feel at seeing her.

But she refused. "Your father is not kindly disposed towards us, mamma said, and that's why you may not come for a visit to Helenenthal. Your father would perhaps send me away."

He replied, with a deep blush, " My father would not do that," and felt much ashamed.

She cast a glance towards the Haidehof, which lay scarcely a hundred yards from the road. The red fence shone in the sunshine, and even the gray half-ruined barns looked more cheerful than usual.

" Your house looks very nice," she said, shading her eyes with her left hand.

"Oh yes," he answered, his heart swelling with pride, "and there is an owl nailed to the door of one of the sheds. But it shall become much nicer still," he added after a little while, seriously, "only let me begin to rule." And then he set to work to explain to her all his plans for the future. She listened attentively, but when he had finished she said again,

" I am tired—I must rest;" and she wanted to sit down on the edge of the ditch.

"Not here in the blazing sun," he cautioned her; "we'll look out for the first juniper-bush we can find."

She gave him her hand, and let him drag her wearily over the heath, which undulated with mole-hills like the waves on a lake, and near the edge of the wood there were some solitary juniper-bushes, which stood out like a group of black dwarfs above the level plain.

Under the first of these bushes she cowered

down, so that its shadow almost entirely shrouded her slight, delicate figure.

"Here is just room enough for your head," she said, pointing to a mole-hill which was just within the range of shade.

He stretched himself out on the grass, his head resting on the mole-hill, his forehead covered by the hem of her dress.

She leaned back on the bush in order to find support in its branches.

"The needles don't prick at all," she said; "they mean well by us. I believe we could pass through the Sleeping Beauty's hedge of thorns."

"You—not I," he answered, lifting his eyes to her from his recumbent position; "every thorn has pricked me. I am no fairy prince, not even a simple Hans in luck, am I?"

"That will all come in time," she replied, consolingly, "you must not always have sad thoughts."

He wanted to reply, but he lacked the right words; and as he looked up, meditatively, a swallow flitted through the blue sky. Then involuntarily he uttered a whistle as if he wanted to call it, and as it did not come, he whistled again, and for a second and third time.

Elsbeth laughed, but he went on whistling—first without knowing how, and without reflecting why; but when one tone after the other flowed from his lips, he felt as if he had become very eloquent all of a sudden, and as if in this manner he could say all that weighed on his heart and for which in words he never could have found courage. All that which made him sad, all that which he cared about came pouring forth. He shut his eyes and listened, so to speak, to what the tones were saying for him. He thought that the good God in heaven spoke for him, and was relating all that concerned him, even that which he had never been clear about himself.

When he looked up he did not know how long he had been lying there whistling, but he saw that Elsbeth was crying.

"Why do you cry?" he asked.

She did not answer him, but dried her eyes with her handkerchief and rose.

Silently they walked side by side for a while. When they reached the wood, which lay thick and dark before them, she stopped and asked,

"Who has taught you that?"

"Nobody," he said; "it came to me quite naturally."

"Can you also play the flute?" she went on.

No, he could not; he had never even heard it: he only knew that it was the favorite pastime of "old Fritz."

"You must learn it," she said.

He thought it would probably be too difficult for him.

"You should try all the same," she counselled him; "you must be an artist—a great artist."

He was startled when she said that: he scarcely darcd to follow out her thoughts.

When they had reached the other side of the wood they separated. She went towards the White House and he went back. When he passed the juniper-bush where they had both been sitting all seemed to him like a dream, and henceforth it always remained so to him. Two or three days elapsed before he dared to say anything of his adventure to his mother, but then he could contain himself no longer; he confessed everything to her.

His mother looked at him for a long time and then went out; but from that time she used to listen secretly to catch, if possible, some notes of his whistling.

The two children often walked home together, but such an hour as the one beneath the juniper-bush never came to them again.

When they passed it they used to look at each other and smile, but neither of them dared to propose sitting down again beneath it.

There was also no further mention of the flute-playing between thcm, but Paul thought of it often enough in secret. It seemed to him likc something divine, unheard of—like the science which taught the table of logarithms. Ah, if he had been clever and gifted like his two brothers; but he was only a dull, stupid boy, who might be glad if others allowed him to help them.

He often asked himself what such flute-playing

sounded like, and what kind of people they were who were initiated into the mysteries of it. He formed a high opinion of them, and thought that they must always cherish high and holy thoughts, such as arose in his own mind occasionally when he was deeply absorbed in his whistling.

And then came the day when he was to see a flute-player face to face.

It was a dreary, stormy afternoon in the month of November. It began to get dark already as he left school and slowly walked along the village road to go home. Issuing from the public-house, which used to be frequented by all the rogues of the neighborhood, wonderful sounds met his ear. He had never heard the like, but he immediately knew this must be a flute-player. Eagerly listening, he stopped at the door of the public-house. His heart beat loudly, his limbs trembled. The sounds were very much like his whistling, only much fuller and softer. "Such music the angels of God must make at His throne," he thought to himself.

Only one thing was inexplicable to him: how this flute-playing, which sounded so sad and plaintive, could come from such a place of ill-repute. The shouts and the clinking of glasses which sounded in between filled his soul with horror. Sudden rage seized him; if he had been tall and strong he would have sprung into the house and turned all these noisy and drunken people out into the street, so that the holy sounds should not be profaned.

At this moment the door was thrown open; a drunken workman reeled past him, an obnoxious odor issued forth. Louder still grew the noise; the tones of the flute could scarcely make themselves heard above it.

Then he took courage, and before the door was closed pressed through the narrow opening into the inner room of the public-house.

He stood there, squeezed behind an empty brandy-cask. Nobody heeded him.

During the first few moments he could not distinguish anything.

The oppressive atmosphere and the noise had overwhelmed his senses, and the tones of the flute grew harsh and unmelodious, so that they hurt his ears.

In the midst of the yelling and stamping people sat a ragged fellow on an upturned cask; he had a bloated, pimply face, a brandy-nose, and black, greasy hair—a figure, the sight of which made Paul shudder. It was he who had played the flute.

Petrified with horror, the boy stared at him. It seemed to him as if the heavens were falling and the world going to ruin.

The musician now put down his flute, uttered a few coarse words in a rough, hoarse voice, greedily swallowed the brandy which was handed to him by the by-standers, and, beating time with his feet, began playing a vulgar ballad, which the listeners accompanied with loud brawling.

Then Paul fled from the den, and ran and ran till he was perfectly dizzy, as if he wished to escape from his own thoughts.

When he was alone on the storm-swept heath, from the extremity of which a sulphurous streak of evening light was shining, he stopped, hid his face in his hands, and cried bitterly.

In the winter which followed, Paul stopped whistling altogether, and flute-playing disgusted him even more. When he thought of it there stood before his eyes the figure of the outcast who had profaned his yearnings for art.

He did not see Elsbeth any more. With the beginning of the cold weather the confirmation-classes had been transferred from the church to the vicarage, and as there was no room there large enough to hold all the candidates, the boys and girls were taught separately. Sometimes he saw Elsbeth's carriage pass, but she herself was so wrapped up in furs and shawls that her face could not be recognized. He did not even know whether she had seen him.

At this time he had to suffer much vexation from the brothers Erdmann, who knew how to torment him beyond endurance. He was perfectly powerless against them, for each of them was twice as strong as he; besides, they always attacked him both at the same time, and while one held him the other pinched. Not that they were thoroughly vicious; on the contrary, they knew how to practise benevolence and generosity towards others; but his quiet, reserved nature was just what they hated with all their heart. They called him a hypocrite and a Puritan, and when they had thrashed him would say, "There, now go and tell tales of us; that would be just like you."

His rancor against these antagonists grew stronger and stronger. He often reproached himself with behaving in a cowardly and dishonorable manner, and accused himself of having a low, servile nature. One day, when he ran up and down in the snow, he worked himself into such a fury that he resolved to rid himself of these two wicked brothers were it at the risk of his own life. He ran to the stables where the grindstone stood, thawed the frozen water in the tub, and sharpened his pocket-knife till it cut a piece of the thinnest tissue-paper. But when, on the following Monday, he was again thrashed, he had not the courage to draw it from his pocket, and had once more to reproach himself with cowardice. He put it off till the next time; but that was the end of it. From his father, too, he had much to endure. The latter was again taken up with grand plans, and when this was the case he always felt very superior, and in an especially bad humor with Paul, whom he despised for his narrow-mindedness.

"Why has not the tiniest spark of my genius been transmitted to that boy?" he would remark; "how beautifully I could educate him to assist in

6

my plans.   But he is too stupid—everything is lost upon him."   It was now his intention to found a company to make his moor profitable, to bring capital together, and to be himself named director of it all, with a salary of several thousand thalers. Every week he drove into town two or three times, and often did not come home even on the following day.   "It is difficult enough," he would say, when he had slept off his intoxication, "but I'll be even with the niggards!   That Douglas, too, insolent fellow, shall pay for it.   If I only knew how to tackle him.   I will never enter Helenenthal again, were it only that I might not see how the fellow has neglected it—for that he certainly has done—and in town I never get sight of him.   But pay for it—pay for it he shall.   If he does not immediately sign a whole bushel of shares, the devil take him."

Frau Elsbeth listened sadly to all this without saying a word, but Paul used secretly to take down the key of the shed from its shelf, and go off to have mute intercourse with "Black Susy."   He stuck to the belief that she would be the means of saving them.

When the Easter holidays were over, the confirmation-classes were again held in the church. Boys and girls met together after a half year's separation.

Elsbeth had changed very much during the winter.   She almost looked like a grown-up lady now.

She wore a longer dress and her hair was arranged in little curls on her forehead.

Paul saluted her very shyly; he felt as if he were no longer fit for her; but she rose from her seat, walked a few steps towards him, and shook his hand heartily before everybody's eyes. During the ensuing lesson a sheet of paper was circulated among the boys which caused much mirth. On it was written, with all sorts of flourishes:

"Paul Meyerhofer,
Elsbeth Douglas,
Betrothed."

The writing was that of the younger Erdmann. Paul's hand searched for his knife; for a moment he felt as if he could draw it on his neighbor here in the open church. He snatched the paper from his hand and tore it into little pieces.

Elsbeth looked at him wonderingly, and the vicar called him to order. Then he became terrified at his own audacity. The Erdmanns must have understood that on this subject he would not stand any joking, and made no further attempts to tease him about Elsbeth.

The confirmation took place on the last Sunday before Whitsuntide. The night before, Paul could not sleep, and at sunrise quietly got up, put on the new clothes which his good aunt had sent him for this occasion, and took a walk through the quiet yard and over the dewy fields, till he reached the moor. which in its flowery garb lay brightly extended before him.

At the sight of the rising sun he folded his hands and said an ardent prayer. From this day forth he resolved to begin a new and better life, forgive all offences. and love his enemies. as Jesus Christ had commanded. Then he thought of the knife which he had once ground with a view to the Erdmanns; he pulled it out of his pocket and threw it far away over the moor. where it sank down in the swamp with a gurgling sound. Hot tears streamed from his eyes: he thought himself bad and reprobate, and totally unworthy to stand before God's altar: he scarcely dared to go home to the farm; only when the twins came rushing towards him in their brand-new muslin dresses did he feel happier and easier in his mind. He embraced his sisters, and vowed in silence to be a true friend and support to them.

Then came his mother. dressed in a faded silk gown. kissed him on his forehead and cheeks. and held his face between her two hands for a long while. looking fixedly into his eyes. She wanted to say something to him. but she could get out nothing more than " My boy, my dear boy!"

Even his father was in the rosiest humor to-day. He took both Paul's hands in his. and made him a long speech as to how he must learn to look out for what was great in human life. and to emulate him. his father. who, though always pursued by misfortune and plundered by the wickedness of men, had never allowed himself to be discouraged from aspiring to the stars, even in this miserable hole into which adverse fate had let him sink. And he knitted his brows and ruffled his hair, every inch of him grandeur and importance.

Paul kissed both his hands and promised everything. At eight o'clock he saw on the high-road which led across the heath a carriage roll by, the silver ornaments of which sparkled in the morning sun.

For a long time he looked after it. Everything seemed to him like a dream. He felt so exultantly glad that he was almost overpowered by happiness. "How have I deserved all this?" he asked himself; and then he began brooding over what the first trouble would be which would drag him down from this bliss. When the twins announced to him that the carriage stood ready for the drive to church he felt sad and depressed.

In the vicarage garden, where syringa and lilac were in bloom, and where the sunbeams glittered on the lawn, stood two little groups of human beings apart from each other—one black, the other white. The former were the boys, the latter the girls.

Elsbeth, in her snowy muslin dress with a lace handkerchief crossed over her bosom, looked white and graceful as a hawthorn blossom.

Her cheeks were very pale, and she kept her eyes

lowered, and played alternately with her hymn-book and a twig of lilac, both of which she held in her hand.

Paul looked at her for a long time, but she did not see him. She would not be disturbed in her devotion by any worldly thought.

And then the vicar came; the bells pealed, the organ resounded, and the procession, ranged in couples, advanced slowly towards the altar.

Paul walked close behind the two Erdmanns, who in their long black coats looked very solemn and demure. Suddenly the consciousness of his guilt overcame him more forcibly than ever. He bent forward a little, touched them softly on the shoulder, and whispered, with moist eyes,

"Forgive me, I have behaved so badly to you."

They nudged each other and smiled maliciously. One of them half turned round, and whispered, with a face of pathetic misery and a look of injured innocence,

"My son, we forgive you."

Paul felt very well that they were mocking him, but his heart was so full of devotion and love that no mocking could affect him.

The children ranged themselves on both sides of the altar.

Paul sent a shy glance into the body of the church, which was crammed with people, but he could not distinguish anybody.

The hour for the sermon was past. He gazed down before him. All seemed like a dream.

A little later he felt his knees resting on a soft cushion and the hand of the vicar on his head. What he said to him he did not hear. He saw Elsbeth on the other side, crying quietly with her handkerchief to her eyes, and thought,

"Ah, cry away, cry away, you will soon laugh again."

And then he asked himself why people always laughed so much, while on the whole there were so few laughable things in the world.

The organ now intoned the hymn, "Praise ye the Lord, the mighty King of Glory." The chorus of the congregation sounded jubilant, and his gaze wandered up to the sunbeams which fell in iridescent light through the painted church windows like a rainbow.

And while he was gazing at it he suddenly started. Just opposite the cross which crowned the altar stood a dark woman clad in gray, of supernatural stature, looking down upon him with big, hollow eyes. It was the penitent Magdalene.

He felt a cold shudder run through his frame.

"Dame Care," he murmured, and bent his head as if he wished to accept with humility what she might grant him for life.

And when he lifted his eyes again the sun shone more magnificently than before.

Fiery red and emerald green sparkled the rays,

weaving a radiant halo round the gray dame's head.

But she stood there sadly in the midst of all the brilliant radiance, and stared down upon him with her big, hollow eyes.

Then the organ began the finale with swelling chords. A joyful thrill passed through the congregation. The troop of children hastened to throw themselves into the arms of their parents, and a kindly glance greeted him from Elsbeth's eyes.

CHAPTER VIII.

PAUL now began to help with the farming. He faithfully kept the vow which he had made on the morning of his confirmation. He worked like the meanest of his servants, and when his mother begged him to spare himself, he kissed her hand and replied, "You know we have a great deal to make good."

In the evening, when the servants had retired to rest and the twins had frollicked till they fell asleep, mother and son often sat together for hours and planned and calculated; but when some resolution had ripened within them and a gleam of hope shone from their eyes, it often happened that they would suddenly start and let their heads droop with a sigh; but neither of them gave utterance to that which weighed on their minds.

About this time Frau Elsbeth began to age rapidly. Long, deep furrows lined her face, her chin became very prominent, and silver streaks appeared in her hair. Only from the depths of her sorrowful eyes one could still see how beautiful she had once been.

"Yes, you see, I am quite an old woman now,"

she said to her son one morning, as she combed her hair before the looking-glass, "and luck has never yet come."

"Hush, mother, what else am I here for?" he answered, though he did not feel hopeful at all.

Then she smiled sadly, stroked his cheeks and his brow, and said, "Yes, you certainly look as if you had caught luck in its flight! but I won't speak like this," she continued; "what should I do without you?"

Such moments of overflowing love had to satisfy them for a long time, for often months passed by without mother or son daring to say any loving words to each other; their hearts were too sorrowful.

The twins meanwhile grew up—two frolicksome, apple-cheeked tomboys, for whom no tree was too high, no ditch too deep. Their curly brown hair fell over their foreheads in a thousand little ringlets, and beneath them two pairs of eyes peeped out, as full of mischief and as sparkling, both with shyness and impudence, as if a stray sunbeam were laughing out of black forest depths.

The laughter of these two resounded from morning to night through the lonely Haidehaus, and the quietness when they were at school or running about in the open fields was the more oppressive.

It was all the same to the twins whether there was sunshine or storm in the house; their heads were always full of tricks, and when at times their father's storming grew too insupportable and they deemed it more prudent to hide behind the stove, they made up for it there by pinching one another's legs.

They were devoted to Paul, which, however, did not prevent them from quietly claiming as their property the best morsels from his plate, the whitest sheets of paper from his writing-case, and the finest buttons off his trousers, for they used to steal like magpies.

He was very anxious about them, for he feared they would become wilder and wilder, especially as his mother grew more tired and despondent, and left matters to take their own course. But he began his educational experiments at the wrong end. His warnings were of no avail, and once as he was in the middle of a beautiful sermon one of them suddenly jumped on his knee, pulled his nose, and called out to his sister, "Fanny, he is getting a beard."

Then the other one climbed after her, and both of them tried who could pinch him the most. But when he got seriously angry with them, they began to sulk, and said, "Fie, we won't speak to you any more."

He had not seen Elsbeth again since the day of their confirmation, though a whole year had elapsed meanwhile.

It was said she had been sent to town to learn there how to move in society. This word had given his heart a pang; he scarcely knew what it meant, but he vaguely felt that she was farther and farther removed from him.

But it happened one day about Easter-tide that he had to work on a piece of ground which lay removed from the other fields and far away at the edge of the wood. He was sowing the seed himself, and a servant with two horses went harrowing after him.

He wore a big seed-cloth round his shoulders, and watched with quiet pleasure how the grains sparkled like a golden fountain as they sank into the earth. Then it seemed to him that he saw something bright between the dark trunks of the trees, rocking up and down like a cradle suspended in the air. But he scarcely allowed himself time to notice it, for sowing is the kind of work which requires all one's attention.

At length the pause for breakfast came. The servant sat down on a sack of corn, but he himself, feeling hot, went towards the wood to be in the shade.

He threw a passing glance at the suspended cradle, and thought, "That must be a hammock;" but he little cared who was lying in it.

Then suddenly it seemed to him as if he heard his name called.

"Paul, Paul!" It sounded sweet and familiar, and in a soft, clear voice, which he seem to know.

He started and looked up.

" Paul, do come here," the voice called again.

He turned hot and cold, for now he well knew who it was.

He cast a shy look at his working-suit, and began to untie the knots of his seed-cloth ; but it slipped round to the back of his neck, so that he could not reach it.

"Do come as you are," called out the voice ; and now he could see how the upper part of her body raised itself from the hammock, while a book, bound in red and gold, glided from her hands and fell to the ground.

Hesitatingly he approached, trying secretly to wipe his boots in the moss, for the soil of the fields was sticking to them.

She on her part had only this moment perceived that her feet and white stockings showed beneath her dress, and hastily tried to cover them with the shawl which had been put round her shoulders. But she could not pull it from under her arms, and she could think of nothing better than to crouch down quickly so that she looked like a hen, while the hammock swayed to and fro.

Perhaps she might have had the intention to impress him a little with her elegance and freshly-acquired social education, but now, as fate would have it, she did not look at him less blushingly or shyly than he at her.

On his side he observed nothing of her state of mind ; he only saw that she had grown very beauti-

ful, that her hair was twisted up into a very aristocratic knot, and that the bow at her bosom trembled slightly on her rounded form. It was quite
clear to him that she had now grown into a
lady.

A long while elapsed before either of them spoke
a word.

"Good-day," she said, at last, with a little laugh,
and stretched out her right hand to him, for she
soon saw that she had the best of it.

He was silent and smiled at her.

"Help me to pull out my shawl," she continued.
He did so.

"That's it; now turn round."

He did that, too.

"Now it's all right." She had made herself comfortable, thrown the shawl quickly over her feet
again, and was looking up at him roguishly through
the meshes of the hammock. "It's really delight-
ful to be with you again," she said; "you are the
best of them all. Have you also been longing for
me?"

"No," he answered, truthfully.

"Oh, get away with you!" she replied, and,
pouting, tried to turn over to the other side; but
the hammock began to sway too much again, so
she laughed and remained lying as she was.

He wondered inwardly at her being so merry.
He never heard any one laugh like that, except the
twins, and they were children. But this laugh

gave him back his self-possession, for he felt instinctively how much older than she he had grown during the interval.

"I suppose you have been very happy all this time?" he asked.

"Thank God, yes!" she replied. "Mamma is always rather delicate, but that is all." A shadow passed over her face, but disappeared again the next moment, and then she chatted on: "I have been in town—oh dear, what I have gone through there! I must tell you about it at the first opportunity. I have had dancing lessons. I have also had admirers—you can fancy that! They serenaded me under my windows, sent me anonymous bouquets, and verses, too—original verses! There was a student, among others, with a white-braided coat, and a green, white, and red cap; oh, he understood it! The things he would say to you! Afterwards he engaged himself to Betty Schirrmacher, one of my friends, but quite in secret—nobody knows it but myself."

Paul breathed freely again, for the student had already begun to make him uncomfortable.

"And were you not vexed?" he asked.

"Why?"

"At his being fickle to you."

"No; we are above such things," she replied, shugging her shoulders. "Oh, you know—they are all stupid boys in comparison with you!"

He felt quite frightened at the idea of calling a

student a stupid boy, and, above all, in comparison with him.

"My brother is no stupid boy," he retorted.

"I don't know your brother," she said, with philosophic calmness; "perhaps he is not. Oh, I have grown ever so much older," she went on. "I took literature lessons, and from that I learned many beautiful things."

Tormenting envy awoke in him.

"Do pick up that book."

He did so.

"Do you know that?"

In gold letters he read on the red cover the words, "Heine's Buch der Lieder" (Heine's Book of Songs), and shook his head sadly.

' Ah, then you don't know anything! Oh, how much there is in that book! I must lend it to you. There, read that; it teaches one a great deal. And after reading it for a little while one generally begins to cry."

"Is it so sad, then?" he asked, looking at the cover with shy curiosity.

"Yes, very sad; as beautiful and as sad as— as— It only speaks of love, of nothing else; but you feel such a great longing overpower you, and that you would like to fly off to the Ganges, where the lotus blossoms, and where—" She stopped, and then she laughed merrily and said, "Oh, that is too stupid; is it not?"

"What?"

"What I am chattering about."

"No; I could listen to you for my whole life."

"No! could you? Oh, you know—it is so cosey here; I feel so secure when you are near me," and she stretched herself out in the net-work as if she wanted to lean her head on his shoulder.

A strange feeling of happiness and peace came over him, such as he had not felt for a long time.

"Why do you look away?" she asked.

"I don't look away."

"Yes, you do. . . . You must look at me. I like that. . . . You have such earnest, faithful eyes. Oh, I know now what to compare those poems with!"

"Well, with what?"

"With your whistling. That is also so—so—well, you know what I mean. . . . Do you still whistle sometimes?"

"Very seldom."

"And you have not learned to play the flute either, I suppose?"

"No."

"Oh, fie! If you love me, you will learn it. . . . I will give you a beautiful flute next time."

"I have nothing to give you in return."

"Oh yes—you shall give me all the songs which you play. And when your heart is very sad . . . well, only read that book; everything is in there."

Paul looked at it from all sides. "What a wonderful book it must be!" he thought.

"And now tell me something about yourself,"

7

she said. What are you doing? What are you working at? How is your dear mamma?"

Paul gave her a grateful glance. He felt he could speak to-day of all that was in his heart; then it suddenly occurred to him that the pause for breakfast was long over, and that the servant was waiting for him with the horses. By noon he must finish, for after dinner the cart was to drive to the town with a load of peat which he had had secretly cut.

"I must go to work," he faltered.

"Oh, what a pity! And when will you have done?"

"At dinner-time."

"I can't wait so long as that or mamma will be uneasy. But in the next few days do come and look here again—perhaps you'll find me. Now I shall lie here for another hour or so and watch you. It looks quite splendid when you walk up and down in your big snowy white cloth and the grain flies round you."

He gave her his hand silently and went away.

"I shall leave the book here," she called after him; "fetch it when you have finished."

The servant smiled knowingly when he saw him come, and Paul hardly dared to raise his eyes to him.

Each time when he passed at his work the place where she was resting in the wood she raised herself up a little and waved to him with her pocket-handkerchief. About twelve o'clock she rolled up her hammock, stepped to the edge of the wood, and called out a farewell to him through her folded hands.

He took off his cap to thank her, but the servant looked the other way and whistled softly, as if he had seen nothing.

During dinner that day his mother could not take her eyes from her son, and when they were alone she went up to him, took his head in both her hands, and said,

"What has happened to you, my boy?"

"Why?" he asked, with embarrassment.

"Your eyes sparkle so suspiciously."

He laughed loudly and ran away; but when at supper she still looked at him — inquiringly and sadly—he was sorry that he had not given her his confidence, and went after her and confessed all that had happened to him.

Then her haggard face suddenly lit up as by a ray of sunshine, and while he crept away ashamed, with glowing cheeks, she looked after him with moist eyes and folded her hands as if in prayer.

He sat up in his room till nearly midnight, his head leaning on his hands. The mysterious book was lying on his knee; but he could not read it, because his father had forbidden him to burn a light at night. He had to wait till Sunday.

He was musing on how she had altered. If only she had not laughed so often; her mirth estranged her from him, and the full blooming life by which she was surrounded removed her far away into that distant country where happy people live. And although she appeared as good and kind as ever, she could not fail to despise him sooner or later because he was nothing but a peasant, and stupid and awkward into the bargain.

A wild tumult of happiness, shame, and self-reproach raged within him, for he thought he might have behaved in a much more dignified manner. An unaccountable fear was mixed up with it all which almost choked him, though in vain he racked his mind to find out whom this fear was connected with.

The next afternoon he could see from the yard, where he was putting up some poles, something white moving to and fro at the edge of the wood. He set his teeth with pain and vexation, but could not make up his mind to abandon his work.

For two days more the white was to be seen there—then it disappeared altogether.

On Sunday morning he took the book of poems out of his box and went with it towards the wood. At dinner-time he was still absent, and in the evening the twins, who were playing at hide-and-seek on the heath, found him whistling under a juniper-bush with the tears streaming down his cheeks.

Thus he translated the "Buch der Lieder" into his own language.

.   .   .   .

A short time afterwards he heard that Mrs. Douglas had been ordered by the doctor to make a prolonged stay in the South, and that Elsbeth would accompany her thither.

"It is all right so," he said to himself. "She will no longer haunt me, then." For a long time he was uncertain whether to send her book back or not; he would have liked to keep it, but his conscience would not allow him. He waited for a favorable opportunity of returning it till he heard that they had gone. Then he was satisfied.

CHAPTER IX.

Five years passed away; five years full of care and trouble.

Paul toiled and moiled; he worked from early morning till late at night; his busy hands were occupied with every sort of labor, and whatever he touched throve. But he scarcely noticed this, for his mind was always taken up with the future.

The same lines of care were on his brow at all times; his eyes were cast down with the same thoughtful brooding expression as if he were looking into his own soul, and often days would pass without his having spoken a single word either at his work or at table.

He went about with the conviction that in reality all his labor was hopeless. He never could reckon on his father's gratitude, and he soon learned to do without it; but it was more difficult to have patience when a whim of his father's spoiled in one hour what he had been working at with great trouble for many weeks.

When his father came home from his journeys it was not seldom that he called him a simpleton and a blockhead in the hearing of the servants, and

would complain bitterly at being obliged to leave his
farm in hands as incapable as his, when his duty—
nobody knew what that duty was—called him away.

Paul was silent at such times, for deep in his
heart he kept the commandment: "HONOR thy
father and thy mother "—" his father for his mother's sake;" so he had reconstructed it. But his
eyes passed with a sombre, searching gaze from
one servant to the other, and whomever he caught
smiling or nudging his neighbor in secret malice
he dismissed next morning.

There was one of the farm-servants who had been
working almost the whole time at the Haidehaus.
His name was Michel Raudszus, and he came from
Littau. He lived in a miserable hovel not far from
Helenenthal, the walls of which were surrounded
by piles of turf, so that the storms should not blow
it down. He had a slatternly wife who had already
been in prison twice, and who sent her children out
to beg.

He was a silent, surly fellow, who did his work
faultlessly and went off without grumbling when he
was not wanted any more, but appeared again
punctually as soon as there was fresh work. Paul
did not like him at first, he was so laconic and reserved, and his sullen behavior had made an uncomfortable impression upon him; but then it suddenly
occurred to him that he behaved in much the same
way himself, and from that hour he had begun to
like him heartily.

Even his father seemed to have a certain amount of respect for him, for though, when drunk, he used to beat the servants, he had never attempted to touch him. It seemed as if the look which the man cast at him from underneath his bushy brows kept him at bay.

This servant was Paul's most faithful helper. He could even trust him to sell the grain in the market, for he always knew how to get the highest prices.

Imperceptibly a great change had come over the silent Haidehaus in these five years. The traces of poverty became more and more rare, and want was less often their guest at table. In the garden, where were pretty flower-beds, the pease and asparagus stood in long rows, and the defective fence had long since been replaced by a new one. The cattle were augmented every year by two or three valuable milking cows, and the milk-cart which drove into the town every morning brought home many a groschen on the first of the month.

That there was no sign of any comfort yet in spite of all this was entirely the fault of his father, who speculated with the greater part of their earnings when he did not spend it in drink.

Paul had secretly contrived that a few thalers at least were saved for his brothers and sisters every month.

His brothers needed money more than ever. Max had passed his last examination, and was now beginning his first year's tutorship at college without salary; and Gottfried, the clerk, was out of situation for several months every year. The two wrote begging letters in every possible key, from the jovial "Fork me out thirty thalers immediately," to the heartrending supplication, "If you don't want me to be ruined, have mercy," etc.

Paul passed many a sleepless night thinking how to help them, and it frequently happened that he deprived himself of something necessary so as to be able to send them the money.

Once Gottfried had written that he had no decent clothes and urgently needed a summer suit. Paul just wanted a summer suit himself, for he had outgrown his old one; sighing, he put the money which he had saved up for himself into an envelope and sent it to his brother; but in the letter accompanying it he mentioned that he was not less reduced in his wardrobe than himself. His brother showed himself magnanimous, and a fortnight later sent him a parcel of clothes and a letter, in which he said: "I enclose an old suit of mine. You, in your humble position, will probably be able to use it still."

Paul had also enabled the twins to have a better education than was to be expected from the very reduced circumstances of his home. He had urged the vicar's wife, who had formerly been a governess, to take them into the private school which she had established for the daughters of well-to-do landowners from the neighboring villages.

The money for the schooling was not the worst of it, and he could manage also to procure their books and copy-books; but it was difficult, very difficult, to keep them nicely dressed, for his pride would not allow his sisters to be behind their friends, and perhaps to be considered as beggar children.

He himself knew too well the feeling of being looked down upon to let his sisters experience the same.

His mother did not offer him any help even in these little feminine cares. She was so much cowed by her husband's abuse that she lacked the courage to buy the smallest trifle on her own responsibility.

"What you do, my son, is sure to be right," she said, and Paul drove to town and was cheated, both by the draper and the dress-maker.

The twins grew up blooming, careless, and saucily merry, without the faintest idea what a tragedy was being enacted in their immediate neighborhood. At ten years old they romped and fought with the village boys, at twelve they went with them to steal pears, and at fifteen graciously accepted bunches of violets from them.

They were known far and wide as the most beautiful girls of the neighborhood. Paul knew this well, and was not a little proud of it; but what he did not know was that they had rendezvous behind the garden fence, and that half the boys who were to be confirmed with them could boast of having kissed their sweet red lips.

CHAPTER X.

IT was in the month of June on a sunny Sunday afternoon.

Trumpet music sounded softly out of the wood. A great festival was to be held there to-day. A wandering band had consented to be hired to give a concert. The country people had come from far and wide, and even the squires had not refused to participate in it, for such a thing did not often happen in this quiet part of the world.

Since the middle of the day a long row of carriages had passed the Haidehof, and old Meyerhofer, who did not like staying at home when anything was going on, had suddenly been overcome by a fit of kindness, and called out to his womenfolk to get ready as quickly as possible; he would sacrifice himself and take them to the festivity.

The twins, who had already for a long time been standing at the window, looking out with eager sparkling eyes, broke out into a loud demonstration of joy. Frau Elsbeth gave them a quiet smile and turned to Paul, who sat silently in his corner and went on cutting little sticks to tie up the flowers, as if all this did not concern him at all.

"Will you not come, too?" she asked.

"Paul can drive," cried Meyerhofer, carelessly.

He thanked them and said that his coat was too shabby, and also he wanted to look after the workmen, who were to come at sunset. The next morning haymaking was to begin.

The twins looked at him, laid their heads together, and giggled; then, when he went towards the door, they hung round him, and Katie whispered,

"Listen; we know something."

"Well, what is it?"

"Something nice," said Greta, mysteriously.

"Out with it."

"Elsbeth Douglas has come home again."

And breaking out into merry laughter they ran away.

Paul at first felt very angry that they dared to mock him; then he sighed and smiled, and wondered why his heart had suddenly begun to beat so loudly.

Half an hour later his family drove away.

"Do join us soon," his mother called down to him from the carriage, and Katie getting into it whispered into his ear,

"I believe they will be there, too."

Now he stood quite alone in the deserted court-yard. The servants had gone to the fields to milk—no human being was to be seen far and wide. The ducks in their pool had put their heads under their wings, and the kennel-dog snapped sleepily at the flies.

Paul seated himself on the garden fence and gazed towards the wood, at the edge of which gay light dresses flitted to and fro, while now and then there was a bright glitter, when the sunbeams were reflected in the harness of the waiting carriage-horses.

The evening came; he was still undecided whether he should venture to follow his family.

A thousand reasons occurred to him which made his staying at home absolutely necessary, and when it was quite clear to him that he ought to remain at home and not go anywhere else he put on his Sunday coat and went to the festival.

It began already to grow dusk as he walked across the sweet-scented heather. His heart was weighed down with secret fear. He did not dare to think out the cause, but as he walked past the juniper-bush, beneath which he once had whistled his most beautiful song to Elsbeth, a pain shot through his breast as if he had been stabbed.

He stopped and reconsidered whether it would not be better to turn back. "My coat is much too shabby," he said to himself; "I can't show myself in any decent society." He took it off and looked at it on all sides. The back was getting shiny at the seams; at the elbows there was a dull silver gloss, and the border on the flaps of the breast even showed a little fringe.

"It won't do with the best will in the world," he said, and then he sat down beneath the juniper-bush and dreamed how smart and elegant he would look if only he could afford a new coat. "But that won't be yet a while," he continued; "first Max and Gottfried must have permanent places, and Greta and Katie must have the ball-dresses they wish for, and mother's arm-chair must be newly done up—" and the more he thought the more other things came to his mind which had a prior claim.

Then again he saw himself in a brand-new black suit, patent-leather shoes on his feet, a fashionable tie round his neck, entering the dancing-room with a careless, distinguished air, while Elsbeth smiled at him very respectfully.

Suddenly he started from his dreams. "Oh, fie! what a fop I am growing!" he scolded himself. "What have I to do with patent-leather shoes and fashionable ties? And now I will just go in my old coat to the wood. Besides, it has almost grown dark," he added, prudently.

Louder sounded the trumpets, and through the branches of the fir-trees joyful laughter met his ears.

A turfy spot in the wood had been selected for the principal scene of the festival. In the middle of it stood the platform for the musicians, on the right the tent of the village innkeeper, who sold sour beer and sweet cake, and on the left a place for dancing was fenced off, the entrance to which cost a groschen more, as one might read on a white board.

Round about in a big circle tables and benches had been placed where the different families enjoyed the supper they had brought with them, and through it all a jubilant, giggling, staring crowd was pressing, eager for either love or a good hand-to-hand fight.

The concert was already finished, the dancing had begun; on the firm, trodden-down moss the couples circled round breathless and stumbling.

. The glow of the sunset lay on the open space, while the wood bordering it was already buried in darkness. Here were the farm-servants and maids from the neighboring hamlets; even the coachmen had left their carriages, because it would have broken their hearts to have looked on at these love-makings from the distance. Every bush, every small tree seemed alive, and out of the darkness came low, amorous tittering.

Shyly, like a criminal, Paul slunk round the festive scene. A fear of strangers had always been his peculiarity, but never yet had his heart fluttered so anxiously as at this moment.

"Is Elsbeth there?" Nowhere in all the crowd were there any traces of the inmates of the White House, but then his family also seemed to have disappeared without leaving any trace. Once he thought the cooing laughter of the twins caught his ear, but the next moment the noise had drowned it.

Twice he had already made the round; then suddenly—his heart threatened to stop from surprise and rapture—he saw, quite close before him, his mother and father sitting in peaceful intercourse at the same table with the Douglas family.

His father rested his elbows on the table, and, red with excitement, talked eagerly to Mr. Douglas. The broad-shouldered giant with the bushy gray beard listened to him silently, at times nodding and smiling to himself. The slender, delicate figure with the sunken cheeks and the blue rings round her eyes, who leaned wearily against the trunk of a tree and clasped his mother's hand with her thin white fingers, that was his godmother, who had always seemed to him like an angel from the other world. But next to her — next to her, the lady in the modest gray dress, her fair hair simply combed back—

"Elsbeth! Elsbeth!" cried a voice within him; and then suddenly a wall of clouds sank down between him and her, and froze his innermost soul, and veiled his eyes with a damp mist.

Opposite to her sat a gentleman with a saucy-looking fair mustache, and still more saucy blue eyes, who bent towards her familiarly, while a smile flitted over her quiet face.

"She will marry that man," he said to himself, with a conviction which seemed to be more than a jealous foreboding. With the clear-sightedness of love he had understood that these two natures harmonized and must seek each other. And perhaps they had already found one another while he himself wasted his days in idle dreams.

He stood there as if stunned, and scrutinized the man who suddenly had rendered it clear to him what he had lost—lost, indeed, without ever having possessed it.

How could he ever have dared to compare himself to this man that, to a hair, was the ideal man of whom he had always dreamed?

Bold and energetic and triumphant (that's what he had meant to be one day), exactly like the strange young man who looked at Elsbeth with his frivolous smile. He also wore patent-leather boots and a fashionable colored necktie, and his suit was made of the finest shining black cloth.

Almost for an hour Paul stood there without daring to move from his position, devouring Elsbeth and her vis-à-vis with his eyes.

The night came. He scarcely perceived it. Long rows of lanterns were lighted, and shed forth an uncertain light on the gay crowd.

" How well I am hidden," thought Paul, and was glad of the darkness into which he had crept. He did not see that two men came walking towards him and were occupying themselves close to him with something on the ground. Then suddenly, not ten steps away from him, a purple red flame

8

flared up and flooded all around in a sea of dazzling light.

He wanted to take refuge quickly in the shade of a tree, but it was too late.

"Isn't that Paul standing there?" called out his mother.

"Where?" asked Elsbeth, turning with curiosity.

"Boy, why are you hanging about in the dark?" shouted his father.

Then he had to come out, in spite of all; and burning with shame, his cap in his hand, he stood before Elsbeth, who leaned her head on her hand and looked up at him smilingly.

"Yes, that's what he always is: a real sneaker," said his father, giving him a clap on the shoulder, and the unknown young gentleman pushed his hair from his forehead and smiled half good-naturedly, half ironically.

Then old Douglas rose, went up to him, and seized both his hands. "Hold up your head, young friend," he called out, with his lion's voice. "You have no reason to lower your eyes — you, least of all the world. He who can at the age of twenty do what you do is a capital fellow and need not hide himself. I won't make you conceited, but just ask who could bear comparison with you. You, perhaps, Leo?" He turned to the young fop, who answered, with a merry laugh,

"You must make the best of me as I am, dear uncle."

"If only there was anything in you to make the best of, you good-for-nothing!" replied Douglas. "This, you must know, is my nephew, Leo Heller, a new edition of 'Fritz Triddlefitz.'"

"Uncle, I'll have my revenge."

"Be quiet, you scoundrel."

"Uncle, I'll wager twenty glasses which of us lies under the table first."

"That's what he calls respect."

"Uncle, you are pinching me."

"Be quiet; just look at this young farmer, twenty years old, who keeps the whole farm going."

"Well, Mr. Douglas, *I* count for something, too," cried Meyerhofer, with a somewhat lengthened face.

"No offence to you," the former answered; "but you have so much to do with your company you naturally cannot bother about such trifles."

Meyerhofer bowed, flattered, and Paul felt ashamed for him, for he well understood the irony of these words.

Mrs. Douglas, smiling, beckoned him to come to her. She seized his hand and stroked it. "You have grown tall and good-looking," she said, in her weak, kind voice, "and you have a beautiful beard."

"But do call him '*Du*,'" interrupted his mother, who seemed to be much easier in her mind than usual. "Paul, ask your godmother."

"Yes — I entreat you," said Paul, stammering and blushing anew.

"God bless you, my son," said Mrs. Douglas;

"you have deserved it," and then her head again sank against the trunk of the tree.

Paul stood behind the bench and did not know what to do. For the first time since he was grown up he happened to find himself in strange society.

His glance met Elsbeth's, who, resting her head on her hand, looked round at him.

"I suppose you won't say 'How do you do' to me at all?" she added, mischievously.

The familiar "*Du*" gave him courage. He stretched his hand out to her, and asked how she had fared during all this long time.

A shade of sadness flitted across her face. "Not well," she said, softly; "but more of that later on when we are alone."

She made room at her side, and said, "Come." And as he sat down near her his elbow touched her neck. Then a thrill went through his body, such as he had never felt in all his life.

Leo Heller shook hands with him across the table, and said, laughing, "To our good friendship, you pattern boy, you!"

"I am, unfortunately, not worthy to be taken for a pattern boy," he answered, innocently.

"Then be glad; I am not one, either. Nothing is more disgusting to me than such a pattern boy."

"Why, then, did you call me so?"

Leo looked at him quite surprised. "Oh, you seem to take everything literally," he said.

"Pardon me, I am so little accustomed to joking," he replied, and a blush of shame rose to his face. In turning towards Elsbeth he saw that she was gazing at him with a strangely earnest, searching look. Then a sudden feeling of bliss rose in his soul. He felt here was one who did not think him stupid or ridiculous, who understood his nature and the laws according to which it manifested itself.

While the three were silent his father, at the other end of the table, continued to expound the plans of his company to Mr. Douglas.

"And if you trust me, sir—but no, you need not even do that — I mean to say, if you will not frivolously forfeit your own chance—one must never stand in the way of one's chance, sir—if you have only just a little spirit of enterprise—oh, then, yes, then, you know, there are hundreds and thousands to be earned; the moor is inexhaustible—why let others grow rich in your stead, sir? On through darkness to light; that's my device. I will strive and fight to the last breath; it is not my own interest which is at stake. It seems to me to be a question for the welfare of humanity. The aim is to win this barren soil for cultivation, to give new life-blood to this whole district, to change the poverty of this country into prosperity—to be a benefactor to humanity, sir."

And in this tone he swaggered on.

Then suddenly he came quite close to Douglas, as if he wanted to put a pistol to his head, crying,

"Then will you take shares in it sir?"

Douglas caught a glance from his wife, who quietly pointed towards Frau Elsbeth, and made him a beseeching sign; then he said, half amused, half angry, "I don't mind."

Paul was again ashamed, for he read in Douglas's face that for him it was only a question of the fun of throwing a few hundred thalers out of the window. He himself knew, too well, that no sensible man could take his father's plans in earnest.

"Have you not seen our girls, Paul?" asked his mother, who now seemed no less constrained than he.

No; he had not seen them anywhere.

"Do go and look about for them; they have gone to the dancing-ground. Tell them not to be too wild, or else they will catch cold."

Paul rose.

"I will go with you," said Elsbeth.

"May I not come too, little cousin?" asked cousin Leo.

"You had better remain here," she answered, lightly, whereupon he declared he should be obliged to kill himself for grief.

"A merry bird," said Paul, with a sigh of envy, as he walked at her side through the crowd.

"Yes; but nothing more," she replied.

"Do you like him?"

"Certainly; very much.

"She will marry him, after all," Paul meditated.

All around people screamed and shouted. A lantern had caught fire, and a troop of young fel-lows endeavored to tear it from the cord. Flam-ing pieces of paper were flying through the air, and the liquid was spirted in all directions.

Elsbeth put her arm in his and bent her head on his shoulder. Again that blissful thrill which he could not explain ran through him.

"There, now I am safe," she said, in a whisper. "Come to the wood afterwards, Paul, I have so much to tell you; there we shall be undisturbed."

And as she said this he felt quite anxious, out of pure joy.

They had come to the dancing-place. The trumpets resounded, and the dancers were spin-ning round and round.

"Shall we dance, too?" she asked, smiling.

"I cannot," he answered.

"That does not matter," she said; "for those sort of things Leo does well enough."

His foolish dreams which he had had under the juniper-bush to-day occurred to him.

"So it is with everything that I fancy to myself," he thought. "I have still one of your books, Els-beth," he said then.

"I know, I know," she answered, looking up at him with a smile.

"Pardon me that I—"

"Oh, what a fidget you are," she jested. "Leo meanwhile has ruined my whole library for me, and wants me now to replenish it for him, because he has nothing more to read."

Leo, and still Leo over again.

"Have you read much that is beautiful in it?" she asked him.

"Once I knew everything by heart."

"And now?"

"Now? Oh, good heavens, I have so much to think of in every-day life—they won't fit into my head any longer."

"Nor into mine, either, Paul. It is because we have seen too much of life; poetry is lost to us."

"To you, too?"

She sighed. "My poor mother," she said.

"What is it?"

"You see, for five years I have been sick-nurse; there are many sad hours, and when the night-light burns, and one's eyes hurt with watching so much, and outside the storm rattles the shutters, many thoughts come to one about life and death, about love and loneliness—well, in short, one makes a book of poetry in one's own head and does not read other people's any more. But come away from this noise; I should like to ask you so much, and here one can hardly hear one's own voice."

"Directly," he said; "I only wanted—"

His eyes wandered searchingly over the dancing-ground, then he heard a man's voice behind him, saying:

"Just look at those two little minxes, mad after men."

Instinctively he turned round, and saw the brothers Erdmann, whom he had not met for years. They had meanwhile been at an agricultural college and become grand gentlemen.

" We'll have fun with them," said the other.

Thereupon they laughingly mixed among the dancers.

Immediately after, Paul, too, saw his sisters. Their mass of brown curls hung loose about their faces, their cheeks were aflame, their bosoms heaved, and their eyes looked wild and eager for love.

" How happy they look—the sweet creatures," said Elsbeth.

Paul gave them a little sermon. They scarcely heeded him, but looked over his shoulders, giggling. And when he turned round he saw the two Erdmanns, who had hidden behind the musicians' platform and were making clandestine signs to them.

The twins by this time had escaped him, and the Erdmanns disappeared as well.

" Come away from here," said Elsbeth.

He consented, but remained as if rooted to the ground.

" What is the matter?" she asked.

He passed his hand across his brow; he could not get those contemptuous words which he had overheard out of his head.

The sisters were young, merry, inexperienced, nobody looked after them; if they should lower themselves in any way, if they—an icy shudder passed through him.

And he, who had vowed to be their faithful guardian, he was going after his own pleasure, he—

"Come to the wood," Elsbeth pleaded again.

"I can't," he gasped.

She looked at him wonderingly.

"I must—my sisters—nobody is with them. Do not be angry."

"Take me back to the table," she said.

He did so.   Neither spoke a word.

Five minutes later he came upon his sisters, who, arm in arm with the Erdmanns, were trying to slip off to the wood.

"Where are you going?" he asked, stepping be-tween them.

They lowered their eyes in embarrassment, and Katie stammered, "We—wanted to go for a little walk."

The brothers Erdmann took the tone of good-fellowship, shook hands with him heartily, and wished most ardently to renew the friendship of their youthful days.   Behind his back they shook their fists at him.

"You will go at once to your mother," he said to the twins, and as they began to sulk he took their arms and drew them away.

The table was half deserted. The Douglas family had left the festival.

Then he went into the wood and reflected on what Elsbeth might have wished to tell him.

But it was not to be — something always came between them.

CHAPTER XI.

It was a midsummer night. The alder-tree sent forth its perfume. The moonlight lay in silver veils upon the earth. There was great rejoicing in the village. Tar-barrels were lighted, and the farm-servants and maids were dancing on the green. The flames sent their glare far over the heath, and the shrill sounds of the fiddle came sadly through the night.

Paul stood at the garden fence and looked out into the distance. The servants had gone to the midsummer-night's fire, and his sisters had not come home yet, either.

They had asked permission to visit the vicar's daughter Hedwig, their playmate, who was an unpretending, quiet girl, in whose company he gladly trusted them.

Now he thought he would wait till they had all come home.

The moonlight drew him out onto the heath. It lay there in midnight silence; only in the heather a linnet chirped from time to time, as if in its sleep. The wild-pinks bent their red heads, and the golden-rod shone as if it wanted to compete with the moonbeams.

Slowly, with hesitating steps, he walked on, sometimes stumbling over a mole-hill or entangling himself in the tendrils of the plants. The dew sparkled before him in shining drops. Thus he came to the region of the juniper-bushes, which looked more elf-like than usual.

The wood stood silent like a black wall, and the moonbeams rested on it like freshly-fallen snow. He found the place where years ago the hammock had hung; in the weird twilight the open space showed through the dark branches. It drew him on and on. Like a palace of dazzling marble the White House, with its balconies and gables, rose before his eyes. Deep silence enshrouded the manor-house; only here and there a dog barked and relapsed into silence directly.

He stood before the trellised gate, not knowing how he had come there. He grasped the bars with both hands and looked in. The wide yard lay yonder before him, bathed in the light of the moon; the big farm-wagons, which were ranged in a row before the stables, stood there in black outline; a white cat crept along the garden fence; everything else lay in deep sleep.

He walked on along the fence. On the ash-heap behind the forge lay some fragments of glimmering coals, which looked in the darkness like burning eyes. Here the garden began. High elm-trees bent their branches over him, and an overpowering perfume of laburnums and early roses floated through the trellis-work towards him. The gravel-strewn paths shone like silver threads through the branches, and the sundial, which had been the dream of his childhood, stood out darkly behind them.

The White House came nearer and nearer. Now he could almost look into the windows. Here, too, all seemed asleep.

He had read here and there in the Liederbuch, too, that the lover used to sing serenades to the queen of his heart on moonlight nights, to the accompaniment of either the guitar or mandolin if this was at all feasible. It had been thus in the beautiful days of chivalry, and in Spain or Italy might still be so. That occurred to him now, and he pictured to himself how it would look if he, Paul the simpleton, were to play the lute here as a knight-errant, crowing longing love-songs at the same time.

At this thought he laughed out loud, and then he remembered that he carried his instrument about with him everywhere. He seated himself on the grass, his back leaning against a post of the fence, and began to whistle — shyly and softly at first, then ever bolder and louder, and as usual when he was entirely given up to his feelings, he at last forgot everything around him.

He awoke as out of a dream when he heard a rustling and creaking of branches at the other side of the fence. He looked round amazed.

Yonder stood Elsbeth in her white dressing-gown with a dark ulster hastily thrown over it.

At the first moment he felt as if he must run away, but all his limbs seemed to be lamed.

"Elsbeth—what are you doing here?" he stammered.

"Ah! what are *you* doing here?" she retorted, smiling.

"I—I was whistling a little."

"And you came here for that?"

"Why should I not?"

"You are right—I am not going to forbid you."

She had pressed her forehead against the trellis-work and looked at him. Both were silent.

"Will you come in?" she asked then—probably not knowing what she said.

"Shall I climb the fence?" he retorted, quite innocently.

She smiled. "No," she said, shaking her head; "they could see you from the window, and that would not do. But I must speak to you. Wait; I will come out and walk a little way with you."

She pushed a loose bar aside and slipped out; then she gave him her hand, and said, "You were right to have come; I have often longed to speak to you, but you were never there." And she sighed deeply, as if the remembrance of sad hours overpowered her.

His whole body trembled. The sight of the maidenly figure, who in her night-garb stood before him so chaste and unconscious, almost took away his breath. His temples hammered, he bent his eyes to the ground.

"Why do you not speak to me?" she asked.

A confused smile passed over his face.

"Do not be angry," he gasped.

"Why should I be angry?" she asked. "I am so glad to have you for once quite to myself. But it is strange—quite like a fairy tale. I am standing at the window, looking at the moon. Mamma has just gone to sleep, and I consider whether I, too, might venture to go to bed, but my thoughts are so restless and my forehead burns—I feel so uneasy. Then suddenly I hear somebody whistling in the garden, so beautifully, so plaintively, as I have only once heard it in my life, and that a long time ago. 'That can only be Paul,' I say to myself, and the more I listen the clearer it is to me. 'But how does he come here?' I ask myself, and as I want above all things to make certain, I put on my cloak and creep down—so—here I am now, and now come, let us go into the wood; there no one can see us."

She laid her arm in his. Silently they walked across the moonlit meadow. And then suddenly she put both her hands up to her face and began to cry bitterly.

"Elsbeth, what is the matter?" he asked, terrified.

She trembled; her soft figure shook with noiseless sobs.

"Elsbeth, can't I help you?" he pleaded.

She shook her head hastily. "It's all right," she gasped; "it will soon be over." She tried to walk on, but her strength failed her. Sighing, she sank down into the damp grass.

He remained standing before her, looking down at her. "Let tears have their course;" that was the rule which he had already often experienced in life. All his timidity had left him. Here was somebody to be consoled, and he was a master at consoling.

When she had grown a little quieter he sat near her, and said, gently, "Will you unburden your heart to me, Elsbeth?"

"Yes, I will," she cried; "I have waited to do so these three long years. So long have I borne it, Paul, and I was almost choked with the burden, and have found no pitying soul in whom I could confide. Yonder in Italy and at beautiful Capri, where everything laughs and rejoices, I have often crept down to the sea in the middle of the night and cried out in my agony, and in the morning I have come back and laughed, even more than the others, for my mother—oh, mother, mother!" she cried, sobbing afresh.

"Be calm; you have me now, to whom you can tell it," he whispered to her.

"Yes, I have you, I have you," she gasped, and leaned her face on his shoulder. "You see I have always known that; but what good did that do me?

9

You were far away; I was often nearly writing to you, but I feared you might have become a stranger to me and would misunderstand me. And since we are back I have only one thought: 'I must confide in him; he is the only one who has known grief; he will understand me.'"

"Tell me what it is, Elsbeth," he urged.

"She will die," she cried out aloud.

"Your mother?"

"Yes."

"Who told you so?"

"The professor in Vienna who examined her. He wore quite a cheerful face before her, and said, 'If you are careful, you can live to a hundred years old;' but afterwards he sent for me, and asked me, 'Are you strong, young lady? Can you bear the truth?' 'I beg you to tell me all,' I answered. 'I must confide it to you,' he said, 'for you are the only one who nurses her.' And then he told me that she might die any day—unless—and then he gave me a number of rules which she must observe about eating and drinking and climate and excitement, and much more. Since that day I tremble from morning to night, and tend her and watch and find no rest. Sometimes the feeling comes over me, and I say to myself, 'You are young and want to enjoy life,' and then I try to be merry and sing, but every note chokes me and I collapse again. Of course, I must show a cheerful face to mother, and to father as well."

"But why do you not confide in him?" he interrupted her.

"Shall his life be poisoned as well?" she replied.
"No; I had rather bear it alone than see him suffer,
too. He has a happy nature, and loves her with
all his soul—otherwise he is sometimes hasty and
excitable, but to her he has never said an angry
word—let him hope as long as he can—I will not
undeceive him."

She leaned her head on her hands and stared
straight before her.

He remembered his mother's fairy tale.

"Dame Care—Dame Care," he murmured to
himself.

"What do you say?" she asked, and looked at
him with great, eager eyes, hungry for consolation.

"Oh, nothing," he replied, with a sad smile; "I
wish I could help you."

"Who could do that?"

"And yet perhaps I can," he said; "you have
only wanted somebody to confide in; you are not
so badly off as you think—indeed, Dame Care has
blessed you, too."

"What does that mean?" she asked.

And then he told her the beginning of that fairy
tale which he had kept in his memory so well.

"And how can one be freed from her blessings?"
she asked.

"I don't know," he replied; "mother never
would tell me the end of the fairy tale. I don't

think, either, there is any deliverance.   Such creatures as we are must renounce happiness of our own free-will, and however near it may be to us we may not see it—something sad always comes between us and happiness.   The only thing we can do is to watch over the happiness of others and to make them as happy as possible."

"But I should like to be a little happy myself," she said, raising her eyes to him trustfully.

"I wish I were as happy as you are," he answered.

"If only this anxiety were not always with me," she complained.

"Anxiety! you must let her be your friend; I have known her all my life, and when I did not know why I quickly found some reason.   It is not so bad, either; if there were no anxiety, one would not know for what purpose one lives.   But only think how contented you might be.   You see nothing but merry faces surrounding you.   Your mother feels happy in spite of all her sufferings, does she not?"

"Yes, thank God," she replied, "she has no idea how ill she is."

"There you see! and your father has no idea of it, either.   No care weighs on them; they love each other, and love you as well.   No angry word is spoken among you, and when your mother at last closes her eyes she will perhaps do so with a smile on her lips, and be able to say, 'I have always been very happy.' Do tell me—what more can you wish for?"

"But she shall not die," cried Elsbeth.

"Why not?" he asked; "is death so terrible?"

"Not for her, but for myself."

"There must not be any question of one's self," he replied, pressing his lips firmly together; "one must just try to bear it the best one can. Death is only terrible when one has waited for happiness all through life and it has not come. Then one must feel as if one had to get up hungry from a richly-spread table, and I should like to save any one I love from that. You see I have a mother, too; she also wished to be happy once, and even yet would like far too much to be so. I am the only one who could take care from her shoulders, and I am not able to do so. What do you think I must feel in this case? I see how she grows old in sorrow and need; I can count the wrinkles on her forehead and cheeks. Her mouth falls in and her chin grows long. It is a long time since she spoke any loud word; from day to day she becomes quieter, and so, quietly, she will die one day, and I shall be standing by and shall say, 'It is my fault; I have not been able to give her one single day of happiness.'"

"Poor fellow," she whispered, "can't I help you at all?"

"No one can help me as long as my father—" he stopped, terrified at the course of his own thoughts.

Both were silent. They sat there for a long time without moving, their twenty-year-old heads leaning on their hands bowed with care. The moonbeams lay like silver on their hair, which the soft wind of the heath ruffled gently.

Then the shadow of a cloud passed over them. They both trembled. They felt as if the sad fairy whom they called Dame Care were spreading her sombre wings over them.

"I will go home," Elsbeth said, rising.

"Go, with God's blessing," he answered, solemnly.

She seized both his hands. "Thank you," she said, softly, "you have done me much, much good."

"And if you need me again—"

"Then I shall come and whistle for you," she answered, smiling.

And then they parted.

As in a dream Paul walked through the dark wood. The fir-trees rustled softly, the moonbeams were dancing on the moss.

"It is strange," he thought, "that they all tell me their woes," and he concluded from that that he was the happiest of them all. "Or the unhappiest," he added, meditatively; but then he laughed mysteriously and threw his cap high in the air.

When he stepped out into the light on the heath he saw two shadows flitting before him which disappeared in the misty distance.

Immediately after he heard something rustle in the juniper-bushes.

He turned quickly round and saw another shadowy couple, who seemed to sink into the ground behind a bush.

"The whole heath seems alive to-day," he murmured; and added, smiling, "of course, it is midsummer night."

Soon after him the twins came home with wild hair and flushed faces. They declared the vicar had told them their fortunes by cards till midnight. They would soon get husbands.

Giggling, they slipped away into their bedroom.

CHAPTER XII.

OLD Meyerhofer revelled in happiness. The promise of the rich Douglas to participate in his undertakings had raised his chances suddenly to a giddy height. The ears which for him heretofore had been closed began to listen to his explanations with eagerness, and in the public-houses, where until now he had been received with a half-ironical, half-pitying smile, he was now considered a great man.

"He will join me with half his fortune," he related; "we are already in communication with Borsig, in Berlin, who is going to furnish us with the necessary machines; we have written to Oldenburg for a technical director, and every day we have inquiries at what price we are able to sell the peat blocks per million."

The consequence was that they pressed him to begin issuing his shares; and when they gathered round him and asked him to reserve so and so many shares for each, he drew himself up proudly and said they would probably remain in private hands.

At home he was busy designing the new headings

for the note-paper of the future firm, and the borrowed money jingled in all his pockets.

Four weeks had passed since that midsummer night, when there came from Helenenthal two cards of invitation: one for Meyerhofer junior and the other for the young ladies.

"For a garden-party," they said.

"Aha! they court our favor already," the old man cried; "the rats smell the bacon."

Paul went with his card—which bore Elsbeth's hand-writing—behind a hay-stack, and there studied each letter of it in solitude for wellnigh an hour.

Then he went up to his garret and stood before the looking-glass.

He found that his whiskers had grown in fulness and only at the cheeks still showed thin places.

"It will do very well," he said, in an attack of vanity; but when he saw himself smile he wondered at the deep sad lines which ran from his eyes, past his nose, down to the corners of his mouth.

"Wrinkles make one interesting," he consoled himself by thinking.

From this hour he exclusively thought about what role he was to play at the party.

He practised before the looking-glass making stylish bows, and every morning looked at his Sunday suit, and tried to hide the shabbiness of his coat by brushing some black color over it.

The invitation had caused a great revolution in

his mind. It was for him a greeting from the promised land of joy, which he, like Moses, had never
seen but from afar. It was not for nothing that
he was twenty years old.

The day of the party arrived. His sisters had
put on their white muslin dresses and fastened
dark roses in their hair. They skipped up and
down before the looking-glass and asked each
other, "Am I beautiful?" And though each willingly replied "Yes" to this question, they hardly
knew how beautiful they were.

His mother sat in a corner, looked at them and
smiled.

Paul ran hither and thither in confusion. He
inwardly wondered how such a joyful event could
cause one such great anxiety. He had prepared
all sorts of beautiful speeches which he intended
to hold at the party: about the welfare of humanity, about peat-culture, and Heine's "Buch der
Lieder." They should see that he was able to
converse amiably with ladies.

The open carriage, a remainder of past splendor,
took the brother and sisters to the party. They
were to return on foot.

As they approached, Paul saw behind the fence
bright-colored dresses flitting through the shrubs
and heard the giggling of merry girls' voices. His
uncomfortable feeling was considerably augmented
by this.

In the veranda Mr. Douglas received them with

a merry laugh. He pinched the sisters' cheeks, slapped him on the shoulder, and said,

"Well, young knight, to-day we are going to win our spurs."

Paul turned his cap in his hand and broke into a silly laugh, at which he felt angry with himself.

"Now *allons* to the ladies!" cried Mr. Douglas, taking the sisters one on each arm, while he himself had to trot behind them.

The giggling came nearer and nearer. Gay men's voices were intermingled with it—he felt as if he were going to be beheaded. And then a sort of veil came over his eyes; indistinctly he saw the crowd of strange faces, which seemed to stare at him from the clouds. His speeches about the turf-culture came to his mind, but there was nothing to be done with them at this moment.

Then he saw Elsbeth's face rise in the mist. She wore a brooch of blue stones and smiled at him kindly. In spite of this smile she never had appeared so strange to him as at that moment.

"Mr. Paul Meyerhofer, the companion of my childhood," she said, taking his hand, and leading him round. He bowed to all sides, and had a vague feeling that he was making himself ridiculous.

"Eh, there is my pattern boy," the cousin's merry voice called out, and all the ladies giggled.

Then he was asked to sit down and was offered a cup of coffee.

"Mamma has gone to lie down a little," Elsbeth whispered to him; "she is not quite well to-day."

"Isn't she?" he said, and smiled in a silly manner.

Cousin Leo had gathered a circle of young ladies round himself, and told them a story about a young lawyer who had been so fond of sweets that, seeing a bag of *pralines* which he was not allowed to have, he had been crystallized into a sugar-loaf. They almost died with laughter over this.

"Oh, if only I could tell such stories," thought Paul to himself, and, as nothing better occurred to him, he ate one piece of cake after the other.

The sisters had immediately been laid hold of by several strange gentlemen; they laughed boldly in their faces, while the quickest repartees flowed from their mouths.

The sisters suddenly appeared to him like beings from a higher world.

"Now we are going to play a nice game, ladies," said Cousin Leo, putting one knee across the other, and leaning back negligently in his arm-chair. "The game is called 'Proposing.' The ladies walk about singly and the gentlemen, too. The gentleman asks the lady he meets, '*Est-ce que vous m'aimez?*' and the lady either answers '*Je vous adore*'—then she is his wife—or she silently refuses him. He who receives the most refusals receives a nightcap, which he has to wear during the rest of the whole evening."

The ladies thought this game very amusing, and

all rose to set to work directly. Paul rose, too, though he would have liked best to remain in his dark corner.

"What can those foreign words be?" he asked himself; he would have liked to inquire of one of the gentlemen, but he was ashamed to betray his ignorance and so to disgrace his sisters. Elsbeth had gone away with the other girls; he would have liked best to confide in her.

He went after the others, quite depressed, but when he saw the first lady coming towards him his anxiety was so great that he quickly left the path and hid in the thickest shrubs.

There was a little wilderness there, as if it might have been in the deepest part of the wood. Nettles and ferns raised their slender stalks, and the un-canny wolf's-milk was competing for supremacy with the burdock. In the midst of this tangled undergrowth he crouched down, put his elbows on his knees, and meditated:

"So that was what people called amusing themselves? It was a good thing that he should learn it for once, but like it he could not. Anyhow, it was nicer at home, and, besides, who could know whether the servants had finished weeding in time —whether the peat had not been piled up too damp? There was much to do at home, while he was lingering about here, entering into silly games like a fool. If it had not been for Elsbeth—but, indeed, what good was she to him? As she smiled at him so she smiled at them all, and if Cousin Leo began with his jokes how bold he was, how he flattered them all. Oh the world is bad, and they are all false—all, all!"

He heard his name being called from the path, but he pressed himself the closer into his hiding-place. Here at least he was sheltered from mockery. An oppressive sultriness was in the air; sleepy buzzing drones were creeping about on the ground. A thunder-storm seemed at hand.

"It's all the same to me," thought Paul; "I have nothing to lose and—the winter rye is in."

It had grown quiet outside—from the distance the clatter of glasses, glass-plates, and teaspoons could be heard, and from time to time it was intermingled with a suppressed laugh.

Paul drew in his breath. The longer he remained in his hiding-place the more dejected he felt; at last he appeared to himself like a school-boy who hides to escape his master's punishment. The smell of the weeds became more intense and more unbearable; an unpleasant moisture came up from the damp ground; like a pale fog it rose before his eyes. Steel-blue clouds rolled up in the sky; the thunder began to resound afar.

"That's what they call pleasure," thought Paul.

There was a rustling in the branches. Heavy drops came splashing down on the leaves; then Paul crept out of his hiding-place like a criminal.

Shouts of laughter welcomed him from the veranda.

"There comes August," one of the gentlemen called out, softly. He had been in Berlin, and had seen the circus there; and the others joined him.

"My honored guests," cried Leo, climbing on a chair, "this pattern boy, called Paul Meyerhofer, has in the most inconsiderate manner withdrawn from the verdict of the assembly. As he foresaw, in his feeling of unworthiness, that most of the refusals would be gathered upon his undignified head, he has in most reprehensible cowardice—"

"I don't know why you speak so badly of me," said Paul, hurt, for he took everything seriously.

A fresh peal of laughter answered him.

"I make the proposition to confer the nightcap on him as a punishment for his crime, and to form a jury for this purpose."

"If you please, I'll take the cap without that," Paul answered, irritated. By this time he had only to open his mouth to call forth fresh mirth.

Solemnly he was crowned with the nightcap.

"I must look very funny, after all," he thought, for they were all dying with laughter. Only his sisters did not laugh; blushing deeply, they looked down in their laps, and Elsbeth looked at him with embarrassment, as if she wanted to ask his pardon.

"August," was again softly whispered from the circle of gentlemen.

Immediately after, the thunder-storm broke forth.

In troops they all took refuge in the house. The young ladies turned pale ; most of them were afraid of the thunder ; one even fainted.

Leo proposed they should form a circle, and that each of them should tell a story; he who did not know any had to give a forfeit.

They agreed to this. The order of precedence was appointed by lot, and one of the gentlemen made the beginning with a merry student's anecdote, which he declared he had experienced himself. Then it was the turn of some young girls, who preferred to pay forfeits, and then he himself was called out.

The gentlemen cleared their throats mockingly, and the girls nudged each other and giggled. Then anger overpowered him, and, knitting his brow, he began at random,

"Once upon a time there was some one who was so ridiculous that people had only to look at him when they wanted to laugh to their hearts' content. He himself did not know how this was, for he had never laughed in his life. . . ."

There was a deep silence all round. The smiles froze on their faces ; first one and then the other looked down upon the ground.

"Go on," cried Elsbeth, nodding to him gently. But a feeling of shame came over him that he thus dared to show his innermost self to these strange people.

"I can't go on," he said, and rose.

This time no one laughed, and for a while there was only a deep, oppressive silence, and then the girl who had been chosen to collect the forfeits came up to him and said, with a polite courtesy,

"Then you must pay a forfeit."

"Willingly," he answered, and detached his watch from the chain.

"An uncomfortable fellow," he heard one of the young gentlemen say low to his neighbor. It was he who had first called up that nickname.

Then it was Leo's turn, who treated them to one of his most racy anecdotes; but the gayety would not come back again.

The rain splashed against the window-panes with a hollow sound; the shadow of black clouds filled the room. It was as if the gray Dame was gliding through the air and touching the laughing young faces with her wings, so that they looked serious and old.

Only when Elsbeth opened the piano and began a merry dance the frozen gayety recommenced.

Paul stood in a corner and gazed at the merry-making. They left him quite to himself; only now and then a shy glance met him.

The twins were flying round the room; their curls were loose, and a wild light sparkled in their eyes.

"Let them romp about," thought Paul; "they must return to misery soon enough." But that there was no misery for them never occurred to him.

10

When Elsbeth was replaced at the piano by somebody else, she came towards him and said, "You are very much bored, are you not?"

"Oh no," he said. "Everything is still so new to me."

"Be merry," she pleaded; "we only live once."

And at that moment Leo came rushing up to her, seized her round the waist, and danced away with her.

"Nevertheless, she is still a stranger to you," thought Paul.

As she passed him again she whispered to him, "Go into the next room; I have something to tell you."

"What can she mean to tell me?" he thought; but he did as he was told.

Half hidden by the curtain, he waited, but as she did not come, every minute the bitterness of his soul increased. He remembered his beautiful speeches about the peat-culture and Heine's "Buch der Lieder," and shrugged his shoulders contemptuously over his own stupidity. He felt as if he had grown years older and maturer in the course of this one afternoon.

And then the questions suddenly arose within him, "What business have you here? What are all those merry people, who laugh and want to please each other, and live thoughtlessly from one day to another—what are all those to you? You were a fool, a miserable fool, when you thought that you had a right to be merry; that you, too, could be what they are."

The ground burned under his feet. He felt as if he were committing a sin by remaining a minute longer in this place.

He slipped out into the hall, where his cap hung.

"Tell my sisters," he said to the servant who was waiting there, "that I am going home to order a carriage for them."

And he breathed as if relieved when the door closed behind him.

The storm had abated: a soft rain came drizzling from the sky, the wind blew refreshingly over the heath, and at the verge of the horizon, where the evening glow paled away, the sheet-lightning of the far-distant thunder-storm shot from fiery, glowing clouds.

As if the wild hunters were behind him, he ran across the rain-soaked road to the wood, whose branches closed above his head with a peaceful murmur. The damp moss sent out its perfume, and sparkling drops fell from the needles of the fir-trees.

When he stepped out onto the heath, and saw the dark outline of his home before his eyes, he stretched out his arms, and cried out into the storm:

"Here is my place—here I belong, and I shall be a rogue if ever again I try to find my happiness among strangers. I swear here that I will reject all vanities and foolish hankerings. I know now what I am, and what is unfit for me shall be lost to me. Amen."

So he took leave of his youth and of his youthful dreams.

CHAPTER XIII.

WHEN he awoke next morning he found his mother sitting near his bed.

"You up already?" he asked, wonderingly.

"I have not been able to sleep," she said, in her low voice, which always sounded as if she were asking pardon for what she said.

"Why not?" he asked.

She did not answer, but stroked his hair and smiled at him sadly. Then he knew that the twins had been telling tales, and that it was grief for him which did not let her rest.

"It was not so bad, mother," he said. consolingly; "they made fun of me a little, nothing more."

"Elsbeth, too?" she asked, with big, anxious eyes.

"No, not she," he replied, "but—" he was silent and turned to the wall.

"But what?" asked his mother.

"I don't know," he answered, "but there is a 'but' in it—"

"You wrong her, perhaps," said his mother, "and look, she sent you this by the girls." She drew from her pocket a long object which was carefully wrapped in tissue-paper.

In it was a flute, made of black ebony, with sparkling silver keys.

Paul blushed with shame and joy; but his joy soon vanished, and after he had looked at the instrument for a while he said, softly, "What must I do with it now?"

"You must learn to play it," answered his mother, with a touch of pride.

"It is too late," he replied, shaking his head sadly; "there are other things for me to do." He felt as if he had been made to drag something dead out of its grave.

"Well, it seems that you cut a nice figure yesterday," said his father, when they met at the breakfast-table.

He quietly smiled to himself, and his father muttered something about lack of feeling of honor.

The twins had big dreamy eyes, and when they looked at each other a blissful smile crossed their faces. They, at least, were happy.

Weeks passed. The harvest was got in unharmed, thanks to Paul's untiring care. It was a better year than it had been for a long time. But his father was already calculating how he could use the profits for his peat speculation.

He bragged on in his usual manner, and the less Mr. Douglas seemed to pay attention to the proceedings, the more he boasted at the inns about the advantage of his partnership.

Having once consented to swindle, he had to

outvie every lie by a new and bigger one. Mr. Douglas might be as patient as he liked; the abuse which was made of his name at last became too much for him.

It was one morning towards the end of August that Paul, who was working in the yard with Michel Raudszus, saw the tall figure of their neighbor walking across the fields straight to the Haidehof.

He was startled—that could not bode any good.

Mr. Douglas shook hands with him kindly, but from under his iron-gray, bushy brows shot an ill-boding look.

"Is your father at home?" he asked, and his voice sounded angry and threatening.

"He is in the parlor," Paul said, depressed; "if you will allow me, I will take you to him."

At the sight of the unexpected guest, his father jumped up embarrassed from his chair; but he recovered himself immediately, and began, in his boasting tone, "Oh, it is a good thing that you are here, sir; I have something urgent to say to you."

"And I not less to you," retorted Mr. Douglas, planting his massive figure close before him. "How is it, my dear friend, that you abuse my name in this manner?"

"I—your name—sir? What do you mean? Paul, go out."

"He may stay here," retorted Mr. Douglas, turning to Paul.

"He shall go out, sir!" cried the old man. "I

suppose I am still master in my own house, sir ?"

Paul left the room.

In the dark passage he found his mother, who had folded her hands and was gazing towards the door with a fixed look. At the sight of him she broke into tears and wrung her hands.

"He will lose us the only friend we have still on earth," she sobbed; then she sank down in his arms, starting convulsively when the threatening voices of the two men fell louder on her ear.

"Come away, mother," he urged; "it excites you too much, and we can't help matters, anyhow."

She let him drag her to her bedroom without resistance.

"Give me a little vinegar," she entreated, "or I shall drop."

He did as she asked, and while he rubbed her temples with it, spoke to her in a loud tone, so that she should not hear the raised voices of the two men.

Suddenly the doors banged; for a while all was quiet—uncomfortably quiet; then the clattering of a chain and the cry of his father, hoarse with fury,

"Sultan—at him !"

" For God's sake, he is setting the dog at him !" shrieked Paul, and rushed into the yard.

He came just in time to see how Sultan, a big fierce mastiff, sprang at Douglas's neck, while his father, brandishing his whip, ran after him.

Michel Raudszus had thrust his hands into his pockets and was looking on.

"Father, what are you doing?" he shouted, tore the whip from his hand, and wanted to go after the dog, but before he could reach the struggling group the beast, strangled by the powerful hand of the giant, lay on the ground stretching out its four paws.

The blood ran down from Douglas's arm and neck. His anger seemed over. He remained standing still, wiping his hands with his pocket-handkerchief, and said, with a good-natured smile,

"The poor beast has had to pay for it."

"You are wounded, Mr. Douglas!" Paul cried, clasping his hands.

"He has taken my neck for a joint of veal," he said. "Come with me for a few steps, and help me to wash myself, so that my womenkind may not be too much frightened."

"Forgive him," Paul entreated; "he did not know what he was doing."

"Will you come back, you wretch?" shrieked his father's voice from the yard. "I suppose you want to make common cause with that forsworn scoundrel!"

There was a convulsive twitch in his neighbor's clinched fists; but he mastered himself, and said with a forced smile,

"Go back; the son ought to stay with the father."

"But I want to make amends," Paul stammered.

"The swindler, the rogue," was heard from the background.

"Go back," said Douglas, with set teeth; "make him keep quiet, or he will do for himself."

Then he began to whistle a march with all his might, in order not to hear the abuse, and walked off with a measured tread.

The old man was raging in the yard like a madman; he threw the stones about, swung the cart-pole in the air, and kicked with his feet right and left.

When he met Paul he wanted to seize him by the throat, but at that moment his mother rushed out of doors with a piercing cry and threw herself between them. She clung to Paul with both arms; she wanted to speak, but the fear of her husband lamed her tongue. She could only look at him.

"Pack of women!" he cried, shrugging his shoulders contemptuously, and turned away; but feeling obliged to vent his rage on somebody, he walked up to Michel Raudszus, who was slowly returning to his work.

"You dog, what are you gaping here for?" he shouted at him.

"I am working, sir," he answered, and gave him a cutting glance from under his black brows.

"What should prevent me, you dog, from grinding you to powder?" the old man shrieked, shaking his fists under his nose.

The servant shrank back, and at that moment

both his master's fists struck him in the face. He staggered back—every drop of blood left his dark face ; without uttering a sound, he seized upon an axe.

But at this moment, Paul, who had been watching the scene with growing anxiety, grasped his arm from behind, wrested the weapon from his hand, and threw it into the well.

His father tried to clutch the servant by the throat again, but with quick resolution Paul seized him round the body, and although the old man kicked and struggled, gathering up all strength, carried him in his arms into the parlor, the door of which he locked from the outside.

"What have you done to your father?" his mother whimpered. She had beheld this deed of violence petrified with horror, for that her son could attack his father was to her perfectly incomprehensible. She looked shyly up at him, and repeated, wofully, "What have you done to your father ?"

Paul bent down to her, kissed her hand, and said, " Be calm, mother, I had to save his life."

"And now you have locked him up ? Paul, Paul !"

" He must remain there till Michel has gone," he replied. '' Don't open the door for him, or there will be an accident.''

Then he walked out into the yard. The servant was leaning against the stable door. chewing his black beard, and leering at him viciously.

"Michel Raudszus!" he called out to him.

The man approached. The veins on his forehead had swollen like blue cords. He did not dare look at him.

"Your surplus wages are five marks and fifty pfenning. Here they are. In five minutes you must be gone."

The servant gave him such a terribly sinister glance that Paul was alarmed at the thought that he had suffered this man near him so long without any foreboding; he kept his eyes fixed upon him, for he feared every moment to be attacked by him.

But the servant turned away in silence, went to the stables, where he tied up his bundle, and two minutes later walked out at the gate. During the whole terrible scene he had not uttered a single word.

"That's done! now to father," said Paul, firmly resolved to bear all blows and abuse calmly.

He unlocked the door, and expected that his father would rush upon him.

The old man was sitting huddled up in the corner of the sofa, staring before him. He did not move, either, when Paul came up to him and said, beseechingly,

"I did not like doing it, father, but it had to be done."

He only gave him a shy look askance; then said, bitterly,

"You can do what you like; I am an old man, and you are the strongest."

Then he sank back again.

From that day forward Paul was master in the house.

CHAPTER XIV.

THREE weeks had passed since then. Paul worked like a galley-slave. In spite of that a strange
unrest was upon him. When he allowed himself a
few moments' repose he could not bear to stay at
home. He felt as if the walls were falling in upon
him. Then he rambled about on the heath or in
the wood, or he lingered near Helenenthal.

"If I should meet Elsbeth I think I should sink
into the ground with shame," he said to himself,
and yet he looked about for her everywhere, and
trembled with fear and joy when he saw a female
figure coming towards him in the distance.

He also began to neglect his night's rest. As
soon as all in the house were asleep he crept away,
and often returned only in the bright morning to
go to work again with swimming head and weary
limbs.

"I will make amends—amends," he murmured
often to himself; and when his scythe hissed through
the corn, he said, keeping time with it. "make
amends—make amends." But how to do so was
totally vague to him; he did not even know if Douglas had been seriously hurt by the dog's bite.

Once when he was roving about at twilight on the other side of the wood he saw Michel Raudszus coming from Helenenthal. He carried a spade over his shoulder, on which hung a bundle. Paul looked at him fixedly; he expected to be attacked by him, but the servant only gave him a shy side-glance and a wide berth.

"That fellow looks as if he were brooding over some evil," he thought, looking after him.

Douglas had taken the expelled workman into his service, so one of the laborers said, and when his father heard this he laughed, and said, "That's just like the hypocrite—he will brew something nice for me."

He was firmly convinced that Douglas had given his case into the hands of the law; indeed, he found a certain satisfaction in the thought that he would be judged "unjustly," of course, and as from one day to the other the summons never came, he explained, scornfully,

"The noble lord is fond of respites."

But Douglas seemed willing totally to ignore the ignominy he had suffered; he did not even demand the capital lent on mortgage.

Paul's soul was overflowing with gratitude, and the less he found means to show it the deeper he felt the shame—the more his unrest haunted him.

So one night he again stood motionless at the garden fence of Helenenthal.

Early autumn mists lay on the ground, and the withering grass quivered lightly.

The White House disappeared in the shadows of the night, and only from one of the windows there shone a dull, dark-red light.

"There she is, watching near her sick mother," Paul thought. And as he found no other means to call her he began to whistle. Twice, three times, he stopped to listen. Nobody came, and anxiety rose within him.

With groping hand he searched for the gap in the fence which Elsbeth had shown him once, and when he had found it he penetrated to the inner garden. The branches tore his clothes as, in a sort of wilderness, he crept along the ground to find a path. At last he came to an open place. The white gravel threw out a dim light which shone brighter than the little lamp in the sick-room.

He seated himself on a bench and looked thither. He thought he saw a shadow moving behind the curtains.

Then suddenly all around grew light; the rose-trees were visible in the night; the gravel sparkled, and the gables of the dwelling-house, which had just before stood out in a dark mass, now showed in dark reddish tints, as if the light of dawn had fallen upon it.

Wonderingly he turned round; the blood froze in his veins; a purple flash of fire shot up in the dark sky. The black clouds were outlined with edges of fire, white flames whirled upward, and high above shot the glowing beams, as if there was an *aurora borealis* in the sky.

"Father's house is burning!"

His head fell heavily against the back of the bench; the next moment he raised himself up, his knees shook, the blood hammered in his temples. "On, on! save what is to be saved!" cried a voice within him; and with a wild rush he broke through the bushes, climbed the garden fence, and sank down into the ditch on the other side.

The burning farm glared over the heath like the rising sun. The stubble shone, and the black wood was dipped in a red glow.

The dwelling-house was as yet unhurt; its walls shone like marble, its windows sparkled like carbuncles. The yard was as bright as in daylight. It was the barn that was burning—the barn, filled to the roof with the harvest. His work, his happiness, his hope, lost like this in smoke and flames.

He gathered himself up again; in wild haste he rushed across the heath. When he passed the wood he thought he saw a shadow flitting away which, at his approach, sank flat on the ground. He scarcely heeded it.

"On, on! save what is to be saved!"

Tumultuous screams greeted him from the yard. The farm-servants were rushing about wildly, the maids were wringing their hands, his sisters ran about calling his name.

11

The village had just awakened. . . . The high-road filled with people. . . . Water-buckets were dragged forth, and a rotten fire - engine came also rattling along.

"Where is your master?" he shouted to the servants.

"Just being carried in; he has broken his leg," was the reply. Misfortune upon misfortune.

"Let the barn burn," he called out to others who, losing their heads entirely, were pouring tiny buckets of water into the flames.

"Save the cattle—take care that they do not run into the flames."

Three or four men hurried to the stables.

"You others to the house; don't carry anything out of it."

"Don't carry anything out," he repeated, tearing the objects out of the hands of some strangers who were just dragging them out of the house.

"But we want to save the things."

"Save the house!"

He hurried up the staircase. In passing he saw his mother sitting mute and tearless near his father, who lay on the sofa, whimpering.

Through a trap-door he jumped onto the roof.

"Give me the hose."

On a pitchfork they handed him the metal point of the hose. The column of water fell hissing upon the hot bricks.

He sat astride on the ridge of the roof. His

clothes became hot ; glimmering sparks, which came flying from the barn, settled on his hair. Burning wounds covered his face and hands.

He felt nothing that happened to his person, but he saw and heard everything around him—his senses seemed doubled.

He saw how the sheaves flew up to the sky in fiery flames, and saw them sink down in a magnificent circle; he saw the horses and cows run out into the meadows, where they were safe between the fences; he saw the dog, half-singed, tearing at his chain.

"Unchain the dog," he called down.

He saw little graceful flames, in bluish flickering light, dancing from the roof of the barn to the neighboring shed.

"The shed is burning!" he shouted below. "Save what is in it!"

A few people hurried away to pull out the carts.

And meanwhile the column of water hissed over the roof, made its way to the rafters and splashed over the bricks. Little white clouds rose before him and disappeared, to reappear again in other places.

Then suddenly "Black Susy" came to his mind. She was standing in the farthest corner of the shed, buried among old rubbish.

A pang shot through his breast. Shall she perish now as well—she, on whom his heart had ever placed its hopes?

"Save the locomobile!" he shouted down.

But no one understood him.

The longing to bring help to "Black Susy" seized upon him so powerfully that for a moment he felt he must even sacrifice the house.

"Send somebody to replace me," he called down to the crowd of people, who for the greater part stood idly gaping.

A stalwart mason from the village came climbing up, took off the slates, and so made himself a path up to the ridge of the roof. Paul gave the hose to him and glided down, wondering inwardly that he broke neither arms nor legs.

Then he penetrated into the shed, from which suffocating smoke was already whirling towards him.

"Who is coming with me?" he shouted.

Two laborers from the village presented themselves.

"Forward!"

Into the smoke and flames they went.

"Here is the shaft—seize it—out quickly!"

Creaking and rattling, the locomobile came staggering out into the yard. Behind her and those who had saved her the roof of the shed fell in.

.   .   .   .

The morning dawned. The gray twilight intermingled with the smoke of the ruins, from which here and there flames sprang up to sink down again immediately exhausted.

The crowd had dispersed. Leaden silence weighed upon the farm; only from the scene of the fire there came a soft creaking and hissing, as if the flames, before subsiding, were holding once more murmuring intercourse.

"So," said Paul, "that is done."

Dwelling-house and stables with all the live-stock were saved. Barns and sheds lay in ashes.

"Now we are just as poor as we were twenty years ago," he meditated, feeling his wounds, "and if I had not been roving about perhaps this would never have happened."

When he entered the porch overgrown with creepers he found his mother, with folded hands, crouching in a corner. Deep lines furrowed her cheeks, and her eyes were staring into vacancy, as if she still saw the flames playing before her.

"Mother," he cried, anxiously, for he feared that she was not far from madness.

Then she nodded a few times, and said,

"Yes, yes; such is life."

"It will be better again, mother," he cried.

She looked at him and smiled. It cut him to the heart, this smile.

"Your father has just turned me out," she said; "I entreat you not to turn me out, too."

"Mother, for Christ's sake, don't speak like that!"

"You see, Paul, it has really not been my fault," she said, looking up at him with a pleading expression, "I never go with a light into the stables."

"But who says so?"

"Your father says that it is all my fault and told me to go to the devil. But don't harm him, Paul," she entreated, anxiously, as she saw him flying into a passion; "don't interfere with him again, he suffers such great pain."

"The doctor is coming in an hour; I have sent for him already."

"Go to your father, Paul, and comfort him; you see, I should like to go myself, but he has turned me out," and, crouching down again, she muttered to herself,

"He has turned me out—out."

CHAPTER XV.

UNSPEAKABLE misery had descended on the Haidehof. The father lay in the parlor, on his sickbed, and groaned and complained and cursed the hour of his birth. In milder moments he seized his wife's hand with tearful eyes, and asked her forgiveness for having united her fate to his ruined life, and promised to make her rich and happy in future. Rich—above all things, rich.

It was too late. Mild words from him now made no impression on her. In her tormented heart she already heard the abuse which would inevitably follow them. With withered cheeks and lustreless eyes she walked about, never uttering a sound of complaint, doubly pitiful in her silence.

But no one had pity on her—not even God and eternal fate. She grew more tired from day to day; on her pale, blue-veined forehead the stamp of death seemed already to burn, and the happiness she had longed for through all her life was farther away than ever.

The only one who would have been able to give her some relief was Paul, and he avoided her like a criminal. He scarcely dared to shake hands with her in the morning, and when she looked at him he looked down. If she had been less torpid and less grief-laden she might have had some suspicion, but all she felt in her misery was that she lacked consolation.

Once at twilight, when he was rummaging about as usual after work in the ruins of the spot where the fire had been, she went after him, sat down near him on the crumbling foundation, and tried to enter into conversation, but he avoided her, as he had done before.

"Paul, don't be so hard to me," she pleaded, and her eyes filled with tears.

"I am not doing anything to you, mother," he said, setting his teeth.

"Paul, you have something against me?"

"No, mother."

"Do you think that the fire was caused by my fault?"

Then he cried out loud, clasped her knees, and wept like a child; but when she wanted to stroke his hair—the only caress which had been usual between them—he sprang up, pushed her back, and cried,

"Do not touch me, mother; I am not worthy of it."

Then he turned his back on her, and walked out onto the heath.

Since the moment of his first waking after the fire a fixed idea possessed him which would not leave go of him; the fixed idea that *he* alone had been guilty of it all.

"If I had not been roaming about," he said to himself—"if I had watched the house, as was my duty, this misfortune could never have happened." All his secret yearnings appeared to him now like a crime committed against his father's house.

Like Jesus in Gethsemane, he struggled with his own heart, seeking expiation and forgiveness. But his self-torment did not let him rest anywhere. At all hours the flames were dancing before his eyes, and when he went to bed at night and stared into the darkness, it seemed as if from every chink fiery tongues were jutting forth, as if clouds of black smoke surrounded him instead of the shadows of the night.

He had not been able yet to think about the cause of the fire; the cares which were overwhelming him again were too great to leave any room for thoughts of revenge. The very necessities of life failed them; money for the chemist could scarcely be scraped together. He meditated and calculated day and night, and formed great plans of campaign to collect the most absolutely necessary cash. He also wrote to his brothers, to know whether they could not procure him by their influence a few hundred thalers at moderate interest. They answered, deeply grieved, that they themselves were so over-run with debts that it was impossible for them to reckon on any further credit. Gottfried, the teacher had, indeed, engaged himself a short time ago to a wealthy young lady, and Paul was convinced that it could not have been difficult for him to induce her family to lend him a small sum, but he was of opinion that the dignity of his position would suffer by such a request; he said he should be afraid of compromising himself with his father-in-law if he disclosed his real circumstances too early.

With all this it was a blessing that the ripe harvest had already been sold and delivered, and that the potatoes, for the greater part, were still in the ground; so he could get some ready money, which wou'd be sufficient to cover the most necessary expenses; but how, indeed, was the rebuilding of the barn ever to be contemplated?

In the middle of the ruins—melancholy ruins of charred beams and charred walls—" Black Susy " stood erect with her sooty body and slender neck, the only thing which, except for a few miserable carts, had been saved from destruction.

The twins, who during this sad time had lost much of their merriment, and only in quiet corners still prattled and giggled, went about timidly; and his father, when he for the first time sat upright in his bed and saw the black monster glaring through the window, clinched his fist, and cried,

"Why did they not let that beast be burned?"

But Paul loved her in his heart only the more tenderly. "Now would be the time for you to come to life again," he said, and pulled out the wheel and looked into the boiler. He began to cut little models of lime-wood in the evenings, and one day he wrote to Gottfried :

"Send me a few books out of the school-library on the working of steam-engines. I feel as if much depended on them for our home."

Gottfried was solicited in vain. In the first place, it went against his principles to take books from the library which he did not use himself ; and, secondly, they would not be of any good to Paul, as he was not up in the theory of physics. Then he wrote to Max. The latter immediately sent him a packet, weighing ten pounds, of brand-new volumes, enclosing a bill for fifty marks. He decided to keep the books and slowly to save up the fifty marks. "Nothing is too dear for 'Black Susy,'" he said.

But fresh cause for uneasiness was to befall him.

One morning a carriage came driving up to the farm, in which two unknown gentlemen were sitting with a gendarme, one of whom, a comfortable-looking man of about forty years old, wearing golden spectacles on his nose, introduced himself as a police-magistrate.

Paul was terrified, for he felt very well that he had been concealing many things.

The magistrate first examined the scene of the fire, took a sketch of the foundations, and asked where the doors and windows had been ; then he had all the servants called out, whom he questioned most closely as to what they had done on the day before, and up to the moment when the fire had broken out.

Paul stood near him, pale and trembling, and when the magistrate dismissed the servants to examine Paul himself, he felt as if the end of the world had come.

"Were you in the barn the day before the fire?" the magistrate asked.

"Yes."

"Do you smoke?"

"No."

"Do you remember whether in any way you had anything to do with fire, matches, or such things?"

"Oh no, I am much too careful for that."

"When were you last in the barn?"

"At eight o'clock in the evening."

"What were you doing there?"

"I made my usual evening round before I locked the gates."

"Do you always lock the gates yourself?"

"Yes, always."

"Did you notice anything on that particular evening?"

"No."

"Did you see any one lurking in the neighborhood?"

It flashed like lightning upon him. He only remembered at this moment the shadow which he had seen disappearing into the wood at the begin-

ning of the fire. But that was not in the neighborhood, and, drawing a long breath, he answered
" No."

" Well, now it will come out," he thought; the
very next question would bring his night wander-
ings to the light of day—would betray the secret
that hitherto he had kept in his inmost heart.

But no. The magistrate broke off suddenly, and
said, after a little pause,

" Was not a servant called Raudszus in your
service till a short time ago ?"

" Yes, " he answered, and stared at the magistrate
with astonished eyes. So it was on Raudszus, then,
that suspicion fell.

" Why did you dismiss him ?"

He related the dreadful occurrence minutely, but
took great care that the scene with Douglas, which
had preceded, should remain as much as possible
in the dark. Now, as the first danger was averted,
he had found his tranquillity again.

The clerk took notes eagerly, and the magistrate
raised his eyebrows, as if all were already clear to
him. When Paul had ended, he made a sign to the
gendarme, who turned round silently, and walked
off on the way to Helenenthal.

" Now for your father," said the magistrate; " is
he in a state to be examined ?"

" Let me see," answered Paul, and he went into
the sick-room.

He found his father sitting erect in his bed ; his

eyes sparkled, and on his features there were signs of ill-suppressed fury.

"Let them come," he called out to Paul; "it is all nothing but fiddlesticks—they do not dare to accuse the real one—but let them come in."

He, too, related the scene of the struggle; but just what Paul had concealed, from shame—the quarrel with Douglas, and the setting-on of the dog—he dwelt on before the strangers with boastful loquacity.

The magistrate scratched his head, thoughtfully, and his clerk noted everything down eagerly.

When Meyerhofer came to the moment in which he ought to have spoken of his son's interference, he was silent. He shot a glance at him, in which a world of defiance and anger flamed.

"And what more?" asked the magistrate.

"I am an old man," he muttered between his teeth; "do not force me to confess my own ignominy."

The magistrate was satisfied. When he asked the old man whether his suspicion had not already fallen on Michel Raudszus, he chuckled mysteriously to himself and murmured,

"He may have furnished the hand, the miserable hand, but—" he stopped.

"But?"

"It is a pity, sir, that justice wears a bandage over her eyes," he answered, with a sneering laugh. "I have nothing more to add."

Magistrate and clerk looked at each other, shaking their heads ; then the examination was closed.

"Will Michel Raudszus be arrested ?" Paul asked the gentlemen before they got into their carriage.

"Let us hope that has been done already," the magistrate answered. "He has made all sorts of suspicious allusions when drunk, and what we have learned from you is more than enough evidence to begin a trial against him. Of course many things will still have to be cleared up."

Then they drove away.

Paul stared after the carriage for a long time.

The last words of the magistrate had awakened his anxiety anew, and while weeks were passing and the first steps towards the trial were taken, he sat trembling nervously at home, just as if the verdict would crush him and him only.

Paul, with his mother and sisters, received a summons to the assizes ; it was only to his father that the choice was left whether he would be examined on oath at home for the last time, but he declared he would prefer to fall down dead in the court than to sit at home while the destroyer of his property was allowed to escaped scot-free. Whom he meant by this phrase he left unexplained — only that it was not the accused servant, he gave one plainly enough to understand.

The day of the trial came. Paul had made a portable chair for his father, which saved him walking a step. In this he was lifted into the cart and softly put down on a layer of hay.

It was a miserable rickety cart which brought the Meyerhofer family to the town, for the better vehicles had all been burned. Paul had made it as comfortable as he could. Over the truss of straw, which served for a seat, he had spread an old horse-cloth, which in the course of years had become torn and discolored.

With poverty all around him, the master of the house lay in the cart, groaning and scolding; his wife was enthroned above him, pale and wretched and harassed, as if she were the genius of this ruin. The ever-blooming youth, which even thrives on rubbish, laughed from two roguish pairs of eyes in between, and in front, as driver of this wretched vehicle, sat Paul, and looked sadly before him, for he was ashamed that he could offer no better conveyance to his dear ones, whom for the first time he took out for a long drive all together.

The faint beams of the November sun were lying on the yellow heath; the heather extended among thin yellow grass; here and there glistened pools of rain-water; and single leaves were hanging down from the crippled willows at the road-side like dead summer birds.

"Do you remember how, twenty-one years ago, we were driving along this same road?" Frau Elsbeth asked her husband, and threw a glance at Paul, whom she had at that time clasped to her breast.

Meyerhofer muttered something to himself, for he was no friend to memories—to *such* memories. But Frau Elsbeth folded her hands and thought of many things: it could be of nothing sad, for she sm:'~d.

The nearer the cart approached the end of the journey, the more depressed Paul felt. He stretched himself on his seat and a shiver kept passing through his frame.

That wild night of the fire stood before his eyes with awful clearness, and in the midst of his fear at having to stand and speak before strange people he was overcome with a feeling of happiness when he remembered how he had stood high on the steep roof, surrounded by smoke and flames, acting and ruling as the leading spirit whom all obeyed—the only one who in all the tumult had kept his head clear. " Perhaps I could still be as courageous as any man if it should be necessary," he said to himself, consolingly ; but he afterwards sank into still deeper despondency as he contemplated his sad, oppressed, worthless existence. " It will never be otherwise ; it can only become worse from year to year," he said. Then he heard his mother sighing behind him, and what he had just been thinking appeared to him as base, heartless selfishness.

" It is no question of myself," he murmured, and the cart passed through the gate of the town.

Before the red brick law-courts with the high stone staircase and arched windows the vehicle

12

stopped. Not far from it stood a well-known carriage, and the coachman on the box still wore the same tassel which had made such an impression on Paul at the time when he was to be confirmed.

When his father was raised up it caught his eye also.

"Ah, so the vagabond is there, too!" he cried. "I'll just see if he can stand a look from me."

Then Paul, with the help of a policeman, carried him up the steps to the room for the witnesses. His mother and sisters came after them, and the people stopped and looked at the melancholy procession.

The waiting-room for the witnesses was full of people, mostly inmates from Helenenthal. In one corner stood a small party of beggars, a woman with a bloated face, a gay red shawl tied round her waist, in which a little baby slept. A little troop of ragged children were clinging to the folds of her dress. They scratched their heads or secretly pinched each other. This was the family of the accused, who wished to state that their father had been at home that night.

Meyerhofer stretched himself out in his chair and threw defiant glances all around. He thought himself a greater man than ever to-day—a hero and a martyr at the same time.

The door opened, and Douglas appeared with Elsbeth on the threshold. Meyerhofer cast a poisonous glance at him and laughed scornfully to himself. Douglas did not heed him, but sat down in the opposite corner, drawing Elsbeth to him. She looked pale and worn, and had a shy, timid manner, that might arise from her strange, unaccustomed surroundings.

She nodded with a slight smile to Paul's mother and sisters, and looked at him with a meditative glance, which seemed to ask something.

He lowered his eyes, for he could not bear her gaze. His mother made a movement as if to cross over to her, but Meyerhofer seized her skirt, and said, louder than necessary, "If you dare !"

Paul felt as if paralyzed. His knees shook under him; a dull weight pressed upon his forehead which rendered him incapable of thought.

"You will bring shame on her," he murmured incessantly, but without knowing what he was saying.

Inside the court the examation of witnesses began. One after the other was called.

First the workmen; then the public-house keeper in whose house Michel Raudszus had made the suspicious allusions; then the ragged little group in the corner. The room began to empty. Then the name of Douglas was called out. He whispered a few words in his daughter's ear, which probably had reference to the Meyerhofers, and then walked off with long strides.

Her hands folded in her lap, she now sat alone by the wall. A deep blush of excitement burned on her cheeks. She looked very sweet and timid, and her simple, truthful nature was impressed on all her features.

His mother did not take her eyes from her, and at times she looked across at Paul and smiled as if in a dream.

A quarter of an hour elapsed; then Elsbeth's name also was called. She threw one friendly glance at his mother and disappeared through the door. Her examination was not long.

" Mr. Meyerhofer, senior !" the clerk called from the court, and sprang towards them to help Paul in carrying the chair.

The old man panted and puffed out his cheeks; then again he leaned back, moaning low—inwardly rejoicing greatly to be able to play a part so full of effect.

The wide assize court swam before Paul's eyes in a red mist; he indistinctly saw closely-packed faces gazing down on himself or on his father; then he had to leave the court again.

The sisters, who up to now had looked around full of curiosity, began to be afraid. To deaden their fear they ate the sandwiches they had brought. Paul encouraged them, and refused the sausage which they generously offered him.

His mother had retired to a corner, was trembling, and said, from time to time, " What may they be wanting with me ?"

" Mr. Meyerhofer, junior !" sounded from the door.

The next moment he stood in the lofty room filled with people before an elevated table, at which
sat several men with severe and serious faces ; only
one, who sat a little on one side, smiled constantly;
that was the chief-justice, who was feared by all
the world. On the right side of the court, too, on
raised seats, sat a little knot of dignified citizens,
who looked very much bored, and tried to pass the
time with penknives, bits of paper, etc. These were
the jury. On the left side, locked up in the dock,
sat the accused. He was making eyes at the audience, and his face looked as if the whole affair concerned anybody but him. Paul had never seen the
sinister fellow look so cheerful.

"Your name is Paul Meyerhofer, you were born
at such and such a time, Protestant, etc.?" asked
the judge who sat in the middle, a man with a
closely-shorn head and a large, sharply-cut nose
reading the dates from a big book. He spoke in
a pleasant murmuring tone, but suddenly his voice
grew harsh and cutting as a knife, and his eyes shot
lightning at Paul.

"Before your examination, Mr. Paul Meyerhofer,
I call your attention to the fact that you will have
to confirm your statement by oath."

Paul shuddered. The word oath passed through
his soul like a dagger. He felt as if he must throw
himself down and hide his face from all those spy-
ing eyes which were staring at him.

And then he gradually felt a strange change

come over him.   The staring eyes disappeared, the
court vanished in mist, and the longer the clear,
sharp voice of the judge was speaking to him, the
more impressively he heard himself threatened with
heavenly and earthly punishment, the more he felt
as if he were quite alone in the big room with that
man, and all his senses tended so to answer him
that Elsbeth should be entirely left out of the question.

"Now is the moment — now show yourself a
man!" cried a voice within him.   It was a feeling
very like the one he had had while sitting on the
roof: his wits were sharpened, and the dull weight
which pressed on him constantly sank away as if
the chains with which he had been fettered were
taken off.

He related in quiet words what he knew about
the accused, and described his character; he also
mentioned that he had felt a sort of inner resem-
blance between them.

When he said that, a murmur went through the
court, the jury let the bits of paper fall, and two or
three penknives were shut noisily.

"What happened when Mr. Douglas and your
father fell out?" asked the president.

"I cannot tell you that," he answered, in a firm
voice.

"Why not?"

"I should have to speak ill of my father," he answered.

"What does ill mean?" asked the president. " Do you mean to imply that you fear to expose your father to punishment by law?"

"Yes," he answered, softly.

Again the same murmur went through the court, and behind his back he heard the voice of his father hissing, "The degenerate rascal!" But he did not allow himself to be confused by that.

"The law permits you in such cases to refuse to make a statement," the president continued. "But what happened that made your father turn against Raudszus?"

Without hesitation he related the scene; only when he had to confess how he had carried his father into the house his voice shook, and he turned around as if wishing to implore pardon from him.

The old man had clinched his fists and gnashed his teeth. He had to live to see his own son tear the halo of glory from his head.

"And after you had dismissed the servant, did you see or hear nothing of him any more?" asked the president.

"No."

"When you awoke in the night of the fire, what did you see first?" he continued his questioning.

A long silence. Paul put his hands to his forehead and staggered back two steps.

A thrill of pity ran through the hall. No one thought otherwise but that the remembrance of that terrible sight overpowered him.

The silence continued.

"Please answer."

"I did—not—sleep."

"So you were awake. . . . Were you in your bedroom when you first perceived the glow of the fire?"

"No."

"Where were you?"

A long pause. One could have heard a leaf falling to the ground it was so still in the court.

"You were not at home?"

"No."

"Where then?"

"In—the garden—of—Helenenthal."

A surpressed murmur arose, which grew into a tumult when old Douglas, who had sprung up from his chair, cried out in a voice that penetrated through the court, "What were you doing there?" Old Meyerhofer uttered a curse. Elsbeth turned pale, and her head sank heavily against the back of the bench.

The president seized the bell.

"I must beg silence there," he said; "it is I who put the questions. On a repeated interruption I shall have you taken out of court. So, Mr. Paul Meyerhofer, what were you going to do in the garden of Helenenthal?"

At the same moment there arose a fresh murmur in the background, and in the witness-box a circle formed itself around Elsbeth.

"What is the matter over there?" asked the president.

The chief-justice, whose eyes no speck of dust in the court escaped, bent forward and whispered to him, with a meaning smile,

"The witness has fainted."

Then the president, too, smiled, and the whole assembly of judges smiled.

Elsbeth, leaning on her father's arm, left the court.

Now the little man with the sharply-cut features rose—he sat before the accused, and had been playing during the whole time with a bunch of keys—and said,

"I ask the president to adjourn the case for five minutes, as the presence of the witness concerned in this matter is of importance."

Paul sent a shy glance at this man.

The court adjourned.

The five minutes were an eternity. Paul was allowed to sit down in the witness-box. His father continued staring at him with fury in his eyes, but he made no sign that he wished to speak to him.

Elsbeth was brought back into the court, pale as death, and Paul stepped forward again.

"I warn you again," the president began, "to be in all things strictly truthful, for you know that each word of your statement is uttered under oath."

"I know it," said Paul.

"But you have the right, as you know, to refuse any statement if you fear that the same would bring down any punishment upon yourself or your family. Will and can you make use of this right now, as you did before?"

"No."

He spoke in a firm, clear voice, for he had the certainty that Elsbeth's honor would be irremediably lost if he were silent now.

"But if my oath is perjury?" he heard his conscience whisper immediately after; but it was too late.

"Oh! what did you want to do in the garden?" the president asked.

"I wanted—to make amends for the sin committed against Douglas in my father's house."

A murmur of disappointment and unbelief went through the court.

"And for that reason you roamed about in the strange garden?"

"I had a longing to meet somebody, of whom I might have asked pardon."

"And for that you chose the night?"

"I could not sleep."

"And were you driven there by your restlessness?"

"Yes."

"Did you meet anybody in the garden?"

"No."

"Have you been there on any former occasion at the same hour?"

A long pause, then another "no" came from his

mouth, this time softly and hesitatingly, as if wrung from his conscience.

The constraint which weighed on every one began to lessen, the president turned over his papers, and Elsbeth gazed across at him with big lustreless eyes.

"Where were you when you first saw the glow of the flames?"

"About twenty steps away from the manor-house of Helenenthal."

"And what did you do then?"

"I was much frightened, and hastened back immediately to my father's farm."

"In what manner did you leave the garden?"

"I climbed over the garden fence."

"So you did NOT open the door which leads from the garden to the yard?"

"No."

"And didn't you pass the front of the house?"

"No."

A new tumult arose in court. The little man with the bunch of keys rose and said,

"I must ask the president to question Miss Douglas again—regarding what she says she heard that night."

"If you please, Miss Douglas," said the president.

With a long look at Paul she rose. They now stood close together in the wide, crowded court, as if they belonged to each other.

"Where did the steps vanish to which you heard when the glow of the fire woke you?"

"Towards the yard," she replied, softly—hardly audible.

"And did you distinctly hear the handle of the garden gate rattle?"

"Yes."

"Consider well if you may not have been mistaken."

"I was not mistaken," she answered, softly but firmly.

"Thank you. You may sit down."

She went back to her seat with uncertain steps. Since that fatal "no" her eye was riveted on Paul. She seemed to have forgotten by that time all around her.

"When you got over the garden fence, which way did you take?" the president continued, turning to Paul.

"Across the heath."

"Did you pass the wood?"

"No; I ran two or three hundred steps away from it."

"Did you meet any one on your way?"

"I saw a shadow which moved towards the wood, and at my approach disappeared suddenly."

A prolonged stir went through the court; the accused man turned pale, and his eyes assumed a fixed look. The chief-justice did not take his eyes off him.

A few more unimportant questions, and then Paul was allowed to sit down.

His mother and sisters were called, but what they could tell was of no importance. The sisters looked round inquisitively, almost boldly. His mother wept when she had to speak about the moment of her waking.

Paul felt proud and happy that Elsbeth had not been compromised by him. He looked down smiling, and rejoiced at his courage. But when the witnesses were called for their oaths, and he had to lift up his hand, he felt as if a load of a hundred pounds were hanging on it, and as if a low, sad voice whispered in his ear, "Do not swear."

And he swore.

When he sat down the voice said again, "Have you, perhaps, committed perjury?" Instinctively he raised his head. Then he fancied that a gray shadow flitted past him and touched his forehead lightly.

He knitted his brows defiantly. "And supposing I should have sworn falsely, was it not for her?"

For a moment his soul was filled with wild joy at this thought, but in the next already a dull weight lay on his breast, stifling his breath and binding him hand and foot, so that he felt as if henceforth he would never be able to move any more.

He heard the monotonous voice of the counsel, who began his speech. But he did not heed it. Once he started, when the counsel for the defence pointed towards him with his bunch of keys, and cried out in his shrill, querulous voice : " And this witness, gentlemen of the jury, who roams about mysteriously at night in strange gardens, and finds out all sorts of psychological and artificial subterfuges to hide the tender motive of his nightly excursions, can you put any reliance upon him when he says he suddenly saw a shadow appear and disappear ? Shadows which, to put it mildly, can only originate in his overheated brain ? What did he want in the garden, gentlemen of the jury ? I leave it to your penetration, to your experience of life, to answer this question ; and as for the witness, it is his lookout to accommodate his oath to his conscience."

Then he collapsed completely.

The jury returned a verdict of " Guilty." Michel Raudszus was sentenced to five years penal servitude.

At the same moment, when the president pronounced the sentence of the law, a mocking laugh resounded through the court. It proceeded from Meyerhofer. He had got up in his chair and stretched out his maimed hand towards Douglas, as if he wanted to fly at his throat.

As he was carried out of court, he continually cried out,

" They hang the insignificant incendiaries, but the powerful ones are allowed to go scot-free."

The uncanny laughter of the helpless man resounded through the wide passages.

CHAPTER XVI.

Winter came and went. . . . The heath was covered with snow and became green again. . . . The ranunculus lifted up their golden heads. . . . The juniper sent forth its tender shoots, and the warble of the lark sounded from out the blue sky.

Only to the dismal Haidehaus spring would not come. Paul had, indeed, made it possible to procure corn for sowing, and a wooden building already stood erected on the place of ruin, but the hope for better times had still not come. Dull and joylessly he did his duty, and deeper and deeper the lines became traced upon his forehead. He brooded over things by himself more than ever, and the fear that he had committed perjury weighed heavily upon him.

Months elapsed before it was clear to him that his grievance was nothing but idle trifling which originated in his over-anxious stickling at words. He reflected thoroughly on the question which the president had addressed to him, and came to the conclusion that he could not have answered otherwise. It was, indeed, the first time that he had penetrated into his neighbor's garden; what had once taken place on a blissful moonlight night had happened on this side of the fence. What was that to the gentlemen of the law-courts?

"No; I am not a perjurer," he said to himself; "I am only a coward, a simpleton, who is afraid of the mere shadow of a deed. Ought I not proudly and joyfully to have sworn a false oath for Elsbeth's sake? Then I should be somebody; then I should have done something, while now I live on, torpid and discouraged, a farm laborer—nothing more."

And in the brain of this "pattern boy" arose the fervent wish to be a great criminal, just because he felt compelled to prove his own individuality. The hours which he had passed on the roof and in the witness-box now seemed to him the ideal of all earthly bliss, and the harder he worked the idler and more useless he fancied himself.

His father was still kept to his chair, which to all appearances he would never again be able to leave, for his broken leg had healed badly. Idle and grumbling he sat in his corner, turning over an old almanac without interest, and abusing every one who came near him.

Only for Paul he cherished a sort of involuntary respect; he grumbled to himself as often as he saw him, but did not dare to contradict him openly.

And his mother?

She had grown a little more weary, a little quieter, otherwise there was hardly any change perceptible in her; but those who observed more attentively could hear a rustle in the air, as though a vulture were hovering over the Haidehaus and draw ing its circles ever closer and closer, and preparing to pounce down one day on its prey.

She herself heard the rustle very well; she knew, too, what it signified; but she remained silent, as she had been silent all her life.

And happiness had not come yet.

At the beginning of April she took to her bed. "General weakness," the doctor said, and recommended a visit to a place where there were iron baths. She smiled, and begged him not to speak of a watering-place to any one, for she knew that Paul would work himself to death to make this course of treatment possible for her.

Such a course would not really help her. She knew very well what she needed; sunshine! Dame Care had shrouded her too closely with her sombre veil to allow a single ray of sun to penetrate into her soul.

It was now left to the twins to take care of the household. And the work was briskly done indeed; even Paul had to confess that. When they had broken anything, they laughed; when a walk was refused them, they cried; but the crying soon changed again to laughter, and the table was never so promptly served, the milk-pails had never been so bright.

His mother often observed that from her window, and thought, "It is a good thing that I should go away; I am no longer of any use in the world."

About Whitsuntide her sleep began to fail; then fever set in.

"Oh, how expensive quinine is!" sighed Paul, when the servant rode off to the chemist's; and he looked appealingly at "Black Susy," but she did not move. Often the work in the fields had to come to a stand-still, in order that they might earn a few groschen for the household by cutting peat.

His mother began to suffer from palpitations, and desired most earnestly that somebody would sit up with her at night. But the twins, tired out with their day's work, would fall asleep in the evening by the bedside of the invalid, and often sank down right across her bed, so that the feeble woman often had to bear upon her own body the weight of the two healthy girls.

Paul sent his sisters to rest, and took upon himself the office of watching.

"Go to sleep, my son," said his mother; "you need rest more than any of them."

But he remained; and in the May nights, when outside in the garden the flowers were whispering and the perfume of the lilac penetrated through every crack, the two would often sit hand in hand for hours looking at each other, as though they had wondrous things to impart. So it had always been between mother and son. The wealth of their love sought for expression in words, but care had robbed them of speech.

In the morning, when the sun rose, he dipped his head into icy cold water and went to work.

His presence brought peace to his mother, in so far that she could sleep at times when he was by. Then he used to go on tip-toe to his room and fetch down his books on physics, in which the construction of steam-engines was so learnedly and unintelligibly set forth. His head, tired with watching and unaccustomed to any mental work, with difficulty grasped the sense of the mysterious words; but he had time, and indefatigably he worked on, page by page, as a peasant ploughs a stony field.

If his mother opened her eyes, she would ask,

"How are you getting on, my son?"

And then he had to explain it to her, and she pretended to understand something about it.

But if she asked, "Why are you doing this?" he would put on a knowing look, and reply, "I am learning to make gold."

"My poor boy," she would answer, stroking his hand.

One night, immediately after the Whitsuntide holidays, she again could not sleep.

"Read me something from those learned books," she said; "they bore one so nicely. Perhaps they will send me to sleep."

And he did as she asked him; but when he had been reading almost an hour, he saw that she was gazing at him with big, feverish eyes, and was further than ever from sleep.

"So with that you want to make gold?" she asked.

"Yes, mother," he answered, confusedly, for the return of fever made him anxious.

"How will you do it?"

"You will see in good time," he answered, as usual.

But this time she would not be put off. "Tell me, my boy," she pleaded, "tell me now. . . . Who knows what may happen? . . . I should like at least to have that little bit of comfort before I fall asleep forever."

"Mother!" he cried, terrified.

"Be still, my boy," she said; "what does it matter? But tell me, tell me!" she pleaded with growing anxiety, as if in the next moment it might already be too late.

With bated breath and confused words he spoke of the plans which he had in his head: how he wanted to reawaken "Black Susy" to life, so that the moor could be utilized to its innermost depths; but in the middle of his speech, anxiety overcame him; he fell sobbing on his knees before the bed with his face on her breast.

She bade him look up, and said: "It was not right of me to make you anxious. If God so wills it, all may turn out differently yet. What you tell me has given me great joy. I know that if you

take anything in hand, you do not soon let it drop.
I only wish I could live to see it."

So, gently, imperceptibly, she restored his courage; as to herself, she had nothing left to hope
for.

Another night when, overtired, he had fallen
asleep in his chair, she called his name.

"What do you want, mother?" he asked, starting up.

"Nothing," she said. "Forgive me, I ought to
have let you sleep. But who knows how long we
shall still be able to talk together? I should like
to make the most of the time."

This time he was too much overcome with sleep
to understand the meaning of her words. He sat
down closer to her and took her hand, but his eyes
closed again directly.

She thought he was awake and began to speak.

"I was once a very merry young creature, not
very different from your sisters. . . . My heart was
nearly ready to burst with joy, and my eyes always
gazed into the distance, as if from there something
unspeakably beautiful would come—a prince, or
something of that sort. Once, too, I began to love
—with that other kind of love, that great heavenly
love which comes upon one like fate. But he would
not have me; he was fair and slender and had a
blemish on his chin. I always longed to kiss the
spot, but could never do it. He saw my love well
enough, and, one day, when he was especially dar-

ing, he took me in his arms and fondled me, and then let me go again. But I was happy; it made me glad that he had once held me in his arms."

She stopped, her eyes sparkled, a rosy, almost maidenly blush tinted her cheeks; she had grown wonderfully young again. Then she saw that he had fallen asleep, and sadly relapsed into silence.

When he awoke, Paul said, "It seems to me, mother, that you were telling me something."

"You must have been dreaming," she said, smiling; but her thoughts meanwhile had been wandering back through her whole life, seeking in every corner of her memory for the remnants of joy which lay concealed there.

"I don't really know," she said, "why I have been so sad all my life. When I come to think of it, a great misfortune has never really happened to me. Of course it was not nice when we had to leave Helenenthal, and when I saw the room lit up blood-red by the burning barn, it gave me a bad enough fright, but, on the whole, life has treated me tolerably well. I have reared all you children, I have not lost one by death—we have always had food and drink, too. Father has sometimes grumbled, it is true, but that is always the case in married life; you will find it so yourself some day. You children have always loved me. You boys have grown up able men, and the girls will be able women, if God wills it, and you keep your eye upon them. What more do I want?"

And so this poor woman, who was gradually being harassed to death, worried herself to discover *what* was harassing her to death. Slowly Dame Care lifted the veil from her head that Death might breathe in her face.

And one evening she died. . . . Her eyes closed; she scarcely knew how herself. The doctor who was called in spoke of weakness, anæmia. It is only sentimental people who say in such cases, "She died of a broken heart."

The twins knelt at her bedside, crying bitterly; their father, who had been carried in in his chair, sobbed aloud, and tried to bring her back forcibly to life. . . . Paul stood at the head of the bed biting his lips.

"I was right, after all," he thought; "she died before luck came. She has had to get up hungry from the table of life, just as I said."

He wondered that the pain he felt was not so great as he had fancied it would be. Only the confused thoughts about all sorts of stupid things flitting through his head like bats at dusk showed him the state of his mind.

It struck midnight; then his father said, "We will go to rest, children ; let him sleep who can ! . . . Hard days lie before us."

He embraced the twins, shook hands with Paul, and had himself carried to his room.

"How good father is to-day !" thought Paul; "he was never like that while she was alive." His sisters clung to his neck, sobbing, and implored him to watch near them, they were so afraid.

Paul spoke to them consolingly, took them to their room, and promised to come and look after them within an hour.

When at the end of this time he stepped to their bedside with a candle in his hand he found them fast asleep. They lay locked in a close embrace, and on their rosy cheeks the tears were still wet.

Then he went to his father's door to listen, and when there, too, he heard no sound, he crept on tiptoe to the room where the dead slept. For the last time he would watch by her side.

His sisters, on going away, had spread a white handkerchief over her face; he took it off, folded his hands, and watched how the flickering light played on her waxen features. She was little changed; only the blue veins in her temples were more prominent, and her eyelashes threw deeper shadows on the haggard cheeks.

He lit the night-light, which during her illness had been burning at her bedside every night, seated himself on the chair in which he always used to sit, and thought he would say a quiet prayer for the dead.

But suddenly it flashed through his mind that he had forgotten to send to the joiner to come early and take the measure.

It was to be a simple pine-wood coffin, painted black, and round it a garland of heather, for she had loved the delicate, unpretending little plant above all others.

"What will the coffin cost?" he went on thinking, and was suddenly struck with terror, for he had nothing to bury the dead with. He began to count and calculate, but could come to no conclusion.

"It is the first time that she wants anything for herself," he said, softly, and thought of the faded dress which she had worn from year's end to year's end.

He added up all that he could get together in a hurry from outstanding debts, but the sum was not sufficient by half to cover the expenses of the funeral.

The three cart-loads of peat, too, which he could send into town to-morrow and the day after, would make but little difference.

Then he took a piece of paper and began to calculate the expenses :

A coffin	15 thalers.
The place in the church-yard	10 thalers.
For the verger	5 thalers.
Linen for the shroud . . .	2 thalers.

Then the expenses of the funeral, which his father undoubtedly would wish to have conducted as grandly as possible :

10 bottles of port-wine	10 thalers.
1 box of cigars . . .	2 thalers.
2 small casks of beer . . .	2 thalers.

Ingredients for the cake : the flour they had in

the house, but sugar, raisins, almonds, rose-water,
etc., had to be purchased. How much would these
amount to? He calculated busily, but his additions
would not agree. "Mother will know very well,"
he thought, and was just about to ask her advice
when he saw that she was dead.

He was horrified. Only now, when his imagina-
tion had brought her back to life again, he understood that he had lost her. He wanted to cry out,
but mastered himself, for he had to go on with his
calculations.

"Forgive me, darling mother," he said, stroking
her cold cheeks with his right hand. "I cannot
yet mourn for you; I must first lay you under the
earth."

.   .   .   .

The funeral was to take place three days later.

As Paul had foreseen, his father could not be
prevented from arranging a great festivity. He
had sent invitations to all his friends in town, on
beautiful glazed paper with a black edge as wide as
your finger. Therein he had given expression to
his grief in well-chosen, elegant phrases, and had
nowhere forgotten to provide his signature with an
elaborate flourish.

In the evening, just when the remains were being
laid in the coffin, his two brothers arrived. They
had not been at home for many years, and Paul
almost failed to recognize them. Gottfried, the
tutor, a dignified man with a severe expression of

countenance and somewhat portly appearance, had on his arm a young lady veiled in black—his betrothed, who with a wondering glance took stock of the low, miserable rooms, and endeavored to show a face at once friendly and full of grief as the situation demanded. Max, the merchant, came behind them. He looked rather dissolute; his smart-looking mustache gave him an air ill-befitting the feelings of a newly-orphaned son, and his mourning was more evident in discomfort than in grief.

Both brothers solemnly embraced their father, and the young lady visitor bent down and kissed first his hand and then his forehead. Then they greeted the twins, who in their black dresses were looking fresher and sweeter than ever. They had overlooked Paul, who stood at the door and fingered his cap in confusion.

At last Gottfried asked, "Where is our brother?"

Then he stepped shyly forward and stretched out his hand.

Three pairs of eyes rested on him searchingly.

"If I were but once outside!" he thought, and as soon as he could get away he went out to work in the stables.

Gottfried followed him thither. Paul was alarmed when he saw him come, for he did not know what he should talk about to this aristocratic man.

"Dear brother," the latter said, "I have a favor to ask you. Could you not provide a brighter room for my betrothed? She feels herself rather crowded in the girls' room."

"I will give her my attic," said Paul.

"You would oblige me if you would do that."

Then he addressed a few more questions to him about their mother's illness, about the cattle, and about the mortgage which lay on the estate.

"You poor creatures," he said; "you have evidently had many a care. But did you endeavor to make the last days of our sainted mother as easy as possible?"

Paul assured him he had done all that was in his power.

"I am glad of that," his brother replied, in a severe tone; "it would have been a sad neglect of your duty if you had not done so. And now come, let us go together to visit the remains of our sainted mother, that she, looking down from heaven, may see us all united."

He took Paul's hand and drew him into the room in which his mother rested peacefully among flowers and burning candles, and where the others were already assembled.

Paul remained standing at the door timidly. He would have given much to be alone with his dead mother for one moment, but as that was impossible he softly crept out and looked through the window from outside, as if he were one of the lookers-on from the village who were standing there.

A little later Max came to him and led him confidentially aside. "I have a favor to ask you, dear boy," he said; "my throat is quite parched with the dust of the journey and with crying. Could you procure me a drop of beer?"

'Paul answered that there were two full casks, but that they were only to be tapped next morning for the funeral.

"Just give me the tap," Max answered; "I am an expert. The beer in the casks will be just as fresh to-morrow as it is to-day."

And when Paul had done his bidding, he turned his back on him and went away.

At eleven o'clock the candles round the coffin were blown out—every one retired to rest.

Paul found that there was no bed left for him, and climbed into the hay-loft, where he sat upright all night buried in thought.

At ten o'clock in the morning the first guests arrived, and, indeed, such guests as had neither accepted the invitation nor been expected at all. When Paul saw them coming his first thought was, "Have I provided enough food and drink?" and the more the carriages came rolling into the yard, and entire strangers kept stretching out their black-gloved hands to his family, the more a voice seemed to say to him, "There won't be enough."

His father had again one of his days of grandeur. He sat in his portable chair as if on a throne, his two eldest sons like vassals near him, and allowed himself to be admired in his grief.

Whenever a new guest came up to him he pressed the proffered right hand in both of his, as if *he* were the one to console, bent his grief-stricken head, and spoke broken words in a voice stifled with sobs, such as: "Yes, she has gone! gone! she's gone! There is no balm for the wounds of the heart! May heaven make amends to her for the grief earth has caused her!" and so forth.

In between he called out to Paul, "My son, you do not provide any wine! My son, remember to offer our guests some refreshment."

Paul ran from one to the other like a waiter, anxiously counting the bottles, which diminished rapidly, and envying his sisters, who, in their fine black dresses, could quietly sit in a corner and cry to their hearts' content, while the strange sister-in-law consoled them. He had not thought of the mourning-dresses in his calculation at all, and it was great good-luck that the merchant sent them on credit, otherwise his sisters could not have appeared at all.

He himself did not look like a mourner in his simple gray suit, and most of the guests who did not know him went quietly past him, and only noticed his existence when he offered them wine and cigars.

In the yard a number of women assembled who had loved his mother on account of her quiet, simple manners, and who now wanted to follow the cortege without really belonging to the mourners.

The sharp eye of his father soon discovered them.

"Paul, my son," he cried, "go out and urge the ladies to enter the house of mourning."

Paul obeyed this order with hesitation, for he did not know how to word the invitation. When he stepped out onto the threshold his first glance fell on Elsbeth, who, in a mourning-dress, stood among the village women and carried a wreath of white roses. And when she saw him her eyes filled with tears.

For a moment he felt as if he would like to press his head against the folds of her dress and cry there; but others stood near her, staring at him. He made an awkward bow, and said, "My father begs you—would you like to see the dead?"

The women slowly went into the house; only Elsbeth lingered.

"Won't you come in, too?" he asked.

"My poor dear Paul," she said, and seized his hand.

He shut his eyes and staggered back two steps.

"Do come," he said, mastering himself again; "look at her, she has always loved you so much."

"Paul, my son, where are you?" sounded his father's voice from the interior of the house.

"Paul," she said, hesitating, with rising tears "you must not despair; there are still others who— love you."

"Oh yes," he said, "I know—but come, I must pour out the wine."

She sighed deeply; then she timidly went in after him, and mixed again with the other women.

"Paul, come here!" beckoned his father, who to-day seemed to fancy himself the master again; and when Paul bent his head to him, he whispered in his ear, "I hear the wine is finished. What does that mean? Will you shame us all?"

"I think there are a few more bottles," Paul answered.

"Make them last till the vicar comes; but you must also offer a glass to the women. Do you hear?"

"Oh, if only the vicar would come soon," sighed Paul, and tried hard to fill the glasses only half.

And at last the vicar came. The whole assembly pressed into the room where the dead woman lay in her coffin. The place was bathed in sunshine, and checkered lights which had found their way through the waving linden branches played merrily on the marble-white face.

Paul helped to carry his father's chair to the head of the coffin; then he withdrew to a quiet corner behind the mourning assembly where he could rest a little, for he was tired with much running about.

But they would not let him rest. "Where is the youngest son?" asked the vicar, who wanted to gather the whole family round him.

"Paul, my child, where are you?" called his father.

Then he had to come forward, and took his place close to the head of the coffin, near his father's chair.

A low murmur passed through the assembly, and some looked embarrassed, as if they would say, "So that is a son, too? Then we have made a mistake there."

The dancing sunbeams caught the vicar's attention, and he took them as the text for his sermon. The earthly sun was indeed shining brightly and full of joy; but that was nothing—that was utter darkness compared with the heavenly sunshine. Then he praised the dead, and praised also those left behind, especially the faithful husband and the two eldest sons as the proud pillars of the house; there was also a spare morsel for Paul, the servant, whom his master had found faithful unto death.

It was only a pity that he understood nothing of this honeyed praise. Lost in thought, he stared before him. His look rested on the silk bow which stood out from his mother's cap, and which moved gently when the draught, caused by the vicar's waving arms, glided over it. It resembled a white butterfly that moves its wings to rise into the air.

Then a hymn was sung and the lid placed on the coffin. At this moment there sounded from the background a heart-rending cry, "Mother, mother!"

Startled and astonished, every one turned round. It was Elsbeth Douglas who had uttered it. Now she lay fainting in the arms of her neighbor.

Paul understood her well. She had thought of the moment when the lid would be laid over her own mother's face. And he vowed to himself he

14

would then be at her side to comfort her. His father also looked up, and on his features the question was clearly written: "Is she, too, here?"

Elsbeth was taken into the next room, and two women remained with her until she recovered.

But the uplifted coffin was borne staggering out of the door till it found rest on the hearse.

Paul seized his cap. Then Gottfried, pressing to his side, put something soft and black into his hand.

"At least tie this crape round your arm," he whispered to him.

"Why?"

"People might think you did not want to wear mourning."

Paul started at this thought and did as he was told. Afterwards he was grieved to have been thus shamed by his brother. and only much later it became clear to him which of them had worn the deepest mourning.

The cemetery lay in the midst of the heath. Three solitary pine-trees indicated it from afar, and along the edge of the wall surrounding it thick thorn-hedges bloomed.

Thither the sad cortege went; the sons followed immediately behind the coffin, the father, with the twins, behind them in a little carriage.

Paul stared straight before him; he thought of the sand through which he was wading — of the wine—of Elsbeth—of his father's portable chair—

and of the heather wreath, which had been half detached from the coffin and was dragging behind.

He resolved to take care that it should not be lowered into the grave with the coffin.

By the grave he felt nothing but a violent burning pain in his temples, and while the vicar was giving the benediction it suddenly occurred to him that instead of the wine he might very well have given beer. Then he had to look after the twins, who in their grief did foolish things, and wanted to spring into the grave after the coffin. He took them in his arms kissed them, and made them lay their heads on his shoulder. They did so, closed their eyes, and breathed as if asleep.

When the first handful of earth was rolling down on the coffin he had a feeling of disgust, as if skittles were being played in his head, and when the bare hillock began to arise, he thought, " To-morrow already there must be some green turf put round it."

The crowd dispersed, his father was carried back to his carriage, and the three sons walked home. Max and Gottfried spoke in low, solemn tones of their earliest recollections of the dead. But Paul was silent, and thought, " Thank God, they have laid her under the sod !"

A feverish activity was still working in his brain —he had as yet understood nothing, had not wanted to understand—but when he entered the yard which, with its shingle-roofed stable, and with the

recent traces of the fire, lay gray and desolate before him, it suddenly came upon him as with a
lightning-flash, like a totally new idea, " Mother has
gone !"

He turned round, groped with his hands in the
air, and, as if thunder-struck, sank to the ground.

CHAPTER XVII.

THE summer passed away, and autumn in its garb of mist came creeping over the heath. Red sunbeams wandered wearily along the edge of the wood, and the heather lowered its purple head. At this time in the Haidehaus, which till now had been quieter than usual, strange sounds began to be heard. Like the knocking of hammers and the tone of bells at the same time, they sounded far over the heath in strict rhythm, at times louder, at times softer, but always with a harmonious echo, which slowly died away into the air.

The villagers stopped, wondering, on the road. One of them asked, "What is going on at Meyerhofer's?"

And another said, "It almost sounds as if he had built himself a forge."

"He will never forge luck," said a third, and they separated, laughing.

The father, who as usual had sat in his corner yawning and grumbling, started up at the first sound, and called the twins to account for it. But they knew nothing either, but that quite early that day a workman had come from the town with files, hammers, and a solder-box, and had had a long conference with Paul, who held in his hand all sorts of plans and designs. They quickly ran to look, and this was what they found :

Behind the shed stood " Black Susy," surrounded with a wooden scaffolding like a lady in her crinoline, and on the scaffolding Paul and the foreman climbed busily about, hammering, examining, and screwing in rivets.

Full of wonder, the twins looked at each other, for they guessed that something grand was in preparation; but they did not deem it necessary to bring these tidings to their father, for they remembered that two little letters they had written had to be quickly and secretly taken to the post by the servant-girl.

Paul, however, stood high up on " Black Susy's " round back, leaning against the slender chimney, and looked longingly towards the moor, like Columbus about to discover a new world.

The first steps on the hazardous road were taken.

In the long, sleepless nights which followed his mother's death, when grief held his soul in iron claws, he had fled from the melancholy image of the deceased to his books. Like a mole he burrowed his way through the dark theories, and when his head buzzed and his body became exhausted from the exciting brain-work, he would cry out to himself, " Her last hope shall not be disappointed !" Then he stretched his limbs, and a new impulse of energy flashed into his brain, and on and on he went, working restlessly till the iron riddle solved itself harmoniously, till each lever was transformed into a muscle, each tube into an artery, contrived on the wisest plans, like a human body by the spirit of the eternal Creator.

Weeks and months passed. Meantime his mind was so completely absorbed by this thirst for knowledge, this desire to create, that all that which had previously harassed him vanished like a distant shadow. His mother's image became more and more peaceful, and seemed to smile upon him. The harvest became multiplied in the barn as if carried thither by invisible hands, and on the day when the last bundle of oats was unloaded before the stack he clapped his hand to his forehead and exclaimed, " It seems to me only yesterday since I saw the first ear !"

The more his knowledge increased and ripened, so much the more the anxiety to succeed arose in his soul. When he wrote to the blacksmith, his heart beat like that of a student before his examination. He shunned bringing his deeds to the light as though to mention them were a crime, for he feared being laughed at. But the constant hammering proclaimed the news to the world.

The new foreman had to sit at their own table, and the father marked his disapprobation of him by refusing to greet his entrance, and muttering a great deal into his plate about fools and parasites.

But nobody heeded him, and the work quietly proceeded. According to Paul's directions, the machine was taken to pieces and sounded in every one of its minutest parts. The faults which a professional engineer would have discovered at the first glance, these two men had to search out and explain to each other with the greatest trouble. A dispute between them would often last for hours, like meetings of the senate.

Once the foreman asked, impatiently, "Why the devil do you not send the thing to a workshop to be repaired?"

Paul started. That, indeed, was an idea! It seemed to him quite a new one to-day, and yet it had often come into his mind before. But he had never liked to yield to it, for it seemed to him too daring and absurd; and, besides, he was too much afraid they might return "Susy" as "past mending." He was like that peasant woman who preferred doctoring her husband to death herself to being told by the doctor "he cannot be saved."

When it had grown dark, and the workmen and servants had ceased working, he used to poke about the work-room aimlessly for another hour or so, simply because he could not tear himself away from "Susy." He would have liked best to stand near her as watchman until the morning. He liked to carry with him under his arm some of his plans or a book. This, also, was aimless, for it was dark —he only wanted to have everything nicely in order. All this happened in great secrecy, for no one had a firmer conviction that Paul was a fool than Paul himself.

One evening, when he was searching in the dark for one of his books to take there with him, he put his hand upon something long and round, carefully wrapped up in tissue-paper in the farthest corner of a drawer.

He could feel in the darkness how he blushed. It was Elsbeth's flute. How was it possible that he had so seldom bestowed a thought upon it or upon the giver? The fair form that he had seen for the last time on the darkest day of his life had gradually faded from his mind as his existence passed into the shadowy realm of sorrow, and now at last, from sheer trouble and care, she had become to him like a shadow herself.

For the first moment he could scarcely recall her features. It was only little by little that her image presented itself to his mind.

He took the flute instead of the books under his arm, crept away to the shed, and sat down on the boiler. He fingered the keys with curiosity; he also put the mouth-piece to his lips, but did not dare to produce a sound, for he did not want to disturb any one's sleep.

"It would be nice," he said to himself, "if I could play all sorts of sweet melodies and think of Elsbeth all the while; I could then once more pour out my heart to her, and feel that I, too, was something in the world. But, then, *am* I in the world for myself alone?" he asked himself, absently laying hold of one of the crooked handles. "As this crooked handle turns and turns without knowing why, and in itself is nothing but a piece of dead iron, so I, too, must turn and turn, and not ask 'Why!' There are said to be people in the world who have the right to live for themselves, and to mould the world according to their own wishes. But they are differently constituted from me; they are handsome and proud and daring, and the sun always shines upon them. They may even allow themselves the privilege of possessing a heart and acting according to its dictates. But I! Oh, good God!" He paused, and sadly contemplated the flute, the keys of which dimly shone in the dusk.

"If I were such a one," he continued, after a while, "I should have become a celebrated musician. I know very well there are many melodies in my brain which no one else has ever whistled; and when I had attained my end I should have married Elsbeth—and father would have been rich, and mother happy; but now mother is dead—father is a poor cripple—Elsbeth will take another—and I stand here looking at the flute and can't play on it."

He laughed out loud, and then slid to the front, so that he could reach the chimney. He stroked it, and said, "But I will learn to play *this* flute that it'll be a pleasure to hear."

As he sat there he fancied he heard subdued tittering and whispering in the garden. He listened; there was no doubt of it. A pair of lovers were cooing, or, perhaps, more than one pair, for divers voices were intermingled, like the twittering of a number of sparrows.

"The maids keep sweethearts, it seems to me," he said; "I'll show them the way out."

He fetched a whip, which was hanging on the stable door, and climbed over the farthest part of the garden fence to waylay the intruders.

Then suddenly he stopped short as if turned to stone, his eyes starting out of his head, and the whip trembling in his hand. He had distinguished his sisters' voices.

He leaned against the trunk of a tree and listened.

"Does he leave you in peace now?" one of the lovers asked, in a whisper.

"He has too much to do with his machine just now," Greta's voice replied; "even his unpalatable sermons he spares us."

"You have never heeded them, anyhow!"

Greta giggled. "In spite of all his dignity he is only a stupid boy, and he understands nothing about love; as long as I can remember he has hung about Elsbeth Douglas; but do you suppose he has ever once dared raise his eyes to her? She, of course, would not dream of taking such a languishing idiot. There is her cousin Leo — he is quite another fellow."

His heart threatened to stop beating, but he went on listening.

"I can't understand why you obey him at all," said the voice of her lover; "we have always given him a thrashing first, and then let him go, and in return he would beg our pardon. One has only to oppose him firmly. he is such a coward!"

"Just wait a bit, you rogue!" thought Paul, who now knew whom he had before him.

But Greta answered, eagerly: "Oh, fie! he has not deserved that from us. He loves us so much that we really ought to be ashamed to deceive him : whatever he sees that we want he gives us, and I could swear that it is nothing but love that makes him so sad. So one mustn't mind now and then taking a sermon into the bargain, especially if one pays no attention to it afterwards!"

"It's a good thing I know that," thought Paul, and crept round in a half-circle, till he came to the arbor where the other couple were sitting.

There it was very much quieter; only from time to time a kiss or a giggle sounded from the darkness among the trees. Then he heard Kate's voice :

"And why did you dance so much with Matilda last Sunday?"

"That is a horrid calumny," answered the other brother. "What gossip told you that?"

"The vicar's daughter Hedwig told me."

"I like that! She is jealous of you; that's the

whole story. How she looked at me last Sunday!
I thought my hair would be singed."

"Oh, the false girl!"

"Well, don't grieve about that. You are all
false! My sweet little lark, my sunshine, my little
madcap, lay your head on my knee, I want to ruffle
your hair."

"So?"

"No; you are lying on my watch-chain. That's
right! Sing me something."

"What shall I sing about?"

"About love!"

"First earn it, you rogue!"

Then all was quiet for a while. Presently Katie
began to warble, softly,

> "'The nightingale on the lilac-bush
>   Sang night's soft hours away;
> I heard a crash, a gentle push,
>   My window-pane gave way!
>
> "'I ran to see the cause in haste,
>   At night's soft witching hour,
> And there I found a ladder placed—
>   A man stood by my bower.
>   La, la, la!'"

"Go on singing!"

"Oh no, it really is not proper."

"Why, then, did you begin it?"

She giggled and was silent.

"Sing me something else."

"Before I sing give me a kiss!"   A short struggle; then his voice:

"What? first you want one, and then you struggle, you cat!"

"Here I am."

"Leave go! d——n it, you scratch!"

"If you take another girl I will scratch out your
eyes!"

"Anything else?"

"No; I will lie down under a juniper-bush and
starve myself to death.   You must come to my
funeral.   Oh, that will be beautiful!   Now just pay
attention; I know a beautiful verse:

> "'What my love for you is, have you known?
>   There is on the heath a grave all alone;
>   In it a poor dead poet is sleeping,
>   To whom his love has brought much weeping;
>   He sleeps and sleeps in his sombre grave,
>   But sleeps not away the grief love gave.
>   At midnight go to the grave on the heath,
>   And wait till he again shall breathe;
>   He knows the singing and kissing well,
>   And he can tell—'

"Isn't that pretty?"

"Very pretty!   Who taught you that, Kitty?"

"I once found it in a book of songs which belonged to mother.   I almost think she made it
herself."

During this conversation Paul had stood there
stupefied with horror; but when he heard his

mother's name his anger overpowered him, and he cracked his whip over the heads of the couple, so that the withered leaves of the arbor flew rustling about.

With a loud cry they all sprang up. No sooner had the brothers recognized him than they attempted to make off; but the girls clung to them whimpering. They sought protection against their own brother.

"Come here!" he called out to them. Then they left their lovers and flew to one another for mutual protection.

The two Erdmanns receded farther still.

"You stay here!" he cried.

"What do you want with us?" said the elder one, who was the first to recover his impudence.

"You shall answer to me for your conduct."

"You know where we are to be found," said the younger one, and pulled his brother by the coat-tail as a hint to escape with him. But at this moment Paul seized him by the throat.

"Leave go!" he screamed.

"You come into the house with me."

"Oh no; *rather* not," said the elder one.

"I don't know at all what you want with us," said the younger one, who, under the iron grasp of Paul's fist, was not a little frightened. "We love your sisters; we have nothing to do with you."

"And if you love them, don't you know where

the door is, through which you might have come to woo them?   Robbers that you are!"

At this moment Ulrich had torn his brother from Paul's grasp; and before he could collect his senses they both flew in hot haste through the garden, leaped the fence, and disappeared in the darkness of the heath.

Completely stunned, he turned round and saw his sisters crouching behind the trunk of a tree.

"Come!" he said, pointing towards the house, and, sobbing, they followed him.

When they wanted to slip away to their own room, he said, opening the door of the parlor, "In here."   Trembling, they crouched down in a corner, for they did not know what punishment he would inflict upon them.

He lit the candle himself, took up the family album and took out a picture.

"Now come to your room."   Like two returning penitents they crept slowly behind him.

"Who is that?" he asked, in his severest voice, pointing to the picture.   It was a portrait of their mother, taken in early youth, almost effaced by the lapse of time.   But they recognized it very well, and, wringing their hands, fell on their knees before the bed and sobbed pitifully on the pillow.

And then they confessed everything to him.   It was worse than he had ever imagined.

A dreadful silence ensued.   Paul stepped to the window and looked out into the night.

"Thank God you are dead, mother!" he said, folding his hands.

Then they wept aloud, crept up to him on their knees, and wanted to kiss his hands. He stroked their hair. He loved them far too well.

"Children, children!" he said, sinking down in a chair, almost as helpless as they were.

"Scold us, Paul," sobbed Kate.

"No, rather beat us," urged Greta; "we have deserved it."

He passed his hand across his brow. It all still seemed to him like a bad dream.

"How could this have happened?" he murmured. "Have I watched over you so badly?"

"They said they—wanted to—marry us!" Kate gasped out.

"When the year of mourning was over, the wedding was to be," added Greta.

"And if they said that, they shall keep their word," he said, endeavoring to console himself. "Do not kneel to me, children, kneel down before God—you need it. This portrait henceforth shall stand on your little table every night. Will you then still have courage to pursue the path of shame? Good-night."

They rushed after him and entreated him to stay with them, "they were so frightened!" but he disengaged himself gently from them and went up to his garret, where he sat and brooded in the dark. He was so deeply ashamed that he thought he

15

should never more be able to bear the light of day.

The next morning he sent for the foreman and paid him off.

The good man looked up into his face quite aghast. "But now, Mr. Meyerhofer, when all is going on so well?" he said.

"Yes, going on so well," he murmured, thoughtfully. "Shame added to misfortune!—the man is right."

"Something has upset me," he then said, "which has given me a disgust for work. Let us leave it for the moment, and when the time comes I will send for you again."

His father bitterly complained over the disturbance in the night. "What were you storming about in the garden?" he asked. "I heard your voice!"

"Thieves were after the apples," replied Paul.

The twins had red, swollen eyes, and did not dare to raise them from the ground.

"So that's how fallen girls look," thought Paul, and promised to be as strict with them as a jailer. But when he spoke harshly to them for the first time, and they looked up at him with a pained, humble glance, like two penitent Magdalenes, he was so much overcome by pity that he folded them weeping in his arms, and said, "Compose yourselves, children, all will yet be well."

He was under the firm conviction that the two Erdmanns would not let the day pass without coming to the Haidehof. "Their consciences will bring them," he said to himself. He felt so sure of it that after dinner he strongly urged his father, who in his laziness had become very slovenly, to put on his new coat, as visitors of importance were expected. His father yielded, grumbling, and was doubly angry afterwards when he found that the immense exertion had been quite useless.

"They will come to-morrow," said Paul to himself when he went to bed; "they have not had the courage to-day."

But the next day passed, too, without anybody appearing, and so the whole week went by.

Paul ran about the house as if distracted. Every ten minutes he was to be seen standing at the gate and looking out over the heath, so that the servants nudged one another and began to whisper all sorts of nonsense.

"It is a pity," he said to himself, "that I am still so innocent, and have not the least experience in love matters; otherwise I should know what I ought to do."

An agonizing fear began to master him, and he tossed about in his bed unable to sleep.

"I must make matters easy for them," he thought one morning, and ordered the basket carriage, which a short time ago he had bought at an auction, to be got ready, and drove to Lotkeim, the Erdmanns' estate, which they kept up together since their parents' death.

His heart felt a pang of shame and wrath as now, like one soliciting a favor, he entered the estate of those who had already injured him so much through his life. Little was wanting to make him turn round again at the gate, but his hands clasped the reins more firmly, and his lips murmured, "It is no question of what you feel."

He drove across the grass-grown yard, on which high thorn-bushes were blooming, and which was flanked by big, though much-neglected, farm-buildings, and stopped before the house, the shutters of which were painted in black and white circles, probably because they were sometimes used for targets.

"It is no honor to marry one's sisters here; but they can no longer lay claim to much honor," he thought, tying his horse to the entrance rail, for no human soul was to be seen who could have taken the reins; only from a distant shed came the measured sound of the flails.

At the moment that he entered the hall he fancied he heard a confusion of voices and then the opening and shutting of the back doors. Then, suddenly, all was still.

He entered the parlor, in which the remains of their breakfast was standing, and which was still filled with cigar smoke. For some time he stood there waiting. Then a scraggy woman slipped through the door of the next room with an embarrassed grin

"My masters are not at home," she said, without
waiting for his question; "they drove away early
this morning and will not be back for some time."

"It does not matter; I will wait."

The old woman began to chatter and explain that
it would be quite useless to wait; she never knew
beforehand when they would come back; often they
stayed away all night, and so on. Meanwhile he
fancied he heard a dog-cart rattling out of the yard
in the greatest haste. He jumped up, alarmed, for
he thought that his horse had broken loose, but he
saw it quietly standing in its place; then a suspicion arose within him—a suspicion which a minute
before he would have thrust back indignantly.

The old house-keeper did not dare to turn him
out; and, unmolested, but also without food or
drink, he sat there waiting till the evening. When it
was dark he set out on his way home, discouraged
and humiliated.

Next morning he returned, this time also in vain.
The third day he found the gate firmly bolted. A
brand-new padlock was hanging on the hasp. It
seemed to have been purchased especially for
him.

Then he could no longer doubt that the brothers
avoided him on purpose. "They are ashamed to
to look me in the face," he said to himself; "I will
write to them."

But when he took up his pen to compel himself
to write friendly words of reconciliation, such dis-

gust at his own undignified deed overcame him that he crushed it to pieces on the table, and paced about the room, moaning aloud.

"I must first go and collect my strength," he said, and crept noiselessly to the girls' room. They sat at the window, spoke not a word, and stared with white faces into the distance ; then one let her head sink against the other's shoulder, and said, gently and sadly,

"They will not come any more."

"They are afraid of him," sighed the sister.

And then they relapsed again into silence.

"Ah !" he said, breathing heavily, while he crept back to his room, "I knew that would help me."

Then he took a clean sheet of paper and wrote a beautiful letter, in which he expounded to the brothers that he was no longer angry with them— that he would forgive them everything if they would restore the lost honor to his sisters.

"To-morrow they will be here," he said, with a sigh of relief, when he dropped the letter into the box. For the rest of the day he wandered about on the heath, for he did not dare to look any one in the face, so much was he ashamed of himself.

But the Erdmanns did not come.

.   .   .   .

It was on Christmas Eve, shortly before twilight. The heath lay deep in snow, and from the leaden sky fresh masses of flakes were descending. Then Paul saw that his sisters secretly took their hats and cloaks, and tried to make their escape by the back door.

He hastened after them. "Where do you want to go?"

Then they began to cry, and Kate said, " Please, please do not ask us." But he felt a dreadful anxiety arise within him, and, grasping their arms, he said, " I shall follow you if you won't confess."

Then Kate gasped out, sobbing, "We are going to mother's grave."

Horror overcame him that they should go to that holy place; but he took care not to let them see it.

" No, children," he said, stroking their cheeks, "I can't allow that; it would excite you too much; the snow is so deep, too, on the heath, and it will soon be dark."

"But some one must go there," said Kate, timidly, " it is Christmas Eve to-day."

" You are right, sister," he replied, " I will go myself. You stay with father and light a few candles for him. Please God, I shall bring you home some comfort."

They let themselves be persuaded, and went back into the house.

But he put on a warm coat, took his cap, and walked out into the dusk.

"You must lock the gates to-night," he said, before he left the yard, for he had a dull presentiment that he would only come home late at night, were it only for the sake of roaming about in the snow.

The white heath lay silent. Deep under the snow lay the withered flowers, and where a juniper-bush had stood before there was now a little white heap that looked like a mole-hill. Even the stems of the pollard willows were white, but only on the side against which the wind had blown.

Painfully he walked on across the snow-covered heath, at every step sinking in over his ankles. From time to time a crow flew through the air with heavy wings, fighting with difficulty against the snow-storm.

There was no path or road to be seen. . . . The three long fir-trees, which in the distance stood out against the sky like black phantoms, were the only sign by which he could direct his foot-steps.

The golden streak, which for a few moments had flamed upon the horizon, vanished ; lower and lower the shadows were sinking, and when Paul had reached the wall of the cemetery, which towered above him like a ghostly rampart, it had become quite dark ; but the freshly-fallen snow gave an uncertain light, so that he hoped to find his mother's grave soon.

The gate was snowed up—the snow had been heaped up by the wind ; nowhere was an entrance to be discovered.

So he groped his way with difficulty along the hedge. from which, here and there, a black twig stretched forth its sharp thorns out of the white covering, till his arms sank deeper into the snow without meeting any resistance.

From there he forced his way to the inner cemetery.

The firs greeted him with a hollow moan, and a raven which had been sitting in the snow flew up noiselessly and circled round their tops restlessly, like a poor soul that cannot find peace.

When he saw the snow-covered plain in its pale uniformity lying before his eyes a terror overcame him, for he saw no sign by which to distinguish his mother's grave. There was no cross on the mound, for he had not had money to buy one, but the mound itself lay dead under the levelling expanse of snow.

A torturing anxiety seized him; he felt as if he had now lost the very last thing that he possessed in life.

And with a trembling hand he began to grope about in the snow, from one mound to the other— a long row, from among which, here and there, a wreath or a little cypress-tree stood out in the dusk.

"Here rests this one, here that one." He knew almost every grave and who reposed beneath it.

And at last his groping hand hurt itself against a piece of glass that stuck out from underneath. . . . He stopped and felt carefully all round. . . . The fragment must be the one which Greta had carried out in early spring to plant asters in; a piece of a green bottle with sharp-pointed edges—yes, here it was. The faded stalks were still in it. And near it the wreath, the heather wreath, which appeared to be frozen stiff, like a stone ring; he had put it there himself the last time he had been here.

When he saw the little heap of snow, which hid all that was dearest to him, lying so white and still, he fell on his knees, and buried his face in the cool, soft flakes.

"It is all my fault, mother," he lamented; "I have not watched over them, I have let them run wild. Do not judge them, mother, they knew not what they did! . . . But I implore you, mother, show me how to act! Send me only one word from beyond the grave. . . . See, I kneel here and do not know what to do."

And then he suddenly felt as if he had no right to lie in that place; he felt as if the shame which his sisters had brought upon themselves was resting on him, too. He called himself a coward, selfish and lazy, because he had remained inactive for such a long time without daring the worst.

"I will do it, mother, this very night," he cried, springing up. "There shall be no question of myself. I will relinquish the last remnant of pride, if only my sisters can be saved." He vowed it with uplifted arms, and hurried out onto the heath.

For wellnigh three hours he struggled along the snowed-up roads. It might have been eight o'clock when he stopped, tired and breathless, before the gates of Lotkeim.

"To-day they shall not escape me," he said, and as he found the gate locked again, he lay down and crept through underneath the fence, as he had seen dogs do.

The windows of the manor-house were brightly lighted up, but as the curtains had been let down, nothing could be seen of the room inside; only snatches of song and laughter floated out into the open air. The house door stood open. He stopped for a moment in the dark hall to stifle the beating of his heart; then he knocked.

Ulrich's voice called out, "Come in!"

There lay the two brothers, stretched out on a long sofa, the feet of the one near the head of the other, a picture of perfect peace of mind and serenity of soul. Each of them balanced a big glass of grog on the palm of his hand, and before them on the table stood a steaming punch-bowl.

They were so startled at the sight of him that they forgot to get up. They were petrified, and remained lying as they were and staring at him.

"I say!" cried Ulrich, who was the first to recover his speech, and Fritz let his glass fall jingling to the ground.

Then the one stooped down and gathered up the fragments of glass with great zeal.

"You can well imagine why I come," said Paul, slowly stepping to the table in his snow-sprinkled garments.

"No!" said Ulrich, who slowly raised himself.

"No idea," chimed in Fritz, who wisely retired behind his brother's back.

"You received my letter, though?" asked Paul.

"We know of no letter," answered the elder one, staring impudently in his face.

"It probably has been lost in the post," the younger added, hastily.

"Only recollect. It was the 16th of November," said Paul.

Then they remembered vaguely that a letter had been delivered to them.

"But we could not make it out and threw it into the fire," said Ulrich.

"Don't use these evasions," Paul answered; "you know quite well what is expected of you."

They shrugged their shoulders, and looked at each other as if he were speaking Spanish to them.

"I have not come to play comedy with you," Paul continued; "you have taken away my sisters' honor and you must restore it to them."

Ulrich scratched his head and said :

"My dear Myerhofer, that is a bad business and can't be so quickly settled. Just sit down and drink a glass of punch with us; then we shall much sooner come to an understanding."

"Yes, much sooner and more comfortably," added Fritz, getting up to fetch two fresh glasses.

"Thank you," said Paul, "I am not thirsty."

The vague feeling was tormenting him that the

brothers were laughing at him even now, as they had done all his life. Iron fetters seemed to bind his limbs; he now felt himself quite powerless and disabled.

"Well, if you come to us like that," Ulrich retorted, apparently hurt, "then we will not speak to you at all. I have no mind to have my Christmas Eve spoiled."

"And to let the punch get cold," Fritz added.

Paul gazed fixedly from one to the other.

How was it possible that those who had so covered themselves with shame could stand before him so proud and impudent, while he, who only came to ask for his rights, trembled and shook like a criminal!

"And if you go home without any consolation!" cried an anxious voice within him. "Do not make them angry; remember what you have vowed to your mother! There must be no question of yourself."

"Well, will you drink or won't you?" Ulrich called out, angrily.

"There must be no question of yourself," cried the voice again. Then he bowed his head, and said, in a husky voice,

"Well, then, please."

The two brothers glanced at each other and smiled, and Fritz, raising his glass, said,

"Merry Christmas!"

"A merry Christmas," he stammered, and swallowed the hot beverage, almost choking, for he was overcome with disgust.

Now he sat in good-fellowship at the same table with the two brothers, he who ought to have been there as an avenger.

"Well, now to end this affair, dear Meyerhofer," Ulrich began. "What is done cannot be undone. We will not stop to inquire whether we ran most after your sisters, or your sisters after us; anyhow, it is just as much their fault as ours. We love them with all our hearts; they are the prettiest girls in the neighborhood, and we are truly sorry when we think that we have injured their reputation; but that we should marry them now you can't possibly expect of us."

Paul cast a hesitating glance at him, and began, dejectedly, "That is the least that—" he did not get any further; he felt as if the blood was freezing in his veins.

"Don't be ridiculous," said Fritz; and Ulrich continued :

"Look here, we would be willing to do it because we think a lot of them, although they have lowered themselves so much "—a spasm of fury darted through Paul's brain, but he controlled himself; "we would fulfil your wish directly, but first tell us what dowry will you give them ?"

" I have nothing," stammered Paul.

"There it is," answered Fritz.

"And we want money, a great deal of money," Ulrich continued. "I am the eldest, and if I take the estate for myself alone I must pay Fritz so much to enable him to purchase for himself."

"I will work," Paul gasped out, and looked at the brothers in humble entreaty.

"You have worked already for ten years and have not saved anything."

"The fire came and prevented me," stammered Paul, as if he were asking pardon for the misfortune that had happened to him.

"And next year something else will come and prevent you. No, dear friend, we cannot depend upon that."

The fear that he would have to return to his sisters without bringing any consolation sank deeper and deeper into his heart. He was so overpowered that it loosed his tongue, and he cried out, "But for God's sake, listen to reason. I can't do more than work. . . . I will work like a slave. . . . Will work day and night. I will pinch, save, and starve even, and all I earn shall be yours. . . . Just see. . . . I have splendid prospects. . . . The locomobile will soon be repaired . . . and the moor is very lucrative . . . it is fifteen feet deep . . . you can measure it. . . . The cart-load of peat fetches ten marks. . . and the dowry shall be paid to the last farthing in yearly instalments."

He gazed at them with expectant eyes, for he felt sure they would seize this offer directly;

and when they continued silent, he passed his hand despairingly over his forehead, from which the cold perspiration was streaming, and murmured,

"Well, what more can I do? . . . Yes, I *will* do more; I will ask my father to give up the farm to me, and will make it over to you, so that . . . when my father dies one of you will be master there . . . I will go away and take nothing but the clothes I stand up in. Is not that enough for you?"

But still they were silent.

Then he felt as if everything to which his belief had hitherto clung was slipping from him, as if the ground were giving way under his feet, as if he himself were dropped into space. He clasped his hands, his teeth chattered, and he stared at them like a man bereft of reason. "Is it possible, then, you are not willing? really not willing? Can't you understand at all that it is your duty to make amends where you have sinned? . . . Does not your sense of honor tell you that you may not rob others of their honor? . . . Does your conscience let you sleep?"

"Stop!" cried Ulrich, who began to feel decidedly uncomfortable.

"No, I will not stop; I cannot go home like this . . . really I cannot. . . . Have you no idea, then, of the mischief you have done . . . of the misery that reigns in my home?" and he shuddered at the remembrance of what he had left there. "If you knew that you would not be so hard. . . . See, Fritz and Ulrich . . . I have known you both such a long time. . . . We have sat together in school . . . and together . . . we have knelt before the altar . . . you always had an ill-will towards me; I have had to bear much from you. . . . But I will forget everything if only you will make amends for this one thing. You are light-minded, but you are not bad . . . you cannot be bad . . . you, too, have had a mother . . . I have seen her . . . she was standing at our confirmation by the third pillar on the left, and crying just as my mother cried, and my mother—oh, fie!" He interrupted himself, for he felt overwhelmed with shame at having mentioned the name of his saint before these scoundrels; but the fear of having to return home without any consolation made him crazy; but he gulped that down, too, and began again, while his thoughts chased each other through his head. "Only think if you went out now to the cemetery and had sisters . . . who had been betrayed . . . and you had not watched over those sisters sufficiently . . . and you dared not touch the snow that lies on the grave . . . and I were the betrayer . . . what . . . what would you do?"

"We should kill you," said Ulrich, glancing at him contemptously.

He uttered a piercing cry, for he now realized how deeply he lowered himself—how he had dragged his pride and honor in the dust. With clinched fists he rushed upon Ulrich, but the latter barricaded

16

himself behind the table, and Fritz rushed to the next room to call the servant.

Then he staggered out.

The gate was locked as before. He did not dare go back to have it opened, so, lying down flat, he crept under the fence like a dog.

CHAPTER XVIII.

"THE young master leads a very gay life all at once," said the servants; and as everything went as it pleased, they stole one bushel of corn after the other.

Paul meanwhile visited all the festivities and dances in the neighborhood. Any one who saw him appear in that merry crowd with his sombre brow and his scared, searching look, asked himself indeed, "What does he want here?" And many gave him a wide berth, as if a shadow had fallen on their joy.

Paul was quite clear about what he was doing. He had heard that the Erdmanns let no festivity pass without going thither to be merry as wildly as possible.

"I shall know how to meet them," he said to himself; "the night is dark and the heath lonely. They will look into my face and the face of death under God's open sky."

Two days after his last visit to Lotkeim he had driven to the town and bought a revolver: a beautiful six-shooter, one with a long slender barrel. Like a wild animal he lurked about at night in the bushes and hidden paths of the heath when he thought they would pass.

But they did not come. They seemed to have become suspicious, and therefore stayed at home: or, what was still more likely, their money had come to an end.

"I can wait," he said, and continued this mode of life; and when he occasionally spent the evening at home, and sat together with his sisters at the supper-table—a sad, silent meal—he felt terrified each time when he looked up and found his mother's features reflected in the two pale, haggard young faces. It drove him out of the house again.

It was Shrove Tuesday, the last night of the carnival, that a grand ball was to be given in the town hall by the land-owners of the neighborhood.

"I shall catch them there," he said to himself, for he had heard that both the brothers were to be stewards of the festivity.

When dusk approached he ordered his sledge, hid the revolver in the boot of it, and set out on his way to the town.

The sun had been shining all day, and now the sky was all aglow with the last rays of the setting sun. The heath lay shrouded in a blue-gray mist, and sparkling ice-crystals were flying through the clear winter air.

When he passed Helenenthal he saw two sledges moving towards the manor-house laden with fir branches.

"It seems to me they are going to have a festivity there," he murmured, looking after the sledges; and with a sombre smile he added, "I need not be jealous, for to-day I, too, hold a festival."

At six o'clock he arrived in the town, procured himself an entrance-ticket, and remained crouched in a corner of the inn till nine o'clock, absorbed in his own dark thoughts.

When he entered the dancing-room, which was all stir and confusion, he hid himself in the shadow of a pillar, for he felt as though the murderous thoughts that filled his soul were written on his forehead, clearly visible to everybody.

All of a sudden a painful thrill ran through his frame. He had found the brothers; they stood in the middle of the room, proud and radiant, with silken badges on their shoulders, and lilies-of-the-valley in their button-holes, looking at the row of girls dressed in white, who ornamented the walls, with a triumphant smile.

"There, now you are doomed," he muttered with a deep sigh. He felt that there was no retreat for him now. And then he hid in a quiet corner, from whence he could keep his victims in sight. The blazing lights lit up the scene for him as clearly as daylight, but he did not see it; the music fell in full chords upon his ear, but he did not hear it; all his faculties were swallowed up in one wild, blood-thirsty longing.

As he was staring in this way at the crowd, he

heard close behind him a conversation between two portly elderly men.

"Are you going to the funeral also to-morrow?"

"Yes. They say it will be a great ceremony. One ought not to miss it."

"Had she been ill long?"

"Oh, very long. Our old doctor had already given her up years ago. Then she was in the south with her daughter, and after her return lingered on for I don't know how long."

He listened; a dim presentiment arose in his mind. The fir branches. The fir branches.

And one of the voices continued:

"Tell me; the daughter must be quite at a marriageable age now. Is she not engaged yet?'

"She is celebrated for the refusals she deals out," answered the other voice. "Some say she did so in order not to leave her sick mother; others because she has a secret love-affair with her cousin, Leo Heller; you know him."

"Oh, the young good-for-nothing!" said the first voice again. "Last week he lost eight hundred marks at baccarat; the money-lenders have got him well into their clutches, and he keeps a mistress, too. But he is a smart, gay fellow for all that, and quite made to catch goldfish."

And the two voices went away laughing.

Paul had a vague feeling as if he must throw himself down on the ground and press his face in the dust; something rose in his throat; everything began to swim before his eyes. So she had ceased to suffer: the pale, kind woman who had watched over the Haidehof like a good angel, and whom his heart had clung to all his life.

Now that she was dead the way was free to ruin and crime. And Elsbeth? How she had trembled in anticipation of this dreadful moment, how he had vowed to be near her then; and instead of that he was lurking here like a wild beast, blood-thirsty thoughts in his soul—he, the only one in whom her pure soul had once confided.

He shivered. "But what does it matter? She has plenty of people to console her; there is merry Leo, with whom she is said to have a secret love-affair; let him show all his wiles now!" He laughed aloud and scornfully, and as soon as he had made sure that the Erdmanns could not escape him if he waited for them at the road-side, he left the room.

As he drove on in the silence of the moon-lit winter night his soul grew calmer and calmer, and when he saw across the silvery heath the White House gradually rising before him like a monument of marble, he began to weep bitterly.

"Hang it! I am blubbering on like an old woman," he murmured, and whipped his horse till all the bells jingled loudly. They sounded in his ear like the knell of all that was good.

In the wood, behind which a side path branched off to Lotkeim, he halted, tied his horse to a distant trunk of a tree, and took off the bells so that their jingling should not prematurely betray him. Then he took the revolver out of the boot of the sledge and examined the cartridges. Six shots—two for each—no harm in having an extra one.

It was bitterly cold, and his feet were benumbed. He crouched at the bottom of the sledge, so that the fur rug should entirely cover him. It was warm and comfortable underneath it, and gradually he felt a great lassitude coming over him, as if he could have fallen asleep. But then he roused himself again.

"You are not at all in earnest about killing them," he murmured, " or you would feel very differently."

Then he sprang up and cried out in the night, "I *will*, I swear it to you, mother. . . . I will!" And in assurance thereof he shot a ball into the air, so that the echo rolled through the silence awfully and the ravens flew croaking from their nests.

The nearer the hour approached at which the brothers must return home the more nervous he grew ; but his nervousness was not about the bloody deed : he trembled lest at the last moment his hand should fail him, his courage vanish, for they had always called him a coward.

It might have been about four o'clock in the morning, and the moon was already waning, when the sound of bells was heard in the distance—at first softly, then louder and louder. He sprang into the hollow which the driving snow had nearly filled up, and threw himself flat upon the ground. The sledge neared the edge of the wood ; two persons wrapped in furs sat in it—it was they. But how long they were coming !

The sledge drove slower and slower at every step. The bells tinkled faintly, and the reins hung down loosely over the sides of the horse. The brothers were snoring. They were given up to him defenceless.

He sprang forward quickly, seized the horse's rein, and unfastened the harness. The sledge stopped, but its masters slept on.

He stood before them staring down upon them. The hand that held his pistol trembled violently.

"What shall I do with them now ?" he murmured. "I can't kill them in their sleep. They must be drunk as well, otherwise they would have woke up long ago. The best way would be to let them go and wait for the next time."

He was just going to harness the horse again when it darted into his mind that he had sworn to his mother he would kill them.

"I knew very well that I was a miserable coward," he thought to himself, "and should never have the courage for it. I am not even good enough to commit murder."

"But I will do it yet," he murmured, stepped back a few paces, and aimed direct at Ulrich's breast; but he did not pull the trigger, for he inwardly feared he might hurt the sleeping man.

"Shall I do it all the same?" he thought, when he had stood for some while in this position. And then he began to picture to himself what would happen when he had done it and both were lying dead before him. "Either I must shoot myself as well, and leave my father and sisters behind me in misery, or instead of shooting myself I should give myself up to justice to-morrow; then the misery at home would be just as great."

"It is madness, in any case"—so he ended his reflections—"but I shall do it all the same."

And suddenly he saw under Ulrich's fur, which had been a little turned back from his breast, a sparkling array of tinsel stars, such as ladies fasten onto gentlemen's coats in the cotillon.

"So they allowed themselves to be decorated with stars by others, while my sisters are in misery!"

"But first I will speak a few home words to them," he muttered, seized hold by the shoulder of Ulrich, who sat on his side, and shook him violently, so that his head rolled from side to side.

Ulrich started from sleep, and when he saw the dark figure of Paul, with the revolver in his hand, standing close behind him, he began to cry out loud and piteously. The other one woke up as well, and both stretched out their arms in pitiful entreaty.

"What do you mean to do to us?" cried the one.

"Do not murder us!" cried the other.

"Put away your revolver. Have pity on us—have pity!" They clasped their hands, and would have fallen on their knees had not the fur rugs prevented them.

Paul looked at them in amazement. He had always seen them daring and eager for fight, so that now in their terror they seemed to him like entirely different people.

He wished in his heart that they would draw their knives against him, so that he could make use of his revolver in an honest fight. And then suddenly the thought arose in his mind: "If you had only once treated them like this when they were boys, you would have been spared many a humiliation—and your sisters, above all."

Ulrich meanwhile tried to clasp his knees, and Fritz kept on crying out, "Take pity on us—take pity on us!"

"You know very well what I want of you," answered Paul, who now felt freed from all hesitation, and with cold resolution pursued his aim.

"What do you want? say, what do you want? We'll do all you want!" cried Ulrich; and Fritz, who tried to hide behind his brother, seemed suddenly speechless.

"You shall keep your promise, as I will keep mine," said Paul. "I wish you could find courage to defend yourselves, so that at last there might be

a clear account between us. . . . But perhaps it is
best as it is. . . . And now repeat after me what I
say: 'We swear before God and by the memory
of our mother that we will redeem within three
days our promise given to your sisters.'" Trembling and faltering, they repeated the words after
him.

"And I swear to you before God and the remembrance of my mother," he answered, "that I
will shoot you down whenever I find you if you do
not keep your oath. There! now you may drive
on—I will harness the horse to the sledge myself.
Stay where you are!" he repeated when, in spite of
that, they wanted to lend him a helping hand.

They did not stir again, so obedient had they become. And when he had finished, they said, with
great politeness,

"Good-evening," and drove away.

"So that is how to do it," he murmured, throwing the pistol down in the snow and looking after
the sledge with folded hands. "If you rely upon
what is right and honorable, and wish, in the good-
ness of your heart, to turn everything to good, you
are called a coward and treated like a dog. But if
you treat others like dogs from the first, without
considering whether you are in the right or wrong,
you are called brave, everything succeeds with you,
and you are a hero. So that is how it is done."

He shuddered. He was seized with such disgust
towards himself and the whole world. In his own

eyes he appeared so polluted that nothing on earth could ever cleanse him again.

.   .   .   .

The next forenoon he stood in the snow behind the shed and gazed towards Helenenthal, where a dark funeral procession was preparing for its sad journey. Twice he had gone to the stables to tell the servants to get the sledge ready, and each time the word had stuck in his throat.

Now he stood there with his hands folded, watching how the long, black, undulating line crept on over the dazzling-white snowy heath; it grew smaller and smaller, and disappeared at last behind the wood, for the cemetery of Helenenthal lay far off on the way to the town.

"How nice it would be," he thought, "if they would bury her, too, beneath the three fir-trees; then mother would have a good neighbor and—"

He started! As quick as lightning his brain had pictured how, on a beautiful spring evening, he might meet Elsbeth there, who would come and sit near the grave that belonged to her, as he would come to his.

"But it is better as it is," he said to himself; "how could I ever find courage to look into her eyes again?—I, who lurk about the road at night to get husbands for my wretched sisters!"

Then suddenly the twins came running up breathless; they trembled all over and struggled for words.

"What is the matter, children?"

Greta hid her head on his shoulder, and Kate sniffled like a child trying to keep back its tears.

"They have come," they stammered, and then they both began to sob.

"That is a good thing," answered Paul, and kissed them.

"Won't you come into the house?" Katie asked, sucking her apron.

"Where have you left them?"

"They are talking to father."

"Ah! that is a very different thing. Run to your room—I will come in a moment."

"And what a price it cost," he murmured, looking after them; then he gave a glance at Helenenthal, and went into the shed where "Black Susy" stood. "It is time that you should come back to life," he said, stroking her black body; "we shall have to work bravely, you and I, if we want to procure the dowry for the girls."

When he stepped into the house he heard the loud-sounding voice of his father coming out to him.

"I am curious all the same to see how they will behave," he thought, and listened.

"Yes, he is a simpleton, and will remain a simpleton, gentlemen. What I have imagined on a big scale, he accomplishes on a small one in his petty, mercenary manner. It went to my heart when I saw him fidgeting about the machine, as if it were nothing more than a willow-pipe, and meanwhile the farm goes to ruin. Oh, gentlemen! you see me here a cripple, but if I still bore the sceptre, gentlemen, I would coin thousands of thalers out of the ground, no less than Vanderbilt, the American, whose life is written in this almanac in a very instructive manner."

"Couldn't you manage to direct the affairs from your chair?" inquired Ulrich's voice.

"Oh, gentlemen, behold my tears! I shed them for the most ungrateful, the most degenerate child which this earth has ever seen. In this almanac there is the story of a son who, at the risk of his life, fetches draughts of water from the hands of robbers for his parents languishing in the desert. I am not able to offer you even a little liquor, a little ginger brandy with aniseed, which I am so fond of drinking myself."

"In future we will bring some for you," Fritz answered him.

"Oh, why has not God given me two such sons as you are? And fancy, he never consults me, he locks me out of the kitchen. I wonder that I have not been starved out. Well, you know him from a child; was he not always a rough, spiteful creature?"

"Oh yes; there was always something violent about him," said Ulrich.

"And he was always handling pistols and whips, especially behind one's back," Fritz added.

"Especially behind one's back—ha! ha! ha! that

is characteristic, that is his way. Ah, gentlemen, secret malice never brings good, as the proverb in this almanac says, and if Heaven permits me to recover again, you shall see how I will take my revenge—first on the rogue, the incendiary, the villanous fellow, to whom all my misery is due, and then on my dear son who treats his father so badly. I shall disinherit him, hunt him away from the farm. Shall I be right, gentlemen, if I do this?"

"Quite right," both declared.

"How do you do?" said Paul, coming forward.

All three started. His father crouched shyly down in his arm-chair, like a dog who fears the whip, and the brothers stretched out their hands, very embarrassed and very humble, and begged him to let by-gones be by-gones.

"Why not?" he answered, combating his repugnance; "you know the right way now."

When the two brought forward their suit, the old man's boastfulness broke out stronger than ever.

"Gentlemen," he said, repressing his voice so that it might sound more dignified, "your proposal is a great honor naturally, but I am not able to answer it with 'Yes.' First, I must ask for a sufficient guarantee, that I may know what future awaits my daughters, who, by their beauty and amiability, as well as by stainless virtue, are destined for a high position. I have educated them most carefully, and watched over them so lovingly that my fatherly heart cannot decide to give them away without serious consideration."

In this tone he went on boasting till Paul quietly said, "Let it be, father, the matter is already settled." Then he was silent, secretly highly elated to have made such a magnificent speech.

In the afternoon Paul went into his sisters' room and said:

"Children, say a prayer for Frau Douglas, who was buried to-day."

They looked at him with eyes sparkling with joy, and a dreamy smile passed over their faces.

"Have you not understood me?"

"Yes," they said, softly, and looked terrified—they clung to each other as if they feared the rod. He left them alone in their happiness, and stepped out into the clear, cold winter air. "How is it," he thought, "that everybody now fears me and no one understands what I mean?"

The same day he dismissed all the servants, and wrote to the foreman to come back on the morrow to resume work again.

.   .   .   .

During the same week it began to thaw, the work went on quickly, and one Friday evening at the beginning of March "Black Susy" stood there, smart and shiny in her newly-mended garment. Next day the boiler was to be tried, and the wood and coal lay heaped up by the walls of the shed.

Paul, unable to sleep, tossed on his bed. The

17

hours crept slowly by, and a short eternity of the most painful expectation elapsed between midnight and dawn.

"Will she come to life?   Will she?"

The clock struck one.   He could not stand it any longer; he dressed and crept out into the cold, wet March night, a flickering lantern in his hand. The wind caught his clothes and the icy drizzling rain scourged his face.

"Black Susy" glared sulkily out of the dark shed as if she resented being deprived of her last night's rest. . . . The lantern threw a ghostly light over the inhospitable place, and each time it flickered the shadow of the machine danced in grotesque forms on the yellow deal wall.

"Shall I wake up the foreman?" thought Paul. "No, let him sleep; I will have the first pain or the first joy all to myself."

Heaps of coal sank rattling into the great iron jaws.   A little blue flame leaped up, flickered all round, and soon a red glow filled the dark interior. . . . The lantern on the wall shone dimly, as if jealous of the warm, cheerful fire-light.

Paul seated himself upon a coal-heap and watched the play of the flames. . . . The oven-door began to glow and half-burnt cinders to fall, throwing out sparks all round.

Paul could hear his heart beat, and as he pressed his hand upon it to still its tumult he felt Elsbeth's flute in his breast-pocket.   He had found it lying on the locomobile the day the work was begun again, and had carried it about with him ever since.

"I wonder if I shall ever learn that, too?" he asked himself, in tumultuous joy at what he had already accomplished. He put the flute to his mouth and tried to blow it—the minutes passed so slowly that he was forced to try and while away the time. But the sounds which he produced sounded hollow and squeaky—still less could he squeeze out a melody.

"I shall never learn it," he thought. "Whatever I do for myself fails—that is a law in my life; I must sow for others if I want to reap."

But in spite of this he put the flute to his lips again.

"It would have been nice," he thought, "if, instead of heating engines here, I had become an artist, as Elsbeth used to prophesy." A thrill of excitement went through him. "Will she live again? Will she?"

He extracted another shrill sound from the flute.

"B-r-r," he said, "that goes through one's nerves! I shall have to leave love and flute-playing to others."

But at this moment there arose in the body of "Black Susy" that mysterious singing which had remained faithfully in his memory all these years. It sounded as if the fates were singing beneath the ash-tree.

"Ah, that is far better music!" he cried, spring-

ing up and throwing the flute away from him. . . .
The iron door rattled. . . . The glowing jaws swallowed new heaps of coal. The shovel fell clattering to the ground.

"It will wake them up in the house," he thought,
startled for a moment. "But let it, let it," he continued; "their happiness and their future are at
stake."

The singing grew louder and louder; then his joy
came to a climax, so that he began to whistle aloud.
"How nice that sounds! Yes, we understand how
to make music; we are brave musicians, Susy." The
chimney sent forth mighty clouds of black smoke,
which disseminated itself under the ceiling like a
canopy, heaving and sinking as though a storm were
driving it. . . . One of the valves sent forth a hissing sound, and a white cloud of steam spirted up,
which quickly mixed with the black smoke. . . . The
hissing grew louder and louder, the hand of the
manometer went on and on. . . .

"Now is the time!"

With a trembling hand he felt for the lever. . . .
A jerk . . . a swing . . . and whirling, as if driven by
supernatural force, the wheel went round.

"Victory! she lives, she lives!"

"Now they may hear, now they may come!" His
hand pulled at the valve of the steam-whistle, and
shrilly the night echoed her cry:

"I live! I live!"

Then he folded his hands and murmured, softly,

"O mother, you should have lived to see this!" And as he said so it suddenly occurred to him that this, too, was useless — that death was upon him also, crying into his ear,

"You will die! will die! before having lived."

"I have still work to do," he said, with moist eyes. "First, I will see my sisters happy, for if they remain poor they will be treated brutally; then I must see the farm right itself; then death may come."

And, like the black clouds around, years and years of struggling and years of care rose up before his eyes.

With sleepy faces the inmates appeared at the gate of the shed; the sisters came, too, and stood anxiously clinging to each other, in the smoke and the glow of the fire, looking in their white dressing-gowns like two pale roses on the same stalk.

"Here your future is being prepared, you poor things," he murmured, nodding to them.

When the foreman had come, Paul went into his father's bedroom, who stared at him confusedly.

"Father," he said, modestly, though his heart swelled with pride, "the locomobile is in working order; as soon as the ground has thawed the work on the moor can begin."

The old man said, "Leave me in peace," and turned his head to the wall.

Next morning, when the locomobile was pulled

out, a strange rattling, scrunching sound was heard on the threshold of the shed.

"Something has got under the wheels," said the foreman.

Paul looked. There, in a heap of little fragments, broken in half, and pressed quite flat, lay —Elsbeth's flute.

A bitter smile came over his face, as if he meant to say, "Now I have sacrificed to you all that I have; now can you be satisfied, Dame Care?"

Since that day he felt as if the last link between himself and Elsbeth was severed—he had lost her, like his dreams, his hopes, his dignity, his own self.

With hurrahs, "Black Susy" wandered out onto the moor.

CHAPTER XIX.

YEARS went by. The sisters had already long been settled as happy wives, their dowry was paid, and the brothers-in-law had already begun to borrow from Paul.

How silent it was now in the quiet Haidehof. The father could hobble about the house and garden on a crutch, but he had grown much too lazy to wield the sceptre again. Paul did not know what else to do for him, except to have his favorite dishes cooked, not to measure his rations of ginger and aniseed too sparingly, and to present him each Christmas with a new almanac. The old man might have been well satisfied with this, for indeed he needed nothing more—he had even grown too heavy to drive to the town ; but the better his body throve the more imbittered and exasperated grew his mind. He would sit and brood for hours, and it was dreadful to see how in doing so he gnashed his teeth and shook his fists. One of his fixed ideas was that his son kept him under on purpose that he might claim for himself the glory of the great ideas which his father had conceived, and the better the moor paid the more eagerly he calculated what his company would have brought in. He was not sparing with the millions; he had no need to be so.

But something sprang up from the darkest corner of his soul, and that was a plan of revenge against Douglas, which he privately nursed and cherished as his most important secret. Even his sons-in-law, to whom he liked to open his heart, knew nothing of this. Ulrich once said to Paul,

"Take care; the old man is brewing something against Douglas."

"What could it be?" he replied, apparently unconcerned, although he had often felt anxiety on this subject.

Dull, and without interest, Paul lived from one day to the next. His whole inner being was sacrificed to the commonplace cares about property and money, yet without his ever experiencing any joy at the success he attained. There was no longer anybody whom he could make happy, and he worked on without knowing why—as a cart-horse in the traces moves forward, ignorant of what the plough does, which it drags through the briers. Months sometimes passed without his taking one retrospective glance at his soul. He did not whistle any more, either. He feared the torments which overwhelming sentiment called into life, but he looked back on the time when he could commune with himself in the language of music as on a lost paradise.

Often when he compared the result of his work, his toiling, his wakeful nights, to that which he had sacrificed for it, he was overcome by intense bitterness. It seemed to him to have been something unspeakably noble, sweet and blissful, only he could not find the right name for it.

He could rid himself of these black thoughts most successfully by plunging deep into some new work, and then a long time would pass before the fit of melancholy attacked him again.

Meanwhile the Haidehof was thriving more splendidly from year to year; the debt to Douglas was paid off, the crops flourished, and in the meadows thorough-bred cattle were feeding. The whole place was to be rebuilt. The house, stables, and barn all were to be thoroughly renewed. And one spring there came a crowd of workmen of all kinds into the yard. The house was pulled down, and while Paul chose a wooden barrack for his dwelling, his father was easily induced to go over to stay with one of his sons-in-law.

"I shall never come back," he said, taking leave; "I cannot stand the sight of your mad proceedings any longer." But the first to come back in the autumn was the old man. He seated himself comfortably in his own arm-chair, and henceforth added his son-in-law to the list of those he abused. It was very possible they might not have treated him with too much consideration.

"Now I have no longer a place on earth where

I can rest my gray hairs," he grumbled, stretching himself lazily on his cushions.

Next spring it was the turn of the farm buildings; the barn, especially, was to be made an example of rural magnificence, as a monument of that terrible night which had given the death-blow to his mother.

The farmers who now drove across the heath often halted to look admiringly at the smart buildings which, with their red-tiled roofs, impressed them already in the distance, and many a one shook his head thoughtfully and murmured the old proverb:

> "To build and to lend
> Bring cares without end."

"Black Susy" on the moor was sending forth her black clouds of smoke, the knives of the cutting-machine bored themselves deep into the clammy ground, and the press worked slowly and silently like a good-natured domestic animal. A newly-built shed with its white walls looked dazzling in the sunshine, and all round about the long black rows of compressed peat were to be seen. The blocks were hard and heavy, with little fibre and much coal. They easily beat all competition and had a good reputation as far as Koenigsberg.

Paul, who on his business journeys mixed much with strange people, now also enjoyed the happiness of being greeted as a man of consequence, and of being treated by the worthy land-owners as their equal.   But he had no longer any pleasure in it.

When they shook hands with him in a friendly manner, congratulated him upon his success, or requested a visit from him, he asked himself in silence, "Are they mocking me?"   And though he saw well that the gentlemen were quite in earnest about it, he always felt as if freed from a nightmare when they let him go.

"Why did not these kind people come here before," he said to himself, "at that time when I needed them—when each kind word would have been of great advantage to me?   Now I am as insensible as a stone—now it is too late."

But his ambition increased more and more. And as if Heaven itself wished to consecrate it all, it caused the fruit to thrive in such abundance that year (the seventh since his mother's death), sent rain and sunshine so lavishly, each at its proper time, that the people began to feel uncomfortable at all this profusion, and asked each other anxiously, "Can it be for any real good?"

"Something will still come and spoil all—a hailstorm or the like," said Paul, who was always prepared for the worst.   But no; the harvest wagons came in one after the other heavily laden, swaying from side to side, and kept pouring the profusion of golden ears into the granary, scattering grains around until it was full up to the rafters.

But neither did this give pleasure to Paul.   The

more he saw his property accumulate, the more proudly the fruits of his handiwork greeted him, the heavier grew his care. Any one who had seen him slowly walking across the yard, with deep lines in his forehead and bowed head, might have taken him for a man encumbered with debts and very near to ruin.

About this time he read in the newspaper that Elsbeth was betrothed. The name of Elsbeth Douglas and Leo Heller stood side by side in letters full of beautiful flourishes.

He did not feel any sharp pain, he was not even startled; only a smile of melancholy satisfaction played round his mouth, as if he were murmuring to himself, "I always said so!"

And then he remembered the document which had once been circulated in church by the younger Erdmann to vex him, and which sounded just the same, only that his own name had stood there instead of the strange one. And that certainly made a difference.

He had not seen her for years. Although their properties lay so close together there had been no meeting between them. The White House still gleamed just as brightly over the heath and overlooked his window as at the time when the longing to wander thither had arisen in his childish heart, but the magic glitter which surrounded it then, and for fifteen years after, had now vanished, extinguished by the deepening shadows of every-day life.

"May she be happy!" he said, and considered himself comforted by this wish.

Next Sunday the harvest festival was celebrated in the church. Paul sat in his corner, and listened to the tones of the organ and the vicar sending up praise and thanksgiving to Heaven. The sun shone through the painted windows in a thousand bright colors, just as it did on the day when he and Elsbeth were confirmed; but there, too, sad and sombre in her ash-colored garments, stood the gray woman, still gazing down upon him with her big, hollow eyes.

"I, too, am celebrating a harvest festival to-day, the harvest festival of my youth," he thought, "but mine is scarcely a too happy one."

The service was at an end. With a triumphant song the organ dismissed the joyful worshippers, who crowded together under the yews in the shady church-yard to shake hands and congratulate each other.

As Paul came down the steps he saw Elsbeth only a few paces before him, on the arm of her betrothed.

She seemed older, and looked pale and delicate. When her look met his she turned a shade paler still.

He trembled all over, but his eyes did not quit her face. In confusion he raised his cap; and at the same place where fifteen years ago they had spoken the first words to one another, they now passed each other in silence and like strangers.

CHAPTER XX.

"Whatever is the matter with father?" said Frau Kate Erdmann to Frau Greta Erdmann, as they were both driving along the road on the way to visit their old home and take the opportunity at the same time of telling their brother all that weighed on their minds.

The old man stood crouched up in a corner behind the barn, and was busying himself over a heap of straw which lay there. When he heard the rattle of the dog-cart he stopped in alarm and rubbed his hands like some one who wished to appear unconcerned.

The two sisters looked at each other, and Greta said,

"We must give Paul a hint of this."

Oh, they had become very reasonable, these two wild girls! not less so inwardly than outwardly; their truant brown curls were combed smoothly behind their ears, and the sparkling eyes had a weary look in them, as though they now knew how it feels to sit in a lonely room and cry one's heart out.

Frau Kate, indeed, had three strapping boys, and

Frau Greta had already hopes of a fourth; and every one knows "Maternity renders weary."

Paul was not at home; he was working on the moor; but their father came towards them with a cunning laugh, swinging his crutch, and crying out, "Can't I run again like a youth?"

Frau Kate expressed her admiration and Frau Greta agreed with her.

"It goes first-rate," he laughed; "the day before yesterday I even went as far as Helenenthal.

They looked at him in surprise, and almost in terror, for since he was forced to leave it he had never been there again.

"How were you received?" asked Frau Greta.

"Who? What? Oh, you think perhaps I went for a neighborly visit? You are real geese! I would sooner be the guest of your watch-dog and try to take his mutton-bone away."

"But what did you do there, then?"

"I peeped through the gate and looked at the clock and then I came home again. How long do you think it takes me to walk there? just guess."

They had no idea.

"An hour and a half, just like a professional runner. . . . Indeed," he looked down meditatively, "if one had anything to carry, it might take two."

"And you went only to find that out?"

"That was all, my love, that was all!" and his eye sparkled meaningly.

Then they seated themselves in the veranda,

which Paul had had erected before the door, on the
model of the White House. The old house-keeper,
who had formerly managed the Erdmanns' estab-
lishment, and who after they were married had emi-
grated to the Haidehof, had to go into the kitchen
to make coffee and waffle cakes, and as their father
did not know what to talk about to his daughters,
he abused Paul and his sons-in-law. To-day he
did it less from absolute love of abuse than from
old habit; his thoughts seemed to be wandering
somewhere else, and while he spoke he wriggled on
his chair with uncomfortable activity.

"Let us go in," said Kate; "we must look after
household matters a little, and the wind is blowing
us away here."

"There will be a storm to-night," said Greta. And
then they both turned round terrified, for the laugh
which the old man gave sounded so very strange.

"Let there be a storm," he said, a little embarrassed; "that won't matter at all. There are storms
in married life too, sometimes, are there not?"

In Kate's face there lurked something of her old
mischievous look, but Greta drew down the corners
of her mouth, as if she were going to cry. She
seemed not quite to have got over the last.

"Yes, autumn will be early this year," she said,
with a touch of melancholy.

The old man whistled "Wenn die Schwalben
Heimwarts Ziehn" (When the Swallows Homeward
Fly), and Katie said:

"Let autumn come ; the barns are full."

"Thank God!" tittered the old man, "they are full."

The sisters put their arms round each other, and pressing their foreheads against the window panes, looked out into the sunny yard, from which clouds of dust were whirling to the sky. . . .

At dusk Paul came home, black as a nigger, for the peat-dust, which the wind had been blowing about, had settled on his beard and face.

He mutely shook hands with his sisters, looked sharply into their eyes, and said, "You shall tell me all about it afterwards."

Greta looked at Kate, and Kate looked at Greta ; then they suddenly laughed aloud, and, seizing him by both shoulders, danced about the room with him.

"You will make yourselves black, children," he said.

"My sweetheart is a chimney-sweep," hummed Greta ; and Kate sang the second verse, " My sweetheart comes from the nigger's land."

Then they kissed him and ran to the looking-glass to see whether the kiss had left a mark.

When he had gone out to make himself tidy, Greta said, "It's funny that he has only to look at one and all is right again."

And Kate added, "But he is more silent himself to-day than ever."

"Paul, be good," they said, caressingly, as they sat together at the supper-table ; "we may only

18

come here on such rare occasions!... show us a friendly face."

"Have you forgotten what day it is?" he answered, stroking their hair.

They started, for their first thought was of the anniversary of their mother's death, but they breathed freely again, for that fell near Midsummer-day.

"Well?" they asked.

"To-day, eight years ago, our barn was burned down!"

All were silent; only their father chuckled and laughed to himself. . . .

It began to grow dark; over the heath there still gleamed a streak of red light, which was reflected in a fiery glow upon the white table-cloth. The storm rattled at the shutters.

It was a good thing that the house-keeper now entered the room. She was a garrulous woman, who had always much news to relate.

"Well, Frau Jankus, what have you to tell us?" called out Kate to her, who was glad to shake off the nightmare of remembrance.

"Oh, dear madam," cried the old person, "don't you know yet? There are great goings-on in the church to-day. The whole village is making wreaths; over the altar they have hung a whole garland of rare tea-roses, and on each side the most beautiful oleander trees are placed.

"Why, what's the matter?"

"A wedding is the matter! Miss Douglas's wedding will be to-morrow!"

The two sisters started, exchanged a quick glance with each other, and then looked at Paul.

But he was rolling a crumb of bread between his fingers, and looked as if the story did not concern him in the least.

The sisters exchanged another glance and nodded significantly. Then, with the same impulse, they both seized his hands.

"Children, you tear me to pieces," he said, with a feeble smile.

"Ah, then there will be *polterabend* there to-day?" asked their father, growing quite lively all of a sudden.

"Probably, probably!" answered the old housekeeper. "Not long ago I saw a troop of children go by quite laden with old flower-pots and rubbish."

"At our wedding they showed more moderation," said Greta, and both sisters looked at each other and smiled dreamily.

"That's a splendid coincidence," muttered the old man, and rubbed his hands.

"Why splendid?" asked Paul.

"Oh, I only meant . . . coincidence—the same day that they burned down our barn. Just tell me, Paul—you were awake—what hour might it have been when you saw the flames rise?"

"It might have been one o'clock."

"Well, you ought to know. Though what the

business really was that took you to Helenenthal that night passes my comprehension, but it is all right, quite right! now I know the exact hour."

"Then you know a great deal!" said Greta, laughing.

"So I do!" he answered, sulkily. "You'll see, my little daughter, you'll see!"

Kate was about to come to her sister's assistance, but Paul made them a sign, secretly, to leave the old man in peace.

Soon after, the sisters took leave.

"You wanted to tell Paul that father has secrets behind the barn," said Kate, when they were both sitting in the dog-cart.

"Yes that is true!" she answered, made the driver stop, and beckoned to Paul. But the old man, who, in his distrust, always liked to hear everything that was said, thrust himself in, and so they had to leave it unsaid.

When Paul, on his usual evening round, came into the kitchen, he saw how his father was negotiating with the house-keeper for an earthen pot.

"What do you want the pot for, Mr. Meyerhofer?" asked the old woman.

"I also am going to celebrate *polterabend*, Frau Jankus," he replied, with a hollow laugh. "Perhaps they will give me some of the wedding-cake.

The old woman nearly died of laughing, and his father limped off to his bedroom with the pot, locking the door carefully behind him.

The whole house had retired to rest; only Paul still paced up and down in the dark yard.

"So to-morrow will be her wedding," he thought, folding his hands. "If I were a good Christian I ought to say a prayer for her happiness. . . . But I am not such an inert fellow yet, by a long way. . . . I believe that I once loved her very much, more than I knew myself. . . . How can it have been that I became a stranger to her?" He thought and thought, but could come to no right conclusion.

The moon rose over the moor—a great blood-red disk—which spread an uncertain light all over the yard. . . . The storm seemed to be augmenting. . . . It whistled round the corners and howled through the trees. . . .

"If a fire were to break out to-day it would not content itself with the barn only," thought Paul; and then it occurred to him that he must send a reminder to the agent, to hasten the insurance. "For one never knows what might happen during the night. . . . I will go to sleep"—he concluded his reflections—"to-morrow is another day, and a wedding day, too."

He went on tiptoe to the bedroom, which he had prepared for himself near that of his father's, so as to be at hand if anything should happen to the old man. He lighted no candle, for the full moon, rising higher, already shone brightly into the room.

"I wonder if you will sleep to-night?" he thought

an hour later. The shadows of the storm-blown leaves led a wild dance on his counterpane, and in between the light of the moon quivered like little tongues of white flame.

"On that midsummer night the moon shone just as bright," and then he remembered how white Elsbeth's dressing-gown had looked, peeping out underneath her dark cloak.

"That was the finest night of my life," he murmured, with a sigh; and then he decided to go to sleep, and drew his blanket over his head to strengthen his resolution. . . .

Some time after, he thought he heard his father get up softly in the next room and limp out at the door. . . . He could distinctly hear how the crutch clattered on the stone flags of the hall.

"He will come back directly," he thought, for it often happened that his father got up in the night.

With that he fell into an uneasy doze, in which all sorts of terrible dreams chased each other through his head. When he next came to full consciousness the moon was already high in the heavens; her beams now scarcely illumined his room at all, but the garden and yard lay bathed in light.

"Strange—it seems to me as if I had not heard father come back," he said to himself. He sat up and looked at the watch that was hanging over his bed.

"Eight minutes to one." Two hours had elapsed meanwhile.

"I suppose I was fast asleep," he thought, and was about to lie down again. Then the house door, caught by the storm, slammed noisily to, so that the whole house shook.

He jumped up, terrified. What is that? The house door open, father not back yet? The next moment he had thrown on his coat and trousers, and with bare feet and bare head rushed out.

The door which led from his father's bedroom into the hall stood wide open. Pale with anxiety, he stepped towards the bed—it had not been used; only on the foot of it there was an impression on the feather quilt. So his father had been sitting there without stirring for more than an hour and a half—evidently waiting till he himself was asleep.

What in the name of Heaven did all this mean?

His look wandered searchingly round the room. The worsted slippers in which his father generally crept about the house were thrown in the corner, but the boots, which for months had been standing there unused, were gone.

What? Did his lame father want to go for a ramble in the middle of the night? His heart almost stopped beating. He rushed out into the yard.

It was as clear as daylight, only as far as the shadow of the barn extended night still reigned.

The storm howled among the trees, the glistening white sand was whirled in the air; otherwise all was silent and deserted.

He hastened through the garden—no trace of him—to the back of the stables—still no trace of him. Ah, what did this mean? The gate open? Where had he gone? The dog near him whined; he hastily unfastened his chain. "Seek for your master, Turk. Seek!"

The dog sniffed about on the ground and ran to the front of the barn, where the bundles of straw were lying piled up like pale mountains of sand along the wall.

The moonlight was dazzling on the whitewashed wall, and lay bright and glittering on the ground. One might have found a pin by its light. There was nothing to be noticed, except in one place the straw seemed disarranged.

But stop! how does the ladder come here, which is leaning against the wall? The ladder which but two hours ago was lying flat along the inside of the fence?

Who has taken it from its place?

And, by heaven!—what is this?—

Who has opened the window of the loft, which he himself had bolted from the inside before the barn was filled with the sheaves?

Below, at the foot of the ladder, the ground looked moist, as if a liquid had been spilled. An odor of petroleum rose from the spot.

With trembling hands he seized the straw which

was strewn on the ground. Yes, it was wet, and the obnoxious odor communicated itself to the fingers that touched it.

He felt his knees tremble under him, a dull, terrible foreboding clouded his senses. With difficulty he raised himself up and mounted the ladder, till he reached the window of the loft.

The dog whined below.

" Seek for your master, Turk. Seek !"

The animal broke out into a joyous howl and ran sniffing round and round, till he seemed to have found the scent.

Paul gazed at him. He was trembling feverishly, in agonizing suspense.

The way the animal took was through the gate. Then it really had been his father who had opened it.

But then—then. Which way would he turn?

" Seek for your master, Turk. Seek !"

The dog again gave a short howl, and then ran with great speed down the path towards Helenenthal.

Helenenthal! What does father want in Helenenthal? Ah, did he not say a short time ago that he had been there one afternoon for an experiment? For an experiment! And how strangely and unpleasantly he laughed when he said it.

And to-day, too. How mysterious his behavior had been! And when they were speaking of the barn catching fire, what did he mean by the words that it was a splendid coincidence to-day? Why to-day? Whatever happens, I must find the solution of this riddle ere it is too late!

He looked around, seeking help.

As his hand was groping mechanically in the dark aperture he laid hold of the handle of a tin can which stood hidden there among the sheaves. It was the petroleum can, which he had freshly filled yesterday. And on whose advice? Who was it who came and said,

"Father, father, for Jesus' sake, what do you want to do at Helenenthal?"

And now, how much is there still in it? It is scarcely half full.

As he unconsciously went on groping about, he came upon some boxes of matches which lay by the can.

This opened his eyes; he gave a terrible cry. "He is going to set Helenenthal on fire!"

Everything swam before his eyes, and he would have fallen backward from the ladder had he not clung to the framework of the window.

All was clear. His father's confused talk, his laughs, his threats.

But there was yet time. The old man could only creep along on his crutch. He might throw himself on his horse, and gallop after him.

"Saddle a horse!" he called out through the dark, and sprang down from the ladder. Then suddenly it shot through his brain—

"Why did father ask so minutely about the time years ago? Would his revenge be executed at the same moment? Good heavens! then all is lost. I told him one o'clock was the hour, and it is one now."

Mad fear seized him — again he climbed the ladder.

In the next moment the flames would rise over there.

Is it not burning there already? No, it is only the moon that shines on the windows of the White House. Heavenly Father, is there no salvation, no mercy? If a prayer, if a curse could have the power to lame the out-stretched hand! Who will warn him, who will give him a sign to turn back?

But there are the flames. No. Perhaps in another second the fiery glow will rise to the sky.

"Elsbeth, awake!"

It will flame up as it did then, eight years ago, when the blood-red reflection paralyzed all his faculties, as he roamed in the garden of Helenenthal. If to-day, as at that time, a fire were to rise on the heath, or that his father's hand might be stiffened in the midst of his criminal purpose.

Oh, God in Heaven, let a miracle happen! Let a fire break out on the heath, as it happened before—as happened before.

There *must* be a fire! And there must be a fire here! If lightning would but strike the roof of his own home, so that the flames might cry out to his father, "Stop, stop!" Ah, why is it such a clear, starlight night? Why is there no threatening cloud upon the horizon? Perhaps he is even now stretching up to the thatched roof. Perhaps he is now striking the match. In another moment all warning will be too late.

There must be a fire! There must be a fire here!

And there is no torch that I could swing to warn him!

"There must be a fire! There must be a fire here!"

And as he looked around with eyes starting from his head, there suddenly flashed upon him an idea as bright as the fire he was longing for.

He shouted with joy.

"Yes, that's the thing. The terror will benumb him. It must be saved. Saved at any price."

With both hands he seized the can, and swinging it round him, poured its contents on the piled-up sheaves.

He grasped the matches. There is a soft hissing, the storm howls through the opening, and the flame shoots up high into the air, a whistling, hissing roaring is heard. The fire has already reached the roof.

He rushes back into the yard, which still lies silent before him.

"Fire! fire! fire!" he cries, to wake the sleepers.

In the stables, where the farm - servants sleep,

there is a great stir, shrieks come from the servants'
rooms.

The roof is already wrapped in a fiery mantle.
The tiles begin to crack, and fall rattling to the
ground. Wherever there is an outlet a fountain of
flame immediately spirts up towards the sky.

Hitherto he had been standing in the yard all
alone, watching his terrible work with folded hands;
but now the doors were torn open, and the farm-
servants and maids rushed screaming into the
yard.

Then he sighed, relieved, as at a duty accomplished, and walked slowly into the garden to avoid
meeting anybody. " I have worked long enough,"
he murmured, slamming the gate behind him. " To-
day I will rest!"

With lagging steps he went along the gravel-path
like one tired out, murmuring incessantly: " Rest!
rest!"

His glance wandered wearily around; the garden lay before him, bathed in a sea of light caused
by the moonbeams and the flames, and the shadows of the storm-driven leaves danced before his
eyes like something supernatural. Here and there
a spark fell upon the path before him, looking like
a glowworm. He searched for the darkest arbor,
and hid in its farthest corner. There he sat down
on the turfy seat and buried his face in his hands.

He wanted neither to hear nor to see anything
more.

But a dull feeling of curiosity made him look up after a while; and as he raised his eyes he saw the flames arch over the house like a crimson, white-edged canopy, for the storm was blowing that way.

Then he knew all was lost.

He folded his hands. He felt as if he ought to pray.

"Mother! mother!" he cried, his eyes full of tears, stretching out his arms to the sky.

Then, suddenly, a strange change came over him. He felt quite happy and free, the heavy load which had weighed on his mind all these years had vanished, and, with a deep breath, he drew his hands along his shoulders and arms, as though he longed to rid himself of the sinking fetters.

"There," he cried, like one from whose heart a burden is taken, "now I have nothing more, now I need care no longer. I am free, free as the birds in the air."

He hit his forehead with his fists, he cried, he laughed. He felt as if an undeserved, unheard-of happiness had descended upon him from heaven.

"Mother! mother!" he shouted, wild with joy. "Now I know how your fairy tale ends. I am released! I am released!"

At this moment the frightened lowing of the cattle fell upon his ear, and brought him back to his senses. "No, you poor animals shall not perish on my account," he cried, springing up; "I would rather die myself."

He hurried to the back door of the house, where the servants were eagerly carrying out the furniture.

"Look at master!" they exclaimed, weeping, and drew each other's attention to his bare feet.

"Leave that alone!" he cried. "Save the animals!"

An axe lay on the path. With it he broke open the back door of the stables, which led into the fields, for the yard was already a sea of flames.

As in a dream he sees how the garden and field are filling with people. The village fire - engine comes rattling along; the road to Helenenthal, too, becomes alive.

Three, four times he rushes into the flames, the servants behind him, then he sinks down, fainting with pain, in the middle of the burning stables.

A shriek, a piercing shriek from a woman, causes him to open his eyes once more.

Then it seemed to him as if he saw Elsbeth's face vanishing in mist over his head, then it was night again round him. . . .

CHAPTER XXI.

At the first streak of dawn a sad procession went across the autumnal heath, on the way to Helenenthal. Two miserable wagons crept slowly, one behind the other. In them was found room for all that remained of the Haidehof.

In the first wagon, wrapped in blankets among the straw, lay the master, terribly burned, unconscious. . . . The pale, trembling woman who anxiously bent over him was the playfellow of his youth.

In this state she fetched him home at last.

"We will take him to one of his sisters," Mr. Douglas had said; but she had laid her hands on Paul's breast, from which the singed rags hung down, as if she wanted to take possession of him for evermore, and had answered:

"No, father, he is coming with us."

"But your wedding, child—the guests?"

"What is the wedding to me?" she replied; and the gay bridegroom stood by stupefied.

In the second cart lay the few pieces of furniture which had been saved: an old chest of drawers, a few drawers with linen and books and ribbons, earthen-ware dishes, a milk-pail, and his father's long pipe.

But where was the latter?

The only one who might have given an explanation lay there unconscious, perhaps already struggling with death.

Had he taken to flight? Had he perished in the flames? The maids had found his bedroom empty, and no trace of himself.

"I suspect no good of him," said old Douglas; "he was always inclined to madness, and if we find his bones to-morrow beneath the ruins I shall be quite convinced that he set fire to the barn himself, and then threw himself into the flames."

However, just as they were driving through the gates of Helenenthal they heard a dog howling piteously near the barn, and saw a strange cur with his fore-paws on a dark mass lying there, and from time to time pulling at something that looked like the end of a garment.

Douglas, surprised, ordered the cart to stop, and walked up to it. There he found the person they were seeking—a corpse. His features were horribly distorted, and his arms still half uplifted, as if he had been suddenly turned to.stone. Near him lay a broken pot, and a match-box was swimming in a pool of petroleum, which was flowing down the wheel-ruts as in a gutter.

Then the gray giant folded his hands and murmured a prayer. When he came back to the cart

19

he trembled all over, and his eyes were full of tears.

"Elsbeth, look here," he said, "there lies the body of old Meyerhofer. He wanted to set fire to our property, and God has struck him dead."

"God does not set barns on fire," said Elsbeth, and looked back at the burning farm, from which a dark-blue smoke was rising in the chilly morning air.

"But is it not through God's providence that we were saved?"

"If any one saved us, this one did," said Elsbeth.

"What? would he have sacrificed everything, would he have become an incendiary—only—to—"

"Ask him," she said, hoarsely, and in the growing anxiety of her heart she folded her hands on her breast and groaned aloud.

"Heaven grant that he may ever be able to answer again," murmured Douglas. Then he ordered the servants to bring the old man's body into the house. He had already sent for a doctor; he himself would drive to the sisters and give them the news.

The guests, horror-stricken, came rushing out to the cart, which stopped before the flower-decked veranda.

"Elsbeth, how ill you look! Elsbeth, spare yourself," cried out her aunts, and tried to take possession of her.

"Go away!" she said, and repulsed the caressing hands with a movement of horror.

Then the gay bridegroom, who during this night had played such a lamentable part, came to her and tried to persuade her to leave the helpless body. But she looked at him with an absent, wandering glance, as if she did not remember ever to have seen him before. Depressed and discouraged he left her alone.

The aunts, wringing their hands, hurried to old Douglas, who was walking up and down before the stables awaiting a conveyance. His powerful chest heaved, his white, bushy brows were knitted, and his eyes shot lightning. A storm seemed to be passing over his soul.

"Have pity," cried the women; "make Elsbeth rest; she must recover herself; she looks as if she were going mad."

"If it is as she says," he muttered to himself, "if he has sacrificed all his belongings. . . . Plague you, leave me in peace!" he cried to the women who surrounded him.

"But think of Elsbeth," they called out. "At twelve o'clock the vicar comes, and what will she look like?"

"That's her lookout!" he shouted. "Let her be, she knows quite well what she is doing."

At the same moment that Paul was lifted from the cart a troop of servants came from the gate carrying his father's corpse.

One after the other the two bodies were carried into the White House, and the dog went whining and sniffing after them. It was a sad procession.

Elsbeth had Paul carried into her own bedroom, locked the door, and seated herself near the bed.

Vainly the aunts implored to be let in.

At eleven o'clock the doctor came, and declared himself willing to stay with his patient till next morning. He had evidently come prepared for it, for he was an old friend of the house and one of the wedding guests. Meanwhile they were to telegraph for a nurse.

"May I not stay with him?" asked Elsbeth.

"If you can," he answered, astonished.

"I can," she answered, with a mysterious smile.

The aunts knocked again. "Spare yourself, child," they cried through the chink of the door; "you must dress — you must go to the register-office. The vicar has come."

"He can go away again," she answered.

There was a murmur outside; the bridegroom, too, was giving his advice.

"What will you do, my child?" said the old doctor, and looked searchingly into her eyes. Then she sank, weeping, on her knees by the bed, seized Paul's powerless hand and pressed it to her eyes and mouth.

"Is that your firm resolution?" the old man asked. She nodded assent.

"And if he dies?"

"He will not die," she said; "he must not die."

The doctor smiled, sadly; "Very good," he said, then, "stay with him a while, and renew the compresses every two minutes. I will insure quiet meanwhile."

Soon the carriages were heard coming to the door and leaving the yard. An hour later the doctor re-entered the sick-room. "The house will soon be empty," he said; "the ceremony is put off."

"Put off?" she asked, anxiously.

The old man looked at her and shook his head. The human heart showed itself to him every day in new complications.

.   .   .   .

For weeks the patient lingered between life and death. The nervous fever which had set in seemed to take away all hope.

Elsbeth scarcely left his bedside. She did not eat, she did not sleep; her whole life seemed to be engrossed by the care of her beloved one.

Her old father let her alone. "She must cure him," he said, "so that I can question him."

The gay cousin began to feel that his position was not an enviable one, and, after he had allowed his uncle to pay all his debts, left Helenenthal.

Old Meyerhofer's body had been fetched by the twins the day after the fire. His mysterious death made a great sensation; the newspapers in the capital spoke of it, and what he had not attained through his whole life—to be celebrated as a hero—was granted to him in death.

But all this time the law was hanging over Paul's head awaiting his recovery.

CHAPTER XXII.

THE lawyer for the defence had ended. A murmur went through the wide court of the assizes, the galleries of which were crammed with spectators.

If the accused did not spoil the effect of the brilliant speech by an imprudent word he was saved.

The president's answer resounded unheard.

And now the eye-glasses and opera-glasses began to click. All eyes were directed to the pale, simply-clad man who was sitting in the same dock where, eight years ago, the vicious servant had sat.

The president asked whether the accused had anything more to add to strengthen the proof of his innocence.

"Silence! silence!" was murmured through the court.

But Paul rose and spoke—first, low and hesitatingly, then every moment with greater firmness.

"I am heartily sorry that the trouble my defender has taken to save me should have been useless; but I am not as innocent of the deed as he represents."

The judges looked at each other. "What is he at? He is going to speak against himself."

He said: "Anxiety made me nearly unconscious. I then acted in a kind of madness which at that moment rendered me incapable of calculation."

"He is cutting his own throat!" said the audience.

"I have all my life been shy and oppressed, and have felt as if I could look nobody in the face, though I had nothing to conceal; but if this time I behave in a cowardly manner, I believe I should be less able to do so than ever—and this time I should have good reason enough for it. My defender has also represented my former life as a pattern of all virtues. But this was not so, either. I lacked dignity and self-possession; I passed over too much as regards both other people and myself, and that has always rankled in my mind, though I was never clear about it. Too much has weighed upon me to enable me ever to breathe freely as a man should if he does not want to grow dull and care-laden. This deed has made me free, and has given me that which I lacked so long; it has been a great happiness to me; and should I be so ungrateful as to deny it to-day? No; I will not do that. Let them imprison me as long as they like. I shall abide my time and begin a new life.

"And so I must say I have set fire to my belongings in full consciousness; I was never more in my senses than at the moment when I poured the petroleum over my sheaves; and if to-day I were to be in the same position, God knows I should

do the same again. Why should I not ? What I
destroyed was the work of my own hands—I had
created it after long years of hard toil, and could
do with it what I liked. I well know that the law
is of a different opinion, and therefore I shall
quietly go to prison for my time. But who else
suffered by the injury except myself? My sisters
were well provided for, and my father—" he stopped
a moment, and his voice shook as he continued—
"yes, would it not have been better if my old father
had passed the last years of his life in peace and
tranquillity with one of his daughters than where I
am now going ?

"Fate would not have it so. A stroke killed him,
and my brothers say that I was his murderer. But
my brothers have no right at all to judge about that ;
they neither know me nor my father. All their lives
they have been concerned with themselves only,
and have let *me* alone care for my father, mother,
and sisters, house, and farm, and I was only good
enough when they wanted something. They turn
away from me to-day, but they can never be more
estranged from me in the future than they have always been in the past.

"My sisters "—he turned towards the witness-
box, where Greta and Kate sat crying with covered
faces, and his voice grew softer as if from suppressed tears—"my sisters won't have anything to
do with me any more, but I gladly forgive them ;
they are women, and made of more delicate metal ;

also, there are two men standing behind them who find it very easy to be indignant at my monstrous deed. They have all abandoned me now—no, not all "—a bright look crossed his face—"but that need not be mentioned here. But one thing I will say, even though I be considered a murderer—I do not repent that my father died through my deed ; I loved him more when I killed him than if I had let him live. He was old and weak, and what awaited him was shame and dishonor—he lived such a quiet life, and would have miserably dwindled away here; surely it was better death should come to him like lightning that kills people in the middle of their happiness. That is my opinion. I have settled it with my conscience, and have no need to render account to any one but to God and to myself. Now you may condemn me."

" Bravo !" cried a thundering voice in the court from the witness-box.

It was Douglas.

His gigantic figure stood erect, his eyes sparkled beneath his bushy brows, and when the president called him to order he sat down defiantly and said to his neighbor, " I can be proud of him—eh ?"

CHAPTER XXIII.

Two years later, on a bright morning in June, the red-painted gate of the prison opened and let out a prisoner, who, with a laugh on his face, was blinking his eyes in the bright sun, as if trying to learn to bear the light again. He swung the bundle which he carried to and fro, and looked carelessly to the right and the left, like one who was not decided which direction to follow, but for whom, on the whole, it was unimportant whither he strayed.

When he passed the front of the prison building he saw a carriage standing there which appeared known to him, for he stopped and seemed to be reflecting. Then he turned to the coachman, who, in his tasselled fur-cap, nodded haughtily from the box.

"Is anybody from Helenenthal here?" he asked.

"Yes; master and the young lady. They have come to fetch Mr. Meyerhofer."

And directly after was heard from the steps, "Hey, holloa! there he is already—Elsbeth, see! there he is already."

Paul jumped up the steps, and the two men lay in each other's arms.

Then the heavy folding doors were opened softly and timidly, and let out a slender female figure,
clad in black, who, with a melancholy smile, leaned
against the wall and quietly waited until the men
unclasped each other.

"There, you have him, Elsbeth!" shouted the
old man.

Hand in hand they stood opposite each other
and looked in one another's eyes; then she leaned
her head on his breast and whispered, "Thank
God that I am with you again!"

"And in order that you may have each other all
to yourselves, children," said the old man, "you
two shall drive home, and I will meanwhile drink a
bottle of claret to the health of my successor. I
am well off, for I retire from business this day."

"Mr. Douglas!" exclaimed Paul, terrified.

"*Father*, I am called—do you understand? Let
me be fetched towards evening. You are now master at home. Good-bye."

With that he strode down the steps.

"Come," said Paul, gently, with downcast eyes.
Elsbeth went after him with a shy smile, for now
when they were alone neither dared to approach
the other.

And then they drove silently out onto the sunny, flowery heath. . . . Wild pinks, bluebells, and
ground-ivy wove themselves into a many-colored
carpet, and the white meadowsweet lifted its waving blossoms, as if snow-flakes had been strewn on

the flowers. The leaves of the weeping-willow rustled softly, and like a net of sparkling ribbons the little streams flowed along beneath their branches. The warm air trembled, and yellow butterflies fluttered up and down in couples.

Paul leaned back in the cushions, and gazed with half-shut eyes at this profusion of charming sights.

"Are you happy?" asked Elsbeth, leaning towards him.

"I don't know," he answered; "it is too much for me."

She smiled; she well understood him.

"See there, our home!" she said, pointing to the White House, which stood out clear in the distance. He pressed her hand, but his voice failed him.

At the edge of the wood the carriage had to stop. Both got out and proceeded on foot.

Then he saw that she carried a little white parcel under her arm, which he had not seen before.

"What is that?" he asked.

"You will soon see," she answered, while a serious smile crossed her face.

"A surprise?"

"A remembrance."

When they entered the wood he perceived something black between the red stems which was hung with garlands.

"What does that mean?" he asked, stretching out his hand.

"Don't you recognize your friend again?" she replied. "She wanted to be the first to greet you."

"Black Susy," he shouted, and began to run.

"Take me with you," she gasped, laughing. "You forget that henceforth there are two of us."

He seized her hand, and so they stepped before the faithful monster that was keeping watch on the road.

"Dear creature," he said, and stroked the sooty boiler, and as they went on he looked back at her every three steps as if he could not part with her.

"I have watched over her well," said Elsbeth; "she generally stands underneath my window, for we have purchased the whole of your father's inheritance that nothing should be lost to you."

When they approached the opposite edge of the wood, he said, pointing to two trees which stood twenty steps away from the road,

"Here is the place where I found you lying in your hammock."

"Yes," she said, "it was there, too, that I found out for the first time that I should never be able to do without you."

"And there is the juniper-tree," he continued, when they stepped out into the fields, "where we—" and then he suddenly cried aloud, and stretched out both his hands into space.

"What is the matter?" she exclaimed, anxiously, looking up at him. He had turned deathly pale and his lips quivered.

"It is gone," he stammered.

"What?"

"It—it—my—my own."

Where once the buildings of the Haidehof rose there now stretched a level plain ; only a few trees spread out their miserable branches.

He could not accustom himself to this sight, and covered his face with his hands, while he shivered feverishly.

"Do not be sad," she pleaded. "Papa would not have it rebuilt before you could make your own arrangements."

"Let us go there," he said.

"Please, please, not," she replied, "there is nothing to be seen except a few heaps of ruins—at another time, when you are not so excited."

"But where shall I sleep?"

"In the same room in which you were born—I have had it arranged for you, and your mother's furniture put in. Can you still say now that you have lost your home?"

He pressed her hand, gratefully, but she pointed to the juniper-bush, which had struck them before.

"Let us go there," she said, "lay your head on the mole-hill and whistle me something. Do you remember?"

"I should think so !"

"How long is it since then ?"

"Seventeen years."

"Oh, heavens, I have loved you so long already,

and in the mean time have become an old maid! And I have waited for you from year to year, but you would not see it. 'He must come at last,' I thought, but you did not come. And then I was discouraged, and thought: 'You cannot force yourself upon him; in reality he does not want you at all. You must come to some resolution.' And to put an end to all my longings, I accepted my cousin, who for the last ten years had been dangling after me. He had made me laugh so often, and I thought he would—but enough of this—" and she shuddered. "Come, lie down—whistle."

He shook his head and pointed with his hand silently across the heath, where, on the horizon, three lonely fir-trees stretched their rough arms towards the sky.

"Thither," he said. "I cannot rest ere I have been there."

"You are right," she replied, and hand in hand they walked through the blooming heather, over which the wild bees were swarming, sleepily humming.

When they entered the cemetery the clock at the White House was striking noon. Twelve times it sounded in short strokes, a soft echo quivered in the air, and then all was quiet again; only the humming and singing continued.

His mother's grave was overgrown with ivy and wild myrtle, and at its head rose the radiant blossom of a golden-rod. Between the leaves rust-colored ants were creeping, and a lizard rustled down into the green depths.

Silently they both stood there, and Paul trembled. Neither dared to interrupt the solemn stillness.

"Where have they buried my father?" Paul asked at last.

"Your sisters took the body over to Lotkeim," answered Elsbeth.

"That is as well," he replied. "She has been lonely all her life; let her be so in death, too. But to-morrow we will also go over to him."

"Will you go and see your sisters?"

He shook his head sadly. Then they relapsed into silence.

He leaned his head on his hands and cried.

"Do not cry," she said, "each one of you has now a home." And then she took the little parcel that she held under her arm, unfastened the white paper of the cover, and there appeared an old manuscript-book with torn cover and faded leaves.

"See," she cried, "she sends you this, her greeting."

"Where did you get it from?" he asked, surprised, for he had recognized his mother's handwriting.

"It lay in the old chest of drawers which was saved from the fire, squeezed between the drawers

20

and the back.   It seems to have been lying there
ever since her death."

Then they sat down together on the grave, laid
the book between them on their knees, and began
to study it.   Now he remembered that Katie, at
the time when he surprised her with her lover, had
spoken of a song-book which had belonged to their
mother; but he had never made up his mind to ask
after it, because he did not want to bring to life
again the painful remembrance of that hour.

All sorts of old songs were in it, copied out neat-
ly; near them others half scratched out and cor-
rected.   The latter she seemed to have reproduced
from memory, or perhaps composed herself.

There was also the one about the poet which
Katie had recited at the time.

And then came one, which was this :

> " Dear child, sleep on ; sleep on, dear child ;
>   Beside thy bed thy mother mild
>   Watches till dreams shall bring thee peace—
>   Sleep on !

> " The little bell whose tones so clear
>   From out the wood resounded here
>   Its silver music soon will cease—
>   Sleep on !

> " Dear child, sleep on ; sleep on, dear child !
>   Without the moon shines soft and bright,
>   A legend tell the linden-trees—
>   Sleep on !

"About the heath the shepherd's son,
  The princess in the White House lone ;
  While leaves are flutt'ring in the breeze—
    Sleep on !

"Dear child, sleep on ; sleep on, dear child !
  Thy rose-bush at the door dreams wild
  Of heath and hill and many things—
    Sleep on !

"Thy little bird upon the sill
  Chirps gently towards thy bed his trill,
  And closes wearily his wings—
    Sleep on !

"Dear child, sleep on ; sleep on, dear child !
  Beside thy bed thy mother mild
  Watches the hour-glass slowly turn—
    Sleep on !

"Thy mother watches—time goes by—
  The midnight hour approaches nigh,
  And then thy father may return—
    Sleep on !"

And then another poem :

I knew a sweet maiden in years that are gone,
Who on the green heath dwelt forsaken and lone.
And longed sore for love—
She looked from her window by day and by night
Her lovely blue eyes glanced out smiling and bright ;
Ah ! she longed sore for love !

'Then by there came riding a bold youthful knight,
  Who asked, ' So strange on me gaze thine eyes bright ?'

'I long sore for love!'
Then he laughed, 'Foolish maiden, wilt come to my
     arms,
There can'st thou rest sweetly, free from all harms,
And there find'st thou love.'

"'Dear heart, dost thou know how forsaken I dwell?
Oh, take me, poor maiden, o'er moor and o'er fell,
But give, give me love!'
When of her company wearied at last,
He said, 'Pretty rogue we've a pleasant time passed,
So hast thou had love!'

"'And of my love art thou weary, dear heart?
So will I stay by thee, nor evermore part,
For I long for thy love.'
But heartily laughed the knight bold and gay,
He saddled his horse and he rode far away,
And left her in sorrow to love.

"And when the time had passed sadly away,
In sorrow her son saw the light of the day,
An offspring of love.
She carried him out in the night on the heath;
'With a kiss, thou poor child, will I do thee to death—
I will kill thee with love.'

"'Do to me, judge, what you will,' then she cried.
'Forsaken am I of the whole world so wide,
And left without love.'
She mounted the scaffold in bridal array,
And said 'Take me hence, thou good God, I pray,
And I long sore for love!'"

Then his two sisters came to his mind, and he

had a feeling as if his mother had known all and forgiven all beforehand.

And directly after stood written, in big letters, this title

THE FAIRY TALE OF DAME CARE.

There was once a mother, to whom the good God had given a son, but she was so poor and lonely that she had nobody who could stand godmother to him. And she sighed, and said, "Where shall I get a godmother from?" Then one evening at dusk there came a woman to her house who was dressed in gray and had a gray veil over her head. She said, "I will be your son's godmother, and I will take care that he grows up a good man and does not let you starve; but you must give me his soul."

Then his mother trembled, and said, "Who are you?"

"I am Dame Care," answered the gray woman; and the mother wept; but as she suffered much from hunger, she gave the woman her son's soul and she was his godmother.

And her son grew up and worked hard to procure her bread. But as he had no soul, he had no joy and no youth, and often he looked at his mother with reproachful eyes, as if he would ask,

"Mother, where is my soul?"

Then the mother grew sad and went out to find him a soul.

She asked the stars in the sky, "Will you give me a soul?" But they said, "He is too low for that."

And she asked the flowers on the heath; they said, "He is too ugly."

And she asked the birds in the trees; they said, "He is too sad."

And she asked the high trees; they said, "He is too humble."

And she asked the clever serpents, but they said, "He is too stupid."

Then she went away weeping. And in the wood she met a young and beautiful princess surrounded by her court.

And because she saw the mother weeping she descended from her horse and took her to the castle, which was all built of gold and precious stones.

There she asked, "Tell me why you weep?" And the mother told the princess of her grief that she could not procure her son a soul nor joy and youth.

Then said the princess, "I cannot see anybody weep; I will tell you something—I will give him my soul."

Then the mother fell down before her and kissed her hands.

"But," said the princess, "I will not do it for nothing; he must ask me for it." Then the mother went to her son, but Dame Care had laid her gray veil over his head, so that he was blind and could not see the princess.

And the mother pleaded, "Dear Dame Care, set him free."

But Care smiled—and whoever saw her smile was forced to weep—and she said, "He must free himself."

"How can he do that?" asked the mother.

"He must sacrifice to me all that he loves," said Dame Care.

Then the mother grieved very much, and lay down and died. But the princess waits for her suitor to this very day.

.   .   .   .

"Mother, mother!" he cried, and sank down on the grave.

"Come," said Elsbeth, struggling with her tears as she laid her hand on his shoulder; "let mother be, she is at peace; and she shall not harm us any more—your wicked Dame Care!"

NOTES.

I TRANSLATION OF THE DEDICATION:

TO MY PARENTS.

FOR THE 26TH OF NOVEMBER.

DAME CARE, the deep gray-veiléd dame,
You know her, dear parents, not only by name;
She came, 'tis thirty years to-day,
And into strange countries she followed your way.
As the November day, sad and dreary and dull,
Lay on the heath in a leaden lull,
And in the willow-trees the wind
Whistled your wedding-dance, rough and unkind.

And when, after hours without any rest,
In Littau's forest you found a nest,
And trembling stood at the threshold so bare,
She entered with you, gray Dame Care,
And waving her arms she blessed the two,
The home you entered, the house and you,
And blessed those two, who, without harm,
Still slept in creation's shielding arm.

The empty cradle that time did mark
Stands under the staircase in the dark,
Indulging in long deservéd rest,
As four times it saw a new little guest.
Then when sun sunk, and all round slept,
From some dark corner a shadow crept,
And staggered dumbly and grew and rose,
And crept with stretched arms to the cradle close.

And what Dame Care then promised to you,
Life has so faithfully made it true
In sighs and weeping and ever and aye,
In troubles of weary working-day,
In pain of so many a sleepless night,
With need and torment ever in sight.

And you are gray, your strength grew lame,
But ever still the deep-veiled Dame
Walks with fixed eyes and blessing hand
All through the poor house, to pass without end
From the tables so poor to the chests so bare,
From threshold to threshold, and blows in the glare
Of the flame on the hearth, and ever and aye
Rivets the weary day to the day.
O dearest parents, don't cease to strive,
And as you had work and cares all your life,
A life so hard and a life so long,
So will at last from Heaven descend
A day of rest when care has an end.

We boys are young, and we can strive,
Our courage is still fresh in life.
We know how to fight with care and need,
And where luck's flower is blooming so sweet.
Soon we return, and when we are there,
We laughingly turn her out, gray Dame Care.

II. Du (*Thou*) and Sie (*You*), pages 68, 115, 116: References to the German use of the former pronoun to denote greater intimacy than the latter implies.

III. August, page 143: Name of the chief clown in the Berlin Circus.

IV. Polterabend, page 275: Evening before the wedding. In some parts of Germany it is customary for the friends of the bride to bring old china or glass, which they smash before her door.

THE END.